# ONE

*Kate*

Four hundred graduation caps soared like a flock of black birds breaking formation. For Katherine Gage, the sight marked the end of the agony of high school. Kate gazed up at the flying headgear and took a deep breath.

It felt like the weight of an anvil had been lifted off her chest. High school had been torture. Maybe it was her own fault that she was an outcast. Would things have been different if anyone had known about the unspeakable childhood trauma that had scarred her? Anyway, she'd been too ashamed to confide in anyone.

As she stared at her euphoric classmates, her mind drifted over the past four years.

By the time she'd entered her sophomore year, Kate had changed. From a gawky, coltish adolescent, she'd blossomed into a young woman. Espresso eyes dominated a delicate face framed by wavy dark hair that fell nearly to her waist. But Kate considered her looks a curse because, suddenly, they'd begun to draw unwelcome attention. She didn't want the attention. She only cared that she had just the right body for riding horses—lean and strong, with long legs and a short upper body.

Unfortunately, the other kids in school didn't ignore her beauty. Hormonal boys asked her out on dates. Cliquey girls tried to include her in their parties or trips to the mall because they hoped having her with them would lure some of the boys their way. Kate politely declined their invitations, always claiming that she needed to study or help her mom with chores.

She assumed that if she turned them down often enough, they'd stop inviting her. She just wanted to be alone. And by the end of sophomore year, she'd figured out how to create more distance from her classmates. She'd learned to make herself invisible.

She grew her bangs out so when she looked down, a curtain of hair hid her face. She wore drab, shapeless clothing, and no makeup. She lost so much weight that her athletic body became scrawny. Like a turtle hiding in its shell, a once-vibrant Kate disappeared inside baggy jeans, oversized sweatshirts, and that wall of raven hair.

She was still polite to the few kids who spoke to her, but she sent a clear message. *Stay away. Leave me alone.* Eventually, the invitations stopped.

But if Kate wanted only to be left alone, things didn't work out so well. As she became more reclusive, her classmates grew antagonistic. They stopped trying to

# SECOND
# CHANCES

# SECOND CHANCES

JANE SAVOIE

The events in this book are fictitious. Any similarity to real events is coincidental and not intended by the author.

Copyright © 2020 Jane Savoie

ISBN:
978 1 7360790 0 3 (print)
978 1 7360790 1 0 (eBook)

Cover photographs by ©matilda553 and ©kiuikson
     (Adobe Stock)
Book and cover design by RM Didier
Typefaces: Athelas, Elina Decor, Grand Central

Printed in the United States of America

*For Rhett*

include her in their activities and labeled her an odd-ball, like Sissy Spacek's character in *Carrie*. It seemed easier to dismiss her and be cruel than to try to understand her.

The girls imitated the way she walked with hunched shoulders and eyes cast down. The bullies from the football team followed her down the hall, taunting her from close behind, whispering, "Horsey, horsey, horsey."

Kate ignored them as best she could. She just wanted to get out of school so she could go to her place of refuge—the barn. The only time she felt like herself, and felt safe, was when she was around the horses.

She connected with them. She trusted them. Animals didn't lie to, manipulate, or use you. If they liked you, you knew it. If they didn't like you, you knew that, too.

The high school principal's voice announcing the names of the graduates brought Kate back to the present. She breathed another sigh of relief that she was finally free of the worst four years of her life. Unfortunately, that freedom came with strings.

Kate had promised her mom that she'd go to college. Lillian Gage knew exactly what it was like to struggle in a minimum-wage job while trying to support two children as a single mother. She waitressed at a coffee shop during the seven-to-three shift and depended on tips to make ends meet. Lillian wanted her girls to have a better life, to have more choices than she'd had. Kate felt like she had to give college a try just to make her mother happy.

After weighing the pros and cons of different schools, Kate chose Johnson & Wales University in Rhode Island. They had a great riding program run by Beth Bradley, who was a J&W graduate. Riding was all Kate had cared about ever since she was a child. So, she'd suck it up and take the other courses just so she could take lessons from Beth.

The other thing she liked about Johnson & Wales was that it was a fairly large school. With close to ten thousand students, the university was big enough that she'd be able to fade into anonymity. Plus, the school was close enough to home that she could live with her mom and not have to deal with college social life. It sounded like the perfect compromise between doing what her mother wanted and avoiding college altogether, which Kate would have preferred.

# TWO

*Kate*

Returning home from her afternoon economics class, Kate searched out her mother. She found her in their living room, sitting in the old red armchair, reading *Better Homes & Gardens* magazine.

Kate stood in front of her and took a deep breath. Then she dove in before she could change her mind.

"Mom, I'm taking a year off from school." She hugged her skinny midriff and went on. "I've sucked it up for two years, and I'm done. I know what I want to do with my life. I've always known. And as much as you hate to admit it, you know, too. For me, everything but riding and training horses is a total waste of time."

Lillian dropped her magazine and stood up. "What? No. You can't quit school. I won't allow it. If you do that, you'll never have a secure career. Do you want to end up waitressing like me?"

Kate backed away from what looked like a standoff

and paced back and forth in their small living room, frustration firing every nerve. But she could feel the resolve in every bit of her. "You've always known what I want to do. It's always been horses, ever since I could walk and talk. Did you really think going to college would change that?"

Lillian's voice dropped a decibel, and her face softened. "Honey, please. College opens up worlds you haven't even considered. Please give it more time. Even if you do end up with the horses, you'll learn so many useful things. Things like accounting and marketing. Those skills will help you in any business—including the horse business."

Kate stopped pacing and faced her mother. "Mom! I've finished all the requirements. I've been exposed to all that. But now they tell I have to declare a major. And just the thought of picking one suffocates me. Is that what you want for me?"

Lillian smiled slightly. "Aren't you being a little dramatic?"

Kate shook her head causing her black halo of hair to ripple down her back. "All I want to do is ride, train, and own my own stable. If the stars and the moon align, I might even earn the right to ride for the U.S. in international competition. A pipe dream, maybe. But it's what you used to tell us: 'Go big or go home.'"

"But sweetheart," Lillian pleaded. "It's so hard to make it as a professional in this business. I've been cheering you on at lessons and horse shows for over ten years. I've learned a lot just from watching, and I see how difficult that life is. Loving horses isn't enough to ensure success."

Kate tugged her bottom lip between her teeth. "But if you want to be happy, you need to be passionate about what you do. I bet if you asked a hundred people if they loved their jobs, probably ninety percent of them would say, 'No. It's just a paycheck. I need to work to pay the bills.' I don't want to spend my life doing something I hate just so I can put food on the table."

Lillian continued to argue her case. "You know perfectly well that the horse industry is a game of chutes and ladders. You white-knuckle yourself up the ladder, and when you almost reach the top, a horse colics. Then you've got a huge vet bill, and you end up flying down the chute with your skirt up over your face. Or the price of hay doubles. The indoor arena needs more footing. Fences need repairing. The trailer needs new tires. Wake up, Kate! The reality is that something always eats away at your profits."

"You're talking worst-case scenarios. I can't believe you're being so negative."

"I'm sorry, dear, but face facts. As the bills pile up, deadbeat boarders and students stiff you. Or you need to work in the barn when staff gets sick or quits without giving notice. Then you're doing barn chores all day long and you haven't got any time for teaching and training."

Kate glared at her. "You're wrong! It doesn't have to be like that."

Lillian tried again. "Listen to me. All the professionals

I've met struggle to keep their heads above water. Think about Fox Hollow Farm. It looks like they have a thriving business, right? They have a full barn and their riders do well at shows. They even take students to Florida for the show circuit in Wellington. But Janice Holcomb told me they almost closed their doors last year because their overhead was so high."

Kate opened her mouth to say something but stopped when her mother extended both palms toward her.

"Kate, listen to me. I want you and your sister to have better lives than mine. Every parent wants that for her children. The horse business sets you up for a lifetime of financial struggle and endless hard work. You'll never be able to retire. Do you really believe you can be the one percent of the one percent who makes it in this field? You're fooling yourself. You need to be an Olympian like Steffen Peters or Beezie Madden."

Kate's eyes narrowed. "Mom, where in the world do you get your so-called facts? I get your point, but you're forgetting something. I have what it takes. I know I do. Even though I only get to ride three times a week at the college stables, Beth Bradley said Gentleman Jim gave me an incredible foundation. She also said I'm really good with difficult horses, that I can do what most riders can't. I'm sure I'll be in high demand."

"Oh, that's just great. You'll ride all the broncs that no one else can handle, and you'll end up hurting yourself. Then you'll really be out of business."

Kate raised her voice to stop her mother from continuing. "Aargh! I'm going to say this one more time, and please try to understand my point of view. I'd rather struggle for a lifetime doing something I love than spend my days in a ten-by-ten cubicle doing something I hate just for a paycheck. Besides, since when does having a job mean any kind of security? Ever heard of downsizing and cutbacks? A nine-to-five job is about as solid as a house of cards in a hurricane."

Lillian tried once again to reason with her daughter. "But at least if you finished college, you'd have something to fall back on. And you wouldn't be spinning like a hamster on a wheel, going nowhere."

"Mom. I know it's not going to be easy and that I have a lot to learn. My head isn't in the clouds. I've researched farms with the best working student programs and sent letters to a couple of trainers on the East Coast. Think of that kind of program as my college education." Kate's eyes shimmered at the thought of apprenticing herself to a top trainer.

"And get this! One of those trainers is Ben Ellis. You've seen him a million times at competitions. I'd die to get a position in his barn. From what everyone says, I'd get the best education ever from him."

Lillian narrowed her eyes. "I agree he seems to take good care of his students, but you know perfectly well that things aren't always what they seem to be. A lot of professional trainers put on a façade when they go to shows or give clinics. It's just another way of luring clients to their barn."

Kate crossed her arms in front of her chest like a kid about to have a tantrum. "In this case, I know for sure that you're wrong. Wheeler and Peter have been with Ben for a long time, and they give me the inside scoop. They tell me everything, from how he runs the barn, to lessons, to what it's like to go to a show with him. It just what I'm looking for."

Lillian continued as if speaking to a child. "Honey. You can't compare your situation to Wheeler's. His grandmother left him such a big inheritance that he'll never have to worry about his future or work a day in his life. For him, horses are a lark. Yes, he loves them, and from what I've seen, he's quite a good rider. But he's lazy. You can't afford that luxury. Please understand what you're getting yourself into if you choose this path."

"I do, Mom. And I love you for your concern. But I want this life. Anyhow, I've already heard from some of the stables that I've written to, and I've set up interviews starting next week. I can hardly wait!"

"But honey. What's the point of applying for a working student position? You don't even have a horse to bring with you."

Kate was prepared for her mother's objection. "Not having a horse might sound like a disadvantage, but you're looking at this the wrong way. As a horseless working student, I'll get to ride lots of different horses instead of just my own. I'll learn how to run a stable without the expense of being an owner. They'll teach me everything about the horse business—veterinary care, stable management, teaching, training, just everything! Wheeler and Peter don't get to do any of those things. They just go to the barn and ride. Not having a horse means I'll learn more and learn faster. So instead of panicking because I'm leaving Johnson & Wales, think of my time as a working student as my higher education."

Lillian's shoulders sagged and she sank back into her chair. "Honey, I just hope your resolve will be enough."

Kate's eyes lit up as she sensed her mother giving in. "It will. You know I learned from you how to never to give up. I'm going to make you proud of me, Mom."

"I'm always proud of you," Lillian continued. "I just want you to be happy. That's all I've ever wanted for my girls. I want you to feel like Stephanie, who loves her job at the gallery. Okay. Let's try it for a year. And we'll revisit the college plan after that. Deal?"

"Deal!" Kate could hardly contain herself as her stomach somersaulted like a Cirque du Soleil acrobat. But, determined to appear like a mature adult who'd made a well-thought-out decision, she gave her mother a huge hug.

Now all she had to do was find the perfect working-student position.

# THREE

*Chris*

When he saw the three horses huddled in a field near the road, Chris Barton slammed on the brakes and pulled his BMW wagon over to the side of the road. He killed the engine and got out, taking in the condition of the two big bays and the smaller chestnut with four white socks that came up to his knees. All three of them were thin, he could see that much. Way too thin.

He looked around to make sure he was alone and ducked under the wire fence. The horses pricked their ears toward him. He kept still, waiting for them to decide whether to approach him or move away. They held their ground. No stranger to horses, Chris approached the leader and gave him a pat. He approached one of the bays and let the horse sniff his fingers. Then he ran his hand over the bay's dull coat and felt every one of his ribs.

"Hey, boy. How are you doing? And where's your water tub?"

Chris wrinkled his forehead and looked around but didn't see any water. He walked away from the horses and searched the field until he came to a tiny stream. If it gets any hotter and drier, this muddy little excuse for a stream will all but disappear, he thought in disgust.

Taking another look at the three horses, he stalked off, muttering to himself, "I'm talking to these people right now. They ought to be arrested."

Chris marched through the field and ducked under the fence again. He strode up to the faded yellow farmhouse, climbed the three stairs up to the porch, squinted through the screen door and tapped on the frame with his knuckles. No response. He banged with the side of his fist.

Just then a woman appeared in the doorway. She was short and chunky, with gray streaks in her brown hair, and wore denim overalls over a black T-shirt. She glared at Chris through the screen.

"What do you want?" she snapped.

Chris removed his cap and suppressed his anger. He knew he wouldn't get anywhere if he came across as belligerent, although every cell in his body was in attack mode. "I'm sorry to bother you, ma'am. My name is Chris Barton. I saw the horses in your field. I really don't mean to pry, but they look like they need help."

"And you need to mind your own business, young man." She started back toward the dark interior of the house.

Chris held up a hand. "Please, wait! I only want to help. What can I do? If you're shorthanded, I can help take care of them. I mean, I live nearby, and I drive over this way almost every day because I'm taking dressage lessons at Erin Miller's place. Can we just talk?"

The woman squinted at Chris. After a sweeping glance that took in his six-foot frame, from his black paddock boots to his sun-bleached hair, she seemed to relax a little. She flicked her hand to warn him to back up a bit, opened the door, and stepped out of her house and over to a wooden bench, where she pushed aside an empty plastic flowerpot and some gardening shears. She balanced on the edge of the seat and looked like she was ready to bolt at any second. "All right. Talk."

In an effort to avoid intimidating her by his size, Chris eased himself down to sit on the top step of the porch. "I'm worried about your horses," he said. "They don't seem to have enough hay, water or shelter."

"Like I said, it's really none of your business. They're doing okay, anyway. What are you, an ASPCA spy?"

One side of Chris' mouth curved up in a lopsided smile. "Hardly. I'm just an animal lover. I'd like to help with the horses if you'll let me."

She barely paused to take that in. "They're fine. The pasture is okay, and there's a stream at the far side of the field. They have a run-in shed, so there's shelter if they need it. They mostly live outdoors, which is great because I don't have to muck stalls."

Chris said, "Please, ma'am. The stream is almost

dried up and they've grazed the pasture down to nothing. I know you can see some green from here, but it's not grass. The only thing left is weeds that they won't eat. I realize you don't know me, but you'd be doing me a big favor if you'd let me help. I can give you references, if you want."

The woman eyed Chris suspiciously. "What's in it for you?"

Chris shrugged his shoulders. "Well, I'm kind of a moth to a flame when I see animals in need. And you look like you have your hands full and could maybe use some help.

At that, the woman ran the back of her hand over her brow. "It hasn't always been like this," she said quietly, almost, he thought, to someone who wasn't there, or maybe to herself.

She looked down at the worn floorboards. "Okay," she said. "It's like this. My ex and I got divorced, and it wasn't pretty. In fact, it's the perfect cliché. He exchanged me for a younger, thinner model. Well, good luck to her. What's to stop him from doing the same thing to her one day? Though I won't lose any sleep over her if he does."

Chris gave her a sympathetic look. "I'm so sorry you're going through that."

Her eyes closed into angry slits. "He blindsided me. I didn't see it coming. But I guess a lot of women tell that story. I can barely function myself, let alone take care of animals. That's why I gave up and just turned them out in the pasture. It looked decent, and I checked out the stream at the far side of the field. I didn't know they'd eaten the grass down to weeds and the stream was drying up. I knew they had the run-in shed. I kind of turned them out...and pretty much put them out of my mind for a while."

For a long moment she was silent. Then she sat up a little straighter on the bench. She nodded her head at Chris and said, "Okay. What do you have in mind?"

Chris jumped up and had to stop himself from hugging her. "Really? You'll let me help? Thank you! Thank you! I'm going to Tractor Supply right now. I'll order some hay and a galvanized tub for water and have them delivered today. You won't have to do anything. I'll be back in a couple of hours at the most. You can trust me. Everything is going to be fine."

# FOUR

*Kate*

In her search for a working student position, Kate had sent letters to several top trainers in New England. She knew she'd have more opportunities if she cast a wider net to include the entire country, but she wanted to stay close to her mother and Stephanie.

When she was writing the letters, Kate could hear her mom's words echo through her mind. She agreed that hard work and detours blocked the road ahead. Kate didn't care. She lived by the adage, "Do what you love, and you'll never work a day in your life."

Within three weeks, a number of farms contacted her by mail. Most of them weren't looking for anyone and wished her luck. But then she got three offers in a row from farms in New England. Buzzing like a kid on a sugar high, she called all three of them immediately to set up interviews.

The first one was at Windsong Stables in Richmond,

New Hampshire. A quick Google showed it was an easy 45-minute drive from home.

The morning of the interview, she dressed in jeans, her Ariat paddock boots, and a hunter green polo shirt. She wanted to look workmanlike but not overdressed.

Butterflies banged around in her stomach so hard she felt nauseated, so she skipped her usual breakfast of oatmeal and toast. Instead she filled a commuter mug with coffee and headed to her mom's car.

As she got behind the wheel, she raised her eyes and gave a silent prayer to the god of ancient cars that the engine would turn over. The last thing she needed was to miss her appointment because the car wouldn't start. Luckily, when she turned the key the often-temperamental motor started right up.

With a thrill rippling through her body, Kate pulled the car out of the driveway and turned left to head to the interstate. As she sipped her coffee, she cued up some classical music and repeated positive affirmations to herself on the way to the farm.

An hour later, she pulled into the parking lot of Windsong Stables. She was nervous about meeting the owner and head trainer, Carlos de la Vega. But she took a few deep breaths and approached the farm with her head held high.

At the door, she scrubbed her feet on a mat until she heard the bristles scraping the soles of her boots clean. She entered the foyer and saw a large white board to her right. It outlined the day's schedule as well as the special needs of certain horses, like wound care or ice boots. It also listed everything from barn chores to veterinary appointments to the farrier's schedule and the lesson times.

Everything about the place appealed to Kate's OCD personality. Then why had those butterflies morphed into bricks?

Something didn't feel right, and Kate thought about bolting. Instead, she cautioned herself to hang tough and stop being so negative.

*Spend the day watching. That will answer your questions.*

She pushed her shoulders back and approached the first person who looked like she worked there. The girl wore a navy polo shirt embroidered with Windsong Stables over the left side of her chest and an intricate WS intertwined on her right sleeve.

"Hi. I'm Katherine Gage. I have an interview for a working student's position today at eleven. Do you know where I should go?

Frowning at the interruption, the girl said, "Follow me. We started lessons at eight-thirty. You can watch until Mr. de la Vega takes a break. Then he'll let you know what to do next."

Kate trailed after the girl to the outdoor arena, where de la Vega was teaching two girls while two others warmed up on their own for their lessons.

The horses gleamed like they were at a competition. They sported white saddle pads embossed with the farm's logo and snowy white polo wraps on their legs.

The girls looked professional in their custom breeches, tall black boots, and crisp riding shirts. They'd tied their hair back into neat buns and secured wayward wisps with bobby pins and hairnets.

Kate shivered with anticipation over what she might learn. But after watching two lessons, the heavy brick in her stomach made perfect sense. The riders never rewarded their horses, but they were quick to punish them with whip or spurs if they did anything that was less than perfect. They treated their mounts like machines. Kate wondered if this place represented the not-so-great barns she'd heard about: The horses existed only as vehicles to bring glory to the stable, their owners and their riders. If you or your family owned a top horse, you possessed a VIP ticket to this world. If not, you might as well be invisible.

Kate liked to win as much as the next person. But she cherished the partnership with her horses more than any ribbon, trophy, or year-end award. Did that meant she'd fail? If you wanted to succeed in this industry, did you have to have a killer instinct and a "win at all costs" mentality? If so, she'd already lost.

The head trainer, Carlos de la Vega, seemed to delight in terrifying his students. He shouted and swore at them. When the younger of the two girls had her back turned, de la Vega looked at the older rider, rolling his eyes. Maybe the younger rider wasn't oblivious after all, thought Kate, because shortly afterwards, the girl left the arena in tears.

Despite his rider's turmoil, de la Vega didn't seem to care. This sort of coach was common enough, Kate knew. It was obvious that as far as he was concerned, the riders he laughed and shouted at needed to toughen up or leave. Most of them bought into his philosophy. He ran one of the most successful show barns on the East Coast. If you wanted to win, you endured verbal and emotional abuse as the price of admission to his elite club.

And not only did you accept his rudeness, but you also kowtowed to him for acknowledging you at all. The riders seemed to prefer insults to being ignored.

All morning, riders came and left the ring without Carlos saying a word to them. It was obvious he wasn't influenced by the amount of money they spent for lessons. Kate assumed he didn't consider them worthy of his help that day. She wondered if his students accepted his behavior as normal. Maybe because they endured it every day, they became immune, and lapped up any crumbs he tossed their way. At least if he shouted, they knew he saw them in the ring.

She silently thanked Gentleman Jim and Beth Bradley for showing her a better way.

How could anyone learn in such a negative atmosphere? She slashed Windsong Stables off her list and left without a word to anyone.

Four days later, Kate visited Fantasy Farm in Mayfield, Vermont.

She raised an eyebrow at the irony of its name when it didn't live up to any of her fantasies. The farm clearly ran on a caste system. It didn't take a genius to see that the boarders who had their own horses belonged to a privileged class. Paying students, who rode school horses, followed them. Grooms and working students were found at the bottom of the food chain.

The staff treated the paying students and boarders like royalty. But the farm treated the working students and grooms like slaves. Watching the activities in the barn, Kate could see than no one showed them any respect.

Kate learned that the working students arrived at five-thirty a.m. to start morning chores and worked non-stop until six in the evening. They wolfed down food whenever possible while dashing from one chore to the next. The routine was pretty demanding: Returning to the barn for night check in the evening, they skipped out the stalls, checked water and hay, and adjusted or added leg wraps, sheets, and blankets.

For housing, the farm stuffed them into a two-bedroom apartment above the barn. In exchange for their work, they rode in one group lesson a week. Kate wondered how often his staff turned over. How could people slave away month after month for practically nothing in return?

Hard work didn't scare her. But she refused to do grunt work six days a week without the benefit of lessons or being treated like a human being.

She escaped Fantasy Farm the same way she'd left

Windsong Stables—without a word. It might be rude to leave without talking to anyone, but she really didn't care.

After visiting both farms, Kate had the nagging thought that maybe her mother was right. You never knew what hid behind the polished facade at the horse shows unless you peeked behind the wizard's curtain. Was everything smoke and mirrors? Had Gentleman Jim and Beth Bradley, with their decency and their love of horses, spoiled her for the "real" world?

The last barn on Kate's list was Ben Ellis' Cherry Hill Farm in Deerfield, Massachusetts. Although discouraged by her first two farm visits, she approached this interview with excitement because her friends Wheeler and Peter kept their horses there.

She knew her friends wouldn't stay if the stable and Ben didn't live up to their reputations. And the thought of having her friends close by was comforting.

Over the years, Wheeler and Peter had gone on and on about Cherry Hill. Kate prayed their stories lived up to the hype. Based on what they said, she knew that Ben's philosophy mirrored her own. According to her friends, he trained through kindness, trust, and building a happy relationship with one's horse.

Ben was a legend in the dressage world. He'd ridden in the 2004 Olympics in Athens and coached riders at many international competitions. He was considered one of the top riders and trainers in the United States, but his real love was coaching. Under his guidance, several riders had secured spots on Olympic, World Equestrian Games, and Pan-American teams.

Wheeler and Peter had told Kate that Ben understood that the person standing on the top of the podium on any given day was the one who had his head screwed on straight. Because he recognized the importance of the mental aspect of competition and getting riders to the ring in the right mindset, he could help riders reach their personal best while many other coaches failed.

Those trainers ignored the psychology of sport and treated all their horses and riders the same. As a result, they had inconsistent results. According to her friends, Ben custom-designed his approach for each rider's needs. He nurtured the insecure ones, ranted at the lazy ones, humbled the arrogant ones, and turned the fearful ones into warriors. He did whatever it took to unlock the potential of each horse and rider, including leading them to the ring and slapping the horse on the butt so they charged forward with confidence. And he did it all with compassion and love for both horse and rider. That's what her friends told her, anyway. Now she had a chance to check it out herself.

As the day of her interview drew closer, Wheeler and Peter insisted they drive Kate there. They didn't want her going alone. So, on a sunny day in late May, they picked her up in Rhode Island and brought her to the stable in Deerfield. The trip zipped by as they consumed cup after cup of coffee and snacked on junk food and gossip.

Wheeler drove through the gates of the farm well after five in the evening. Sugar maples stood like the queen's guards on either side of the long driveway.

Even though she'd seen pictures of the farm, the real thing blew her away. She covered her open mouth with her hands. "Omigod! Look at that!"

She pointed to a life-sized bronze statue of a horse standing on powerful hind legs.

Wheeler chuckled. "Impressive, eh?"

With the wide-eyed wonder of a child on her first trip to Disneyland, Kate said, "The farm is so beautiful! I can't imagine living and working here."

Wheeler and Peter laughed at Kate. "Close your mouth, Chica. You look like an awestruck teenager at her first Rolling Stones concert."

Kate giggled. "Hurry and park, Wheeler. I want you guys to show me around. I'm happy it's late so I can get my first look when we're alone. I don't want everyone to know what a dork I am right off the bat. They'll figure it out in time. This way I can act as sappy as I want and only you guys will know the truth—which you already do!"

Wheeler zipped his Escalade into a parking spot, and the three of them jumped out. "True dat. But we love you anyway."

Each of the boys held one of Kate's elbows and guided her through the main door. Looking up, she almost tipped over backwards while staring up at the domed tongue-and-groove ceiling in the foyer.

"Whoa! I feel like I should say a prayer or something."

The boys got a kick out of looking at the place through her eyes. They'd been at Cherry Hill for so long they took the splendor of the place for granted. After gazing at the ceiling until she got dizzy, Kate bent down to touch the golden brick floor, which was reminiscent of an eighteenth-century church.

Kate laughed at herself. "Still praying here!"

Peter broke the spell. "Beautiful to look at but a bear to sweep, as you'll soon find out. C'mon. We want to show you more and tell you about some of the people before it gets any later. Audrey manages the barn, and Jason is a working student. Melissa helps out part-time when she can. Ben also has two stable hands, Mateo and Phillipe. Louise, another working student, recently left, which is why there's a position open."

Used to dominating the conversation, Wheeler chimed in, "Audrey and the working students get group lessons on school horses six times a week, train the young horses under supervision, and ride the boarders' horses when they're away."

Because it was late, Wheeler and Peter took Kate on a quick barn visit and said they'd show her more the next day. They told her they'd take her on a tour after her interview with Ben, which he'd scheduled for nine. They didn't know if Ben had made other plans for Kate, but if not, they'd be close by, they promised.

After the tour, the three of them went to dinner at Fitzwilly's, a local hotspot. While they wolfed down their food, Kate peppered the boys with questions about Ben, the horses, the farm, the working students, and the boarders.

Finally satiated with food, drink, and answers to Kate's questions, they headed to Wheeler and Peter's apartment. The two had rented a place nearby in Florence so they could live close to the barn. Despite the comfortable guest-room bed, Kate's mind spun at warp speed as she fantasized about riding and training with the famous Ben Ellis.

# FIVE

*Chris*

Chris took the three horses under his wing. As he became a familiar face, Carolyn Tabor dropped her defenses and began to trust him, especially when she saw how he tended to her horses without seeming to have any agenda.

One day she stopped him as he was about to get into his car to leave and invited him onto the porch for a lemonade. Chris took a seat near her. They chatted a bit and, then she told him more of her story.

Carolyn gripped her frosty glass with one hand as she fiddled with the hem of her worn T-shirt with the other. "It's ironic that my ex-husband gave the horses to me as a gift. At one time, they commanded a hefty price. The broodmare is 16 years old. The youngster is her three-year-old son. She's from the Donnerwetter line, which has fabulous temperaments. We bought her because we thought her babies would keep me in horses for years to come. In the meantime, he bought the FEI horse to get me in the ring. He's an eight-year-old Dutch gelding from the Nimmerdor line. We hoped he'd my big-time dressage horse while we trained the youngster."

"Sounds like a great plan, at least in theory."

"I know I'm not doing right by these horses, but I'm stuck with them. I wish I could find someone to take them and give them a good home. If I could do that, they'd be gone tomorrow."

Chris' heart leapt. "Really? Maybe I can help you there, too. Tell me a little more about them."

Carolyn looked off toward the field where the horses were. "From what we were told, the Nimmerdor gelding had a lot of education for such a young horse and a good show record in Europe. But I wasn't very experienced, and that damned horse knew it. When I rode him, he'd get so strong in my hand. I haven't ridden him in almost a year, so he's badly out of shape. The mare has a fabulous temperament and excellent gaits. She's produced several top dressage horses. We hoped the baby would inherit her genes."

Chris made a split-second decision when he heard her story. Trying to find homes for three horses might take some time, so he asked if he could buy them himself. He had no idea what kind of money she'd take. He offered her what he considered a fair price for unfit horses in poor condition.

Carolyn exhaled. "You know what? When we bought them, they were worth a lot more money than that. But, as I said before, I'd almost be willing to pay to someone take them off my hands. So, here's what I propose. Give me a dollar so we can make it legal, and they're yours.

Chris' eyes widened in disbelief. "Seriously?"

"Yes, seriously. I know it sounds crazy, but if I don't place them soon, some organization will take them away from me anyhow. And this way it'll be one less thing I have to cope with."

Chris beamed. "I'm on it. Give me a day or so to make arrangements for them."

As soon as he got home, Chris called Erin Miller and asked her if he could quarantine the horses at her barn, since he took lessons there. Boarding the horses there would be the perfect solution because he could keep an eye on them.

Erin said, "Chris, you're doing a wonderful thing. And I'd love to help. But our farm doesn't have a quarantine barn. If these horses are in such poor condition, they need to be kept separate from others until you're sure they're healthy. I can ask some friends, but it might take a little time to find the right situation."

"I understand," Chris answered. "I just wanted to get them out of their current circumstances as soon as possible. I appreciate your putting the word out."

Erin added, "Why don't you go on some of the forums on the internet? That way you can widen your search.

DressageChat.com is a good place to start."

"That's a great idea! I'll do that right now. Thanks, Erin. See you tomorrow."

After hanging up, Chris opened his computer. He googled DressageChat.com and posted an urgent request. The subject line read, "Help me rescue three horses."

> *I've come into possession of three horses. They're in a dangerously poor state. Can anyone help me house these horses while I nurse them back to health and find people to adopt them?*
>
> *I'll pay all their expenses. My barn can't help because they don't have a place to isolate them.*
>
> *I need a facility with a separate barn so I can quarantine them. They don't seem to have anything contagious, but you never know. I think they're just in very poor condition from neglect. Ideally, the barn should be within thirty minutes of Leverett, Massachusetts, where I take lessons, so I can get there every day.*
>
> *Please message me if you can help or have any ideas of what I can do.*

# SIX

*Kate*

The next morning, Kate, Wheeler, and Peter arrived at the stable just before nine o'clock. The boys hugged her and pointed her toward Ben's office. They wished her luck as they headed off to check on their horses.

Kate mustered her courage and tapped on the door to Ben's office.

She gulped at the rumble of a masculine voice. "Come in."

Stepping through the doorway, Kate said, "Hello, Mr. Ellis. I'm Kate Gage. Is this still a good time for us to get together?"

"Yes, Kate. I'm expecting you," Ben said. He was seated at a desk that was piled with papers. "Have a seat. Let's chat, and then Jason can take you on a barn tour and introduce you to some of our boarders and their horses."

"Sounds good to me."

"Today is Audrey's day off," Ben told her. "She started out as a working student but grew into the manager's position. She's the reason the stable runs like clockwork. While she's gone, Jason can fill you in on your duties. Then you can spend the afternoon checking out lessons. This is a big commitment for you, Kate, so I want you to weigh everything before making a decision. But first, I'd like to ask you some questions. Okay?"

Kate blushed. "Of course."

Ben's eyes swept her features, taking in her flushed cheeks, and he softened his voice. "Why do you want to do an apprenticeship at Cherry Hill?"

Kate's looked down at her hands and said, "Many reasons. But you're the biggest one. I've studied your book from cover to cover, and I love your philosophy."

Kate knew from Ben's book, *The Mind of an Athlete,* that although he believed in the value of persistence and determination, he didn't rely solely on grit. Instead, he showed his riders how to reprogram their subconscious minds.

In the book, Ben explained that programming your subconscious was simple and effective. All you had to do was install new "software" in your mental computer. The new software contained two programs for peak performance—vivid visualization and positive self-talk.

Using this approach, Ben produced many top riders. People demanded his services. Kate would consider herself more than lucky if he accepted her into his working student program. She'd used his ideas about visualization and self-talk for years and been amazed by the results.

Kate admitted, "My copy of your book is so dog-eared. I've underlined nearly every sentence with a yellow highlighter. I suppose it's time to get a new one."

"I'm flattered," Ben said, smiling. "I'll be sure to sign your next copy."

Kate looked at him. "When I read it, I feel like you're speaking directly to me. Like you, I consider the mind as important to training as skills and technique. Probably even more so."

"That's true. It's hard to succeed without the right mind-body connection."

Kate nodded and added, "And like you, I never blame my horse. If he's disobedient, the first thing I do is check that he's not in pain. The next thing I do is check my position in case I'm giving muddy or conflicting signals."

"Well, it sounds like we're on the same page there." He rocked back in his chair and said, "Or maybe you're just a clever 'interviewee.'"

Kate's ears turned red again. She hoped his teasing meant he approved of her answers.

Ben smiled and asked, "So what's your ultimate goal?"

Kate hesitated, and then said quietly, "It's always been my dream to own a barn. In the meantime, I want to learn every aspect of the horse business, from veterinary care to stable management to training to supervising clients and students."

"Didn't the Equine Studies program at the university expose you to all of that?"

"Oh, yes. And Beth Bradley is amazing. But I only got

to go to the farm three or four times a week. That's not enough."

Ben leaned forward and said, "Those are big goals. It'll take quite a bit of time to learn all that. Which leads me to my next question. What type of commitment do you plan to make to reach your goals?"

"My mother gave me a year to follow my dream," Kate said. "She hopes I'll get discouraged and go back to school after I get a taste of this life. But I'm realistic. Even though I've been riding since I was a kid, I know a year is a drop in the bucket. I'm willing to take as long as it takes, and I don't plan to cut corners. So, I'll be here for a long time if you want me. Don't worry. Mom hopes this is a whim, but she'll soon see it isn't."

"Well. Like most mothers, I'm sure she has your best interests at heart."

Kate added, "Yes. She does. But I need to learn how to do my job well and not shortchange the animals or the clients out of my own ignorance. I know that doesn't happen overnight."

"Exactly. By the way, how do you feel about showing?"

Kate bit her lower lip as she considered her answer.

"I've shown most of my life at small shows and I love it. It's great experience and helps me learn how to prepare others for competition. But if you think it's a problem for me to show and juggle my duties, I don't have to compete. I know the job comes first."

Ben surprised her by saying, "You're welcome to show as long as it doesn't interfere with the care of the boarders or their horses. In fact, I like my working students to compete. They learn so many things, from how to organize their time to planning good warm-ups to making split-second decisions in the ring to earn the most points—or lose the least amount of points if things go south."

"You're kidding! That's fantastic! I know I'd learn so much."

"Win or lose, it's a great opportunity," Ben said. "And as long as you learn something new every time you compete, I consider a show successful. We look at the entire picture here—not just placings from any particular horse show."

"That sounds wonderful!" Kate's eyes lit up. At the same time, she worried about how she'd afford show clothes and entry fees. "Who would I show?"

"One of the school horses. They're all seasoned and do their jobs well. If you're lucky, you may even catch some rides on one of the boarder's horses."

"Omigod! That would be amazing."

Ben glanced at her slender body and asked, "Do you have any physical limitations, like back problems or anything, that would make it hard for you to do your work? As I'm sure you know, there's a lot of heavy lifting that goes on in a barn."

Kate opened her arms wide and said, "No, I'm great. I know I don't look all that strong, but I'm as healthy as the proverbial horse."

"That's good to hear. And how do you think you work

with others? That's not always an easy task in a barn full of strong egos. I'm not just talking about co-workers. You'll also have to deal with demanding and spoiled clients. They challenge the best of us."

"I learned to be diplomatic early on," Kate said. "When I was at Jim Bailey's stable, I had to deal with a lot of different personalities."

Ben nodded at her answer. "You're going to need those skills here. Some of our clients will test you more than you can imagine. So, that's about it. Do you have any questions for me?"

"Where would I live? Do you have housing here or do I have to find an apartment?"

"You'll share the apartment above the boarders' wing with Audrey. She'll help you settle into the routine and show you how we like things done. As you know, the horses always come first."

"Of course. How many horses would I take care of?"

"You'll take care of four of the boarders' horses. We limit the number because we like to have the time to pamper them. Of course, there'll be times you have to fill in when Audrey, Jason, Mateo, or Phillipe have a day off or another commitment. But usually, it'll just be four. If we come to an agreement, Audrey will assign your horses to you. She has a knack for making good matches."

"I can't wait to meet her."

Ben continued, "Since Audrey's not here today, this morning I've asked Jason to show you where everything is. Here's the schedule in a nutshell." He swiveled in his chair to point to a whiteboard behind his desk. "Breakfast starts at six. Then you turn the horses out while Mateo and Phillipe clean the stalls. They occasionally help with turnout, but their main job is to do the stalls while the horses are outside."

Kate took notes as she listened to Ben's instructions.

"You'll bring them in around eight. Put them in their stalls for a few moments so they can pee and have a drink. Then start grooming. Check the white board in the tack room every day so you know the order of the boarders' lessons and who to prepare first. The boarders have either private or semi-private lessons in the morning—unless they have a conflict."

"Okay." Kate kept jotting the details in her notebook.

"Start feeding lunch at eleven and let the horses rest while you eat. The group lesson starts at one o'clock. If you stay, you'll start on Jolicoeur. He's a good guy, generous to a fault, and you'll have fun with him. Usually you'll take your lesson on Joe or another school horse, but sometimes you'll ride one of the young horses or one of the boarders' horses if their owners are away. After the group lesson, I teach outside students. Their riders prepare their own horses, so you won't have to groom, tack up or bathe them afterwards. But keep an eye on the students in case they have questions or problems."

"I will, of course."

"In the afternoon, you'll either hand-walk or turn the horses out for a second time, depending on the weather. If it's nice and they can get turned out, use the time to tidy up or clean tack. As you know, there's always something to do in a barn. We feed dinner at four. Then skip out the stalls and sweep the aisles.

"You're free until the evening, which is when you do night check—check the water buckets, give each horse a flake of hay, and check that sheets, blankets and leg wraps all look secure. You, Audrey, and Jason can decide how you want to rotate night-check duties. It doesn't matter to me who has which night as long as someone covers the barn. In any event, it goes without saying that each time you walk by any stall, peek in and make sure all is well even if it's not one of your personal charges. Any questions?"

"Not right now, but I'm sure I'll have a ton by the end of the day. I'll write them down in my notebook, so I don't forget anything."

Kate deliberately held off asking any questions about days off or coffee breaks. She sensed that fishing for what was in it for her or when she got some down time turned off a potential boss. She hoped that focusing on what she could do for the barn would tell Ben a lot about her work ethic.

Ben's chair scraped across the floor as he pushed himself away from his desk and stood up. With the interview over, Kate thanked him for his time, headed out of the office and closed the door behind her. She took a deep breath, but before she could exhale, a young man sashayed up to her.

# SEVEN

*Chris*

Chris held the phone away from his face and stared at it. "Excuse me? Did you say Ben Ellis?"

"Yes. This is Ben. Is this Chris Barton?"

Chris' mind raced, wondering what the well-known trainer could want from him. "Um, yes, it is. What can I do for you, Ben?"

"I'm calling about the horses you want to rescue. My wife, Maria, likes to cruise around the Dressagechat forum. She told me about them last night. Did you find a situation for them?"

"No, I'm afraid not. I stop over there twice a day to make sure they have hay and water, but I haven't found a place yet."

"Well, I might be able to help you. Maria says you'll pay their expenses but that you need a place to quarantine them until a vet says they're healthy. I have a small barn at the back of my property at Cherry Hill. It's far enough away from the main barn so they won't expose other horses to anything contagious."

"You're kidding."

"No, I'm not. Here's what I'm willing to do. I'll give you a free lease for the barn itself. You cover bedding, feed, fly spray system, manure removal, and do all the work. How's your schedule? Will it be hard for you to be there so often to care for them?

Chris was quick to reassure Ben. "It won't be hard at all. I'm a freelancer for the Herald so I can work anywhere at any time, including when I'm at the barn keeping an eye on the horses."

"Well, that's terrific. Oh, and by the way, the barn has three small turnout areas. I haven't been up there for a while, so I'll send some of my staff up to check out the fencing."

Chris could feel his heart beat faster. "Ben! That's amazing. I'm knocked out by your generosity. Thank you hardly covers it. When can I bring them over? As soon as you give me the word, we'll be there."

"My pleasure, Chris. I'll ask my people to go up there today to check things out. I'll call you back tonight with an update."

Early that evening, the phone buzzed again. "Barton."

"Hi, Chris. It's Ben Ellis."

"Hi, Ben."

"Two of my staff went up to the barn to check it out. I told them you'd be using it as a quarantine center for three horses. I expected it to be in good shape because the last people using it were conscientious."

"I see," said Chris, wondering if he was about to be turned down.

"The barn itself needed a little airing out. Audrey and Jason opened the windows and got rid of the cobwebs. They found water buckets and feed tubs and scrubbed them out. They also walked the fence line around the paddocks. Everything looks good, so you can come as early as tomorrow afternoon if that works for you. Call County Line Feed today. That's who we use. They're fast and will deliver supplies in the morning. I'll also call Dr. Roberts to come tomorrow afternoon and have a look at them."

Chris gave a low whistle. "Jeez, Ben. You're a lifesaver."

Ben laughed. "No worries. Let's just get those horses healthy."

# EIGHT

*Kate*

Jason's sudden appearance the moment she left Ben's office startled Kate. She spun around, looking for the welcoming faces of Wheeler and Peter, but Jason put his hands up to stop her.

"Hello, dahling! I'm Jason, your designated tour guide this morning. The boys know I'm taking care of you. They're in the barn getting their horses ready to ride."

Not much taller than Kate, Jason had the undernourished look of someone for whom meals were more of a chore than a pleasure. But his hazel eyes sparkled with humor.

"Oh. Okay. Nice to meet you, Jason," Kate said, catching the guy's out-there-but-harmless vibe.

Jason bowed deeply. "We're going to have so much fun! Follow your fearless leader."

He offered her his hand. Then with mock formality, he twirled her underneath his arm and lowered her into a dramatic dip. Kate giggled and her mouth fell open as she gazed at the vaulted ceiling above her.

"As you can see, this is the rotunda," he said as he snapped Kate upright into a ballroom dance hold.

"The offices are there on the right. Oh. Silly me. You already know that because you just came from Ben's office. But Maria also has an office right there, right next to Ben's. She's Ben's wife. The lunchroom and bathrooms are just past Maria's office. You're free to eat or have coffee in the lunchroom or go to your apartment on your breaks. And those mahogany doors in front of us lead to the viewing room that overlooks the indoor arena. Right this way, my dear."

With Kate in tow, Jason climbed the five steps to the viewing room and flung the double doors open with a flourish so she could step inside ahead of him. She took one glance at the floor-to-ceiling windows facing the indoor arena, the luxurious leather chairs and couch and the heavy wooden tables, and said, "Wow! It's an understatement to call this a viewing room."

Jason watched as Kate wandered around the room. She touched everything to convince herself it was real. Stopping in front of a huge framed poster, she read the words:

> *Winning starts with what the world never sees. It's unending training, well into the night, and mornings in the barn before dawn.*
>
> *It's every step, every motion, and every scoop of*

*feed. Nothing can be left to chance. You strive for perfection. You learn when to push and when to pull back, never asking more of your horse than you would ask of yourself.*

*Because you know in your heart, how strong you finish is determined before you even step into the arena.*

Kate whispered to Jason, "I love that! It's like a prayer."

"Well, that's Ben's philosophy. His main interest is training true horsemen and horsewomen. As far as he's concerned, horsemanship begins in the barn. He hasn't got much patience for the Dressage Queens. You know, those riders who want their horses handed to them and thumb their noses at doing work behind the scenes, where there's little glory or recognition. But he knows he has to pay the bills, so he puts up with them."

Kate nodded and continued exploring the viewing room. Her mouth fell open at the sight of the television on the wall to her left. "Omigod! Check out the size of that TV! I've never seen one that big before. I feel like I'm in a movie theater. I can smell the popcorn from here!"

Jason walked over to it. "Yeah. Cool, huh? We use it to go over our rides and training videos. Sometimes Ben gives lectures in here. We learn a lot that way. As I'm sure you know, horses don't always look the way they feel. Ben's critiques give us a reality check."

"What a great idea. Ben really covers all the bases."

"We also watch top riders to see what they do in the ring. It gives us something to aspire to, and we study how the successful ones deal with mistakes."

"I get that. I totally learn a lot from watching top competitors. I love studying people like Charlotte Dujardin and Isabell Werth. The way they handle competition is such a great image to hold in my mind's eye."

"Yeah. The best riders make split-second decisions and stay calm even when they screw up. Unlike a lot of amateurs, they don't get stuck on the last mistake. They know they can't change what's already happened and thinking about it could mess them up because they can't focus on what's coming up next." He motioned her back toward the door. "C'mon, slowpoke! Let's check out the stables and meet the horses."

"Sounds good to me," said Kate, beginning to relax.

They walked back down the steps, and Jason resumed the tour. "When Ben built the barn, he designed it in a U shape. The viewing room is one short side of the U. There are twelve box stalls on each of the long sides. Ben keeps the school horses and some empty stalls for horses that come in for training on the left. The boarders live over here on the right side."

Kate cocked her head. "Does everyone use the same tack room and wash stall?"

"Oh, no. Each side has its own room for tack and cubbies for the riders' personal stuff. There are two grooming areas in the middle of each row of stalls. It's almost like two separate barns, although there's only one feed room and laundry room. You'll also find two wash stalls at the end of each aisle. You can even use the wash stalls for grooming if a lot of horses have to get ready at the same time. Just be sure not to let any hay or shavings go down the drain or we'll have a big mess."

"That makes sense. I'll be really careful. I can see how much thought Ben put into the layout."

Like a museum tour guide, Jason walked backward up the aisle. "Let me introduce you to our horses. Ben said you'll look after some of the boarders' horses so you'll spend most of your time over here. But as you know, the horses don't read our work assignments or check the clock unless it's time to feed." He guffawed at his cleverness.

Kate's lips tugged upward. "That's for sure."

Turning serious, Jason said, "You have to pitch in wherever and whenever you're needed—even at three o'clock in the morning if there's a colicky horse."

As they approached each stall, the horses moseyed to the front of their boxes. They enjoyed interacting with people, so they came to say hello rather than hiding with their heads in a back corner and ignoring passersby. Jason swung each door open and gave Kate a little history on each one, including the traits that were endearing or, sometimes, made them like special-needs children.

When they got to the third stall, Jason lowered his voice to a whisper and said, "Now don't tell the other horses, but here's my favorite baby." He opened the stall door and Kate found herself looking into the soft brown eyes of a beautiful gray mare.

"Her name is Kamilla. Cathy Demerest owns her.

Kammie is such a character. I'm not really a mare person, but when you find a good one, she'll give you her heart and soul. I'm so lucky that I get to ride her when Cathy can't get to the barn."

Kate stroked the mare's face and said, "Hi, girl. It's nice to meet you. I hear you're a very special lady."

Cammie bumped Kate with her nose as if to say, "Of course I am."

Kate giggled at the mare's pushiness. Turning to Jason, she asked, "How old is she?"

"She's ten and can do everything in the Grand Prix. She's a blast to ride, but like many mares, she's very opinionated. If you don't ask her to do something in the right way, she'll blow you off—like if your timing is a bit off and you ask for flying changes every third stride, she'll randomly throw in changes every second, fourth or even every stride. I think she gets a kick out of it. But she sure teaches you how to be more precise with your aids."

Kate threw her head back and laughed. "I love when they have so much personality."

Jason gently pushed Kammie back so he could close her stall door. "Don't pout, my little princess. I'll be back later, and I'll give you a good spa treatment."

Continuing their way up the aisle, Kate sighed. "They all look so content. That tells me a lot. Anyhow, I can't remember half of what you've told me, but I'm excited about everything. Who do you think I'll take care of?"

Jason cocked his head. "I'm not sure. Audrey will let you know. You might take over Louise's horses. She left a few weeks ago. We've covered her horses since she left, but it's been tough. Mateo and Philippe pitch in when the schedule gets tight, so that helps, but it'll be great to have another pair of hands."

Jason continued the tour by leading her past the wash stall and out the back of the barn. "We have three arenas outside." He pointed slightly to the left and said, "One is here behind the indoor school. Another is behind the school horse wing where we're going next. We also have lessons in the main arena, which runs parallel to the boarders' wing on the right side."

"That's great! That way no one has to deal with too much traffic."

"They all have footing that feels like you're riding on a cloud. The main ring and indoor arena have mirrors along one entire short side. There's also a round pen near the back arena for longeing and work-in-hand. Plus, there are tons of trails and open fields where you can ride. Ben set the entire farm up so well, right down to the placement and the number of turnout areas. He doesn't want us to overuse the pastures. That way the horses always have grass. I hate when I see paddocks that have been eaten down so much that they're just dirt."

Jason gave Kate enough time to take it all in, and then headed over to the other side of the barn. The layout mirrored the boarders' aisle.

As they started to stroll down the aisle, Jason said, "I want you to meet all the horses, of course, but I want to introduce you to Jolicoeur in particular because that's who Ben will probably start you on."

"Oh, yes. He did mention his name. I can't wait to meet him."

"Here he is," Jason said as he swung the first stall door open.

Jason and Kate were greeted by a big chestnut gelding with a huge white star and intelligent, curious eyes. Jason stroked his neck and told Kate, "You're going to love him. Everyone does. We mostly call him Joe, but he's also earned the name 'The Professor.' You couldn't find a better teacher. He knows his job inside and out."

"He's lovely. I'm so excited about getting to ride him."

Jason looked fondly at Joe. "He cracks me up. He can size someone up almost instantly. If he has a beginner on him, he's careful and kind. He won't spook or do anything that might unseat his rider. But if he feels you can handle it, be prepared for a happy buck or a scoot across the ring. He has quite a sense of humor, and it's obvious that he loves his job."

"I know we'll get along great, but I'll be sure to stay on my toes."

Jason slid Joe's door shut, and he and Kate continued down the barn aisle, stopping at each stall so Jason could introduce her to all the horses.

By the time they reached the tack room, Kate was overwhelmed. "I doubt I'll remember anyone's name or quirks by the end of the day. I've already forgotten half of what you've told me."

"Don't worry. I won't quiz you. It's a lot to take in. You'll get to know the horses one at a time as you work with them. There's no rush. We all went through the same thing. Before long you'll know every horse inside and out."

Kate wrinkled her brow. "If you say so. I just hope it doesn't take me too long. There's so much to learn."

"Let's take a brain break, and I'll show you how to get to the apartment. It's above the boarders' wing. Living at the farm makes it convenient to keep tabs on everyone. There are also two baby monitors up there so you can hear what's happening on each side. Just make sure you take Fantastique's feed tub out of her stall before you go to bed. Otherwise, Audrey says, you'll listen to her play drums on it most of the night. Her nickname is 'Reggae Fanny.'"

Kate chuckled. "I love that! Do they all have nick-names?"

"Yeah. Once we get to know them, it sort of just happens. I can't wait 'til you meet Audrey. She's been here about three years. She came as a working student so she could work off her training and housing, but she's grown into the paid manager's job. If you ever have questions about barn protocol, schedules, care, feeding or medicine, ask her. If you stay, which I hope you do, you'll share the apartment with her. Don't let her size fool you. She's a spitfire. And she can ride rings around just about anyone—which, of course, she knows."

# NINE

*Kate*

After her disappointment with Windsong Stables and Fantasy Farm, Kate was delighted by the atmosphere at Cherry Hill. The students welcomed her. The boarders seemed pleasant and helpful. And the owner and head instructor, Ben Ellis, was a skilled and compassionate teacher—not to mention easy on the eyes.

After her tour, Kate Velcroed herself to Jason to study the morning routine. Then she spent the afternoon watching lessons.

Kate loved Ben's techniques. He didn't use a cookie-cutter system. She knew that many barns used one method for every horse and rider. God help you if you didn't fit in. You and your horse fell by the wayside and no one cared about the fallout.

Ben tailored his programs to meet an individual's needs. And he never seemed to raise his voice or get frustrated. It didn't matter if he taught potential team riders or novices. No matter their ability, it was clear that he believed everyone worked hard and therefore deserved his best. As Jason had explained, Ben didn't show favoritism, regardless of the size of his riders' checkbooks or the extent of their talent.

By the end of the day, Kate knew without a doubt that she wanted to be at Cherry Hill. On her way to talk to Ben, she lingered in the barn to say goodbye to the horses and people she'd met that day.

When she finally got to the office, she peeked through the open door. She found Ben huddled over some paperwork in his office. "Excuse me, Mr. Ellis. Can you spare a minute?"

"Of course, Kate. How was your day?"

"Fantastic! I thought I'd have a million questions, but I don't. Usually when it comes to important decisions, I like to mull things over and write out a list of pros and cons. But I don't feel like I need to do that. If you'll have me, I'd like to start as soon as I can."

Ben's face broke into a thousand-watt smile. "Wonderful! You'll make a great addition to our family. But you need to reassure me that you'll agree to at least a one-year commitment. We talked briefly about your mother's expectations. Will that be a problem for you or her?"

Kate shook her head, her mind drifting back to her promise. "Don't worry. I'll make sure it isn't an issue. I can't wait to get started."

"Excellent. Why don't you take a couple of days to get organized and move into the apartment this weekend?

Plan to start on Monday. I don't teach lessons that day, so things are pretty relaxed. It'll be easier for you to learn the routine and familiarize yourself with the horses when things are quiet."

Wheeler and Peter let out celebratory whoops when they heard the news.

Wheeler said, "C'mon, guys. Let's go. The faster we get Kate back to Rhode Island, the sooner we can move her here. I don't know why we didn't bring everything at the same time. Of course Ben would want her. Kate, do you think you'll have a problem with your mom?"

Kate shook her head. "She wants me to stay in college, of course, but she understands what this means to me. She hopes working full time will discourage me, and then I'll make a more sensible decision about my future. She also knows me well enough to realize that the more she fights me, the harder I'll dig in my heels. At least I'm close to home. That's the reason I only looked at farms in New England. I can visit her and Stephanie or they can get to Cherry Hill in less than two hours. It's not like I'm moving to California."

Wheeler laughed. "I can't believe I'll get to see you almost every day just like when we were kids."

Kate hugged her childhood buddy as if her life depended on it. "Me, too! Can you stand it? Ben Ellis accepted me as a working student. I bet tons of people want that position. I'm apprenticing myself to one of the top trainers in the country. He's never gonna get rid of me!"

"Hey, guys!" Peter said. "It's my turn to congratulate the newest member of the Cherry Hill family." He spun Kate around and gave her two proper kisses, one on each cheek.

"Enough mush!" Wheeler laughed and made a sweeping gesture toward the vehicle. "Hop in so we can hit the road!"

# TEN

*Kate*

Early Saturday afternoon, Wheeler and Peter helped Kate pack her few belongings in the Escalade. By midafternoon, they were ready to leave for Cherry Hill.

Lillian and Stephanie followed them out to the car, and mother and sisters hugged each other.

Struggling past the lump in her throat, Lillian said, "I'll miss you so much, Darling! But you're following your heart's desire, so I'm sending you on your way with all my love. Please call me when you arrive so I know you're safe."

Kate blinked back a tear. "Oh, Mom. I love you guys so much, too. And I'm not far away. I'll come home to visit you and Stephanie, and you can come to the farm."

Attempting a smile, Lillian said, "Of course. We'll get together a lot. Try to keep us away! I can't stop thinking about your first lessons. Little did I realize where they'd lead."

Kate thought back to those lessons at Bailey stables. She'd obsessed about and "played" horses since she could walk. And then her mom blew her away one day when she told the girls that she'd signed them up for riding lessons.

The Gage household had always budgeted its money, but Lillian had given the girls as many opportunities as she could. She'd introduced them to everything from sports to the arts. Lillian wanted them to find their passion, and she'd be damned if she'd let her husband's desertion stop her from providing for her girls. One year, they took piano lessons. The next summer, they took ballet lessons. And another time her mom enrolled them in art classes.

Kate reminisced about the summer evening when Lillian announced her latest plan about riding lessons over a cookout of hot dogs and beans.

Kate's eyes opened like saucers as she babbled at her mom, "Riding lessons? When? Where? What do we wear?" Kate danced around the barbecue grill like a whirling dervish, barely able to breathe, let alone eat.

Lillian threw her head back and laughed. "Slow down before you knock the grill over! One question at a time. Yes, riding lessons. Next Saturday. We're going to Bailey Stables in Wayford. The owner, Jim Bailey, gave me a list of what you'll need, and we'll go shopping this week. Stephanie! Wipe that frown off your face. I've saved all winter and already paid for the lessons. It's a done deal, so relax and enjoy it."

After school that Monday, Lillian drove the girls to a consignment tack store and bought them used riding boots. Mr. Bailey required that they wear shoes with heels. He wouldn't let his students ride in sneakers because of the danger of their feet slipping through the stirrups.

As they entered the store, Kate nearly swooned from the heady aroma of leather and gazed at row after row of saddles, bridles, boots, saddle pads, and riding clothes. Any horse-crazy girl would think she'd found heaven on Earth. Kate and Stephanie wandered up and down the crowded aisles as Kate added item after item to her future wish list—breeches, gloves, brushes, halters, helmet, and shirts, and a snazzy riding jacket.

The girls settled down long enough to try on some used boots. Stephanie was happy with a pair of short paddock boots. But Kate insisted she wanted tall boots that reached just below her knees. She'd explained to her mother that real riders wore knee-high boots.

Stephanie frowned at her sister. "You're such a brat. Tall boots cost more than paddock boots. And you're only nine. You'll outgrow them in a year. Don't make mom spend money she doesn't have on something that won't fit after one summer."

Kate stuck her tongue out at her sister. "I've already thought of that. I'll get boots that are too big for me. That way they'll fit for several years. I can stuff the toes with socks until I grow into them."

Stephanie shook her head. "All right. Do what you want, you little monster. You will anyhow."

After trying on several pairs of boots, Kate settled on some well-worn brown boots. Those boots represented all her dreams. She'd even ended up sleeping in them the entire week before her first lesson!

Unfortunately, even after doing all their shopping at the consignment store, Lillian hadn't been able to afford gloves and breeches for both girls. So, they'd gone to Walmart and bought leggings and winter gloves from a sale bin.

The farm supplied protective helmets, and Mr. Bailey had told Lillian to make sure the girls braided their hair or tied it back in workmanlike ponytails.

Lillian grumbled a little about what she thought of Jim Bailey's military stuffiness. But she admitted to the girls that she appreciated his attention to detail and safety. She didn't want Stephanie or Kate to get hurt because of sloppy rules.

After their shopping spree, they grabbed some lunch at McDonald's and then drove home. Kate ran to her room and closed the door so she could savor the moment alone.

She laid the leggings, gloves, and boots out on her bed and stared at them in disbelief and anticipation.

The wait for her first lesson on Saturday seemed like the longest week of Kate's life. Time crept by like a boat dragging anchor. She kept track of the days by marking them off on a calendar in the kitchen. Each night before she went to bed, she'd count down the days. "Four more sleeps until my lesson. Three more sleeps until my lesson."

That special Saturday finally came. Stephanie was calm and thought that Kate was acting like a goof. She told her sister, "I'm older than you and can handle anything that gets thrown my way. Still, why didn't mom sign us up for painting or pottery? Better yet, diving! Horses are smelly and horseback riding is silly."

Kate's eyes widened into moons. "How can you say that? You know I love horses! This is my dream come true."

After breakfast, they headed to their old Chevy Nova for the short drive to Jim Bailey's stable. On the way to the car, Kate bounced on the balls of her feet like she was springing on a pogo stick.

Over the years, her mom had driven past the entrance to the stables many times on her way to do errands. Each time Kate's heart beat faster as she gazed at the navy sign with the gold script lettering that said, "Bailey Stables." She'd squeeze her eyes together and try to will her mom to pull into the driveway. It never happened.

And now she was about to enter that enchanted kingdom. As they drove down the rut-filled dirt driveway, Kate savored the butterflies dancing around in her stomach.

When the road widened into a parking area, Lillian held her breath and gawked at the barn. What probably at one time had been grandiose just looked tired and in need of TLC. Kate reacted differently. The once-majestic stable reminded her of a castle, complete with towers and turrets. It transported her back to a romantic era she'd only read about or seen in the movies.

Lillian pulled into a parking spot. Kate jumped out of

the car and slammed the door behind her.

"Hey, slow down, Sweet Pea!"

But the words fell on deaf ears. Lillian looked at Stephanie, and they giggled at her unbridled enthusiasm.

Ponytail swinging, Kate bounded toward the double doors standing sentry at the entrance to the barn. She skidded to a stop and stared at the doors. They reminded her of pictures she'd seen of Buckingham Palace. She held her breath. If she dared to place even one foot over the threshold, would someone stop her and throw her in the dungeon? Taking a chance, she cracked one door open and tiptoed into the palace.

A rich bouquet of smells—fresh hay, oiled leather, and horses—filled her senses. She inhaled deeply, hoping to draw that fragrance into every pore of her body. If someone could bottle that scent, they'd have the most wonderful perfume ever—among horse lovers, at least.

Then she heard a symphony of sounds. Peaceful munching of hay. Soft nickering. Rustling straw. Rhythmic brushing of brooms across brick floors.

As she stood in the doorway, she gawked at the dusty cherry cabinets adorning every wall. Engraved trophies, plaques, trays, and medals stuffed the cases. Other frames held ribbons buried one on top of another from decades of horse shows. Time had faded the original bright colors of the ribbons and tarnished the trophies. But Kate only saw treasures. She fantasized about having boxes filled with colorful ribbons and cases of silver trophies in her own barn one day.

Rows of framed pictures hung between the trophy cases. Kate squinted at the faded black-and-white pictures of horses jumping big walls and horses and hounds fox hunting. She felt the history of the farm and the riders who'd honed their craft here. As she stopped to study the details of each picture, Lillian and Stephanie caught up to her.

"Jeez, Short Stuff," a breathless Stephanie said. "It's about time you stopped!"

"I'm sorry, Steph. I'm way too excited to slow down."

"Well, I'm sure they have some rule about running in the stable. You don't want to scare the horses, do you? You'll get us kicked out."

A dark veil swept across Kate's face. It horrified her to think she'd get thrown out of her personal nirvana before she'd even had a chance to begin. "Oh, no! I promise not to scare the horses. Besides, we're not even in the…"

The arrival of an elegant man dressed in riding attire and an Irish cap cut her words short. He introduced himself as Jim Bailey and welcomed them to his stable.

Gentleman Jim, as his staff called him, gave them a quick tour of the barn, showing them who they'd ride.

The grooms had cross-tied both horses in the wide barn aisle and prepared them for the girls. Gentleman Jim assigned Stephanie to Old Lady. The bay mare was the perfect mount for beginners. At twenty years old, she did her job like a pro. Her soft eyes reflected volumes of patience, and the white hairs dotting her face highlighted her experience.

He assigned Kate to Little Lady. The mare resembled Old Lady because they were the same color—brown, with a black mane and tail. But because of her youth, she didn't have white hair on her face. And despite being only seven, Little Lady excelled at babysitting novices because of her placid and forgiving nature.

Kate remembered thinking Gentleman Jim lacked creativity when naming his school horses, but she didn't care. She only cared about this magnificent creature in front of her.

As Little Lady's groom tacked her up, Kate approached the mare and gently stroked her neck. Then when she couldn't stand it one more second, she buried her nose in Little Lady's shoulder to inhale the sweet fragrance of horse.

Before leaving for Ben Ellis' farm, Kate felt the nostalgia of that first lesson envelop her like a blanket. Then she snapped back to the present and embraced her mother.

"You're right. Mom, I'm so grateful for all the sacrifices you've made over the years so I could ride."

Her mother hugged her back, blinking away tears. "You're so welcome, honey. Now go pursue your dream with everything you have inside of you."

Wheeler settled behind the wheel of the Escalade as Peter claimed shotgun. Kate climbed into the back seat and turned to look at her mom and Stephanie.

Lillian swiped at the tears in her eyes with the back of her hand and spoke to Wheeler through his open window. "Off with you then, Wheeler. Drive safely. Precious cargo, you know."

Wheeler smiled. "Yes, Mrs. Gage. No worries." Mother and daughters blew kisses at each other and waved as he drove the car out of the driveway. They didn't stop until they couldn't see each other anymore.

Kate turned around to face the front as tears filled her eyes. Kate missed her mom and Stephanie already, but anticipation about this new chapter of her life swept away the pain of leaving. She felt very grown up and couldn't wait to immerse herself in Ben's program.

# ELEVEN

## *Kate*

Once back at Cherry Hill Farm, Wheeler and Peter helped Kate get her stuff out of the car. Since she didn't bring much, they got everything in one trip and climbed the stairs to Audrey's apartment.

When they got to the upper landing, Peter tapped on the door. It flew open as if caught by hurricane-force winds. Mischievous blue eyes in an elfin face greeted them.

Wheeler pushed through the door ahead of the others and ruffled Audrey's pumpkin-colored curls. "Hiya, Munchkin! Wait 'til you see who we brought you. Ta da! This is Katherine Gage, known to most people as Kate. But those of us who love her call her 'Blister Butt' because she'll ride from dawn to dark if you let her. Kate, this is the famous, or should I say infamous, Audrey Rhodes."

Kate held her breath as she prepared for the reaction

she'd endured throughout high school. Would Audrey think she was an oddball? Bracing herself, she peeked through a curtain of ebony hair at the girl who probably only cared that Kate had the right body for working and riding—strong and long.

Kate's shyness didn't faze Audrey. In her typical bulldozer-like fashion, she plowed right through Kate's reserve.

The diminutive girl gave Kate the once over and said, "Welcome, Katie! Come in, come in! I'm so glad you're here. Boy, do we ever need help. Since Louise left, we've been running around like chickens with our heads cut off. Oh, sorry. Does that sound rude? We'd be glad you're here even if we weren't short-handed. The boys say you can ride anything. And they also say you're not afraid to get your hands dirty. That gives you high marks in my book."

Extending her hand, Kate said, "It's nice to meet–"

Audrey chattered on. "Jason probably explained that you'll work in the boarders' wing. Most of the boarders are nice but some are real DQs. You know, *Dressage Queens.* They're pompous, arrogant prima donnas. They expect the royal treatment. Remember, you're a working student, not a working slave. I'll warn you right now. Watch out for Alyssa Smithson. I'm sorry I'm dumping her on you, but Louise took care of her horses, so it makes sense for you to take over. Actually, I find the DQs entertaining. They live in their own world, that's for sure. The stories I could tell you."

It didn't surprise Kate that Audrey couldn't wait to gossip. Kate had been around stables long enough to know that horse people loved juicy rumors. When friends greeted each other, they didn't say, "How are you?" Instead, they asked, "Did you hear that Claire Brenden's horse tore a suspensory ligament because she worked him too hard in deep footing? How stupid was that?" Or, "Did you hear that Anton and Miranda split up?"

Barn life revolved around who slept with whom, who lost a sponsor, who got kicked out of which facility, who dumped their trainer for a new one, or who bought an expensive horse that they couldn't ride.

Friends thought spreading information made them important, and the stories became more bizarre and less accurate with each retelling. If you had your finger on the gossip pulse, people welcomed you at their parties.

When Audrey finally paused to take a breath, Wheeler threw his head back and laughed. "Around the stables, we call Audrey 'Horsemen's 4-1-1.' If you need information, just ask her. She insists she knows everything. When she screws up, we call her 'Horsemen's 4-1-2.'"

Audrey stuck her tongue out at Wheeler. Kate had a suspicion it'd be wise to avoid getting sucked in by the girl's affability. From what little she'd seen and heard, underneath that friendliness lay someone who could be a fierce adversary if she thought she'd been crossed.

According to Wheeler and Jason, Audrey had earned her manager's position in Ben's stable through her intense drive. She'd impressed Ben at shows because, although she rarely rode the most talented horses, she always placed well. As a technician in the ring, she often won simply because she put in mistake-free tests.

Before Kate had a chance to respond to either one of them, a sudden blow from behind nearly knocked her to the ground. She turned to see a golden body wiggling furiously, right down to the tip of her tail.

Audrey laughed at the pup, who almost outweighed her. "Sorry. This is Bella. Isn't she gorgeous? She's ten months old and has no manners and is the love of my life. As you can see, she's beside herself that you came by just to visit her."

Kate squatted down to rub the Golden Retriever's silky head, and the puppy immediately heaved herself onto her back. With legs flailing like an overturned centipede, she insisted on a belly rub. She punctuated her request with one continuous whine that started deep in her throat.

They all laughed at the pup's antics, and Audrey said, "I swear she can hold a gurgle in her throat longer than Barbra Streisand can hold a high note."

Audrey motioned to the left with her head. "C'mon, Katie. I'll show you to your room, and then we can eat. I'm starving!"

Peter puffed out his cheeks like a squirrel gathering nuts for the winter. "You're always starving, Audrey. I think you have the metabolism of a jet engine. If I ate like you, I'd weigh more than my horse." Audrey eyed Peter's waistline and decided he passed muster.

But then she glanced at Wheeler and was quick to warn him to lay off the beer. Audrey never minced words. Whatever came into her head popped out of her mouth. As Kate soon discovered, she'd tell you the truth—whether you wanted to hear it or not.

Wheeler caressed his thickening stomach and laughed. "I'm working on developing a deep seat by emulating the dressage masters."

Wrinkling her nose, Audrey said, "Well, you've made a good start. You're beginning to look like the Pillsbury doughboy. How about you work off some of that by setting the table? Katie, you have a seat and relax. Enjoy it now, because once Monday comes, sitting and relaxing will be a distant memory."

Soon the four sat down to dinner at the cozy kitchen table. Assuming they'd be tired and hungry after their drive, Audrey had made a huge pot of spaghetti and a salad.

"Thanks so much for making dinner," Kate said as she dug in with relish.

Audrey smiled and forked more salad onto her plate. "Being the new girl comes with its own set of challenges, so I just wanted you to relax and feel at home on your first night."

While they ate, Audrey filled Kate in on what she could expect as a working student. "I'm sure Jason already told you about the schedule, but, if not, here's what we do on an average day. We feed breakfast at six. Once the horses finish eating, we turn them out in the paddocks and help Mateo and Phillipe muck their stalls. By eight, we bring them in and start grooming."

"Yup. That's what Jason told me," Kate said, taking a sip of water.

Audrey continued, "Boarders like Wheeler and Peter are on partial care, so they groom and tack up their own horses. Others are on full care, so we do everything for them—groom, tack up, bathe, medicate, wrap legs, and clean tack. As I mentioned before, you'll be in charge of Alyssa Smithson's horses—Celebrity and her new horse, Chancellor. Chancellor arrived from Holland two weeks ago. We're giving him time to recover from the trip and adjust to all the changes in his environment. You won't need to do much with him yet except turnout, hand walking, and grooming. Alyssa won't start hacking him right away—and that won't be until you ride him for several days so she knows he won't be too fresh for her."

Kate interjected, "Is he in the second stall on the right? I think I remember him. He's lovely."

Audrey set her napkin down next to her plate. "Yeah, he is. He hasn't been here long enough for us to know him very well, but he seems very sweet. And I love his wide blaze and all the white on his legs. He showed at Prix St. Georges and Intermediare I in Europe and got good scores. They taught him all the Grand Prix movements while he was there, but he hasn't competed at that level yet."

Kate raised her eyebrows. "Wow! That's pretty cool. I can't wait to see him in action."

"Watch out for Alyssa. She's our premier Dressage Queen. She won't lift a finger to help anyone and loves ordering staff around. Alyssa thinks she's powerful and important, but I think she's pathetic and needy. She'll do her best to put you in what she considers your place. But you'll be fine if you take her with a grain of salt instead of getting offended."

Kate absorbed Audrey's words like a sponge. "Sounds like she's projecting her own insecurity. I've come across lots of riders like that since I was a kid."

Audrey continued, "She cracks me up because she's delusional about her abilities. Alyssa's convinced she's destined for the Olympics. Unfortunately, she doesn't have an ounce of talent. But you never know. With Ben as her coach and those two fabulous horses, anything is possible. Get this. Supposedly she—excuse me, her daddy—spent hundreds of thousands of dollars for each of the horses. Whatever Alyssa wants, Alyssa gets. What a waste of super horses."

Kate stared at Audrey. "Yikes. I should be so lucky to have the money for that kind of horse."

Audrey rolled her eyes. "Alyssa disposes of horses the way you or I would toss out a used razor. If one doesn't work out, daddy buys her a new one. It would never occur to her they don't work out because she can't ride them. It's always the horses' fault."

Kate crossed her arms over her chest. "That's awful.

I hate it when people blame their horses for their own mistakes. It's like they think that the horses spend the night in their stalls plotting and scheming how to sabotage them. Duh!"

Audrey snorted. "I know. Remember, Wheeler? Versace lacked a work ethic. Quartermaster shut down after about fifteen minutes. And lazy Icarus plotted against her. Jeez! I would have given my eyeteeth for any of those horses. Don't you think it's interesting they all had the same issue? It would never occur to Alyssa that she might be the problem. It's obvious to all of us. After all she's the only one at the scene of every crime."

"Yeah. We remember. At least you found them homes with people who appreciated them."

Wheeler flashed a warning look at Kate. "Here's what you need to know where Alyssa's concerned. In her case, DQ not only stands for Dressage Queen. It also means Drama Queen. She's the star of her own soap opera. Make sure you don't cast a shadow on her brilliance. If you do, sooner or later you'll pay the price. Everything in her life happens in Technicolor while we peons live in black and white. She gets hysterical over the smallest things, like if three horses are working in the ring at the same time or if she doesn't like her start time at a horse show. Too much stress for me. She's a walking, talking, bleeding ulcer."

Kate listened intently and took it all in. She found the gossip interesting but didn't take it to heart. Her classmates in high school had labeled and judged her. She wasn't going to make the same mistake with Alyssa. She'd make her own decision about the girl without needing to agree or disagree with the others. Maybe she wasn't really as bad as Wheeler and Audrey made her sound.

Audrey sucked in her breath through clenched teeth and looked at Kate apologetically. "You'll also inherit Cara Griffin's horse, Artisan. We call him Artie. Cara is also a DQ, but she's a different animal from Alyssa. Don't get me wrong. She's a piece of work, too. She'll be sweet to your face. No, let me rephrase that. She'll be *too* sweet. I can't be around her very long or I sink into a diabetic coma. She'll fawn all over you, tell you how gifted you are, and that no one rides as brilliantly as you do. I can't tell if she's ever sincere or if she's just a master bull-shitter. But in either case, she makes me gag."

"At least it sounds like she's not negative," Kate said, sticking up for the girl she hadn't yet met.

"Don't worry. She won't bother you because you're the wrong sex. She has a mad crush on Ben. In fact, most new students end up crushing on him. It doesn't matter to Cara that he's married. She's a total barracuda who flirts shamelessly."

Kate suppressed a shiver. "That must really piss Ben off."

"Oh, sure. But she pisses off Ben's wife, Maria, even more. Luckily Maria knows the score. Ben and Maria hit a rough patch early in their marriage. I'm not surprised. Ben is gorgeous. Imagine what he looked like fifteen years ago? It's tempting to want to be the head trainer's golden girl."

Wheeler and Peter nodded knowingly, but Audrey didn't let them interrupt her rant.

"Many clients have tried to seduce him, and one even succeeded a long time ago. They carried on for about a month. Maria was furious when she found out. She laid down the law to Ben and told him that if he didn't keep his dick in his pants, he could say goodbye to her back as she walked out the door. Ben didn't want to lose Maria. My sources tell me it never happened again. I sure hope not. Anyhow, it seems like they worked through their bump in the road. But Maria still keeps a close eye on the students and staff."

"Who could blame her after that?" Kate asked.

Audrey laughed. "For obvious reasons, Maria can't stand Cara. One day during her lesson, Cara lifted her shirt and flashed her braless boobs at everyone. Maria pitched a fit. After that, she started calling her 'Tutti Frutti' after the German TV strip show from the nineties."

Refusing to be left out of the gossip, Wheeler added, "You'll recognize Cara because she dresses like a slut. I laughed my head off one day when the zipper on her skintight breeches came down during her ride, and she didn't have any panties on. Gross! She'll do anything for shock value. Maria read her the riot act, but it didn't bother Cara. She loves any attention she can get. I bet if they didn't need the money and Ben didn't adore Artie, Maria would have kicked her out a long time ago."

Audrey got up to clear the table. "Anyhow, don't worry about Alyssa and Cara. The important thing is you'll love their horses. You'll even get to ride them when the DQs can't make it to the barn. I don't know much about Chancellor, but Celebrity and Artie are generous and talented. They'll turn themselves inside out to please you. It's worth putting up with their idiot owners to ride those horses. You'll also take care of Jackie Kellogg and her mare Fantastique. You'll enjoy them. Jackie appreciates anything you do to help her. So, no problem there. But I wanted to warn you about our resident DQs. Sorry about dumping them on you."

Kate knew she had to pay her dues, and DQs didn't bother her. She was all too familiar with them because she'd helped out the spoiled little girls who rode at Gentleman Jim's stable. Gentleman Jim had about as much use for the princesses as Ben did for the DQs. But the bottom line for both of them meant they had to run viable businesses and make ends meet. The bottom line for Kate meant being able to work around these creatures she loved.

"Don't worry. I can handle them."

Audrey continued, "Okay. Back to the schedule. We feed lunch at eleven. Our group lesson is at one o'clock. Most days, it'll be you, me, Jason, and sometimes Melissa, who lives in town. Melissa usually rides Kammie. You'll meet her tomorrow. She works at First National Bank, so she can only come on the weekends or on a Monday if it's a holiday weekend like this one. She doesn't have a ton of money, but she's dedicated and pitches in whenever we need an extra pair of hands. Ben helps her out by letting her ride in the group for free. He hasn't said it in so many words, but he considers her lessons therapy for her. She has serious issues, and the horses help. Plus, they love her, and she's a great worker."

Peter piped up and said, "Yeah. She's super nice but thin as a rail. We're convinced she has some kind of eating disorder. For a while no one ever saw her eat. Then last year she actually began coming to dinners with us. We assumed she'd gotten some professional help and worked through what looked like anorexia. But she still didn't gain any weight. I think she substituted one eating disorder for another. No one has any proof, but if you go out to eat with her, she'll leave the table at least once during a meal. She claims she has a small bladder, but we think she's throwing up in the bathroom."

Wheeler said, "Well, if you met her mother, you'd understand why she'd have an eating disorder. The woman is overbearing, to say the least. The only thing Melissa can control is what she does or doesn't put in her mouth."

Audrey rolled her eyes. "Add the pressure of the dressage world to monster-mom, and you have the perfect formula for an eating disorder. I mean whoever decided we should wear white breeches for competition? Why not choose a slenderizing black or navy? Why won't anyone admit that women have round thighs? Jeez. Look at Isabell Werth! It hasn't slowed her down any."

"Yeah, you're right about the pressure." Peter agreed. "Remember what happened to Martha Robbins last year? Martha won a big Prix St. Georges class at the Devon Show in Pennsylvania. She won a pair of custom-made breeches as one of her prizes. She was so excited and ran over to her sleazebag coach, Dietrich Krause, to tell him the news. Krause said, 'That's great! What size are you going to order?'"

Peter pinched his lips together. "Krause's question confused Martha because custom-made breeches don't have standard sizes. She assumed she'd get measured. When she asked him about it, Krause laughed at her and said something like, 'Of course you'll get measured. But I want you to get them two sizes too small and fit into them in four weeks. Then he turned his back to her and snickered with his buddies."

"I remember," Wheeler said. "Martha sputtered something about having a pear-shaped body. She tried to explain that if she dieted until she had thin thighs, the rest of her body would look like she'd just escaped from a concentration camp. Krause's answer to that was to tell her to 'look into liposuction'! Can you imagine? How rude!"

Audrey nodded her head. "Yeah, it's an unforgiving sport. It's easy to fall into the trap of conforming to some absurd standard. Anyhow, you'll meet Melissa tomorrow, and I'm sure you'll like her."

Kate kept her expression blank. "I'm sure I will."

"Let's see. Where was I in the schedule? I keep getting distracted by the boys. Oh, yeah. In the afternoons, we either turn out or hand walk, ride whoever needs exercise, clean tack, do laundry, and feed by four. We do night check around eight or nine. By the time you're done, you'll be ready to fall into bed. If you're like me, you'll sleep like you're in a coma. Before you know it, the alarm will go off at five-thirty and by six, we start all over again."

It sounded great to Kate. She loved to work hard. She thought back to her childhood summers when she mucked out ten box stalls each day in exchange for one five-dollar group lesson a week on a school horse. From the beginning, working around the horses was a labor of love.

Kate had felt sorry for the wealthy little girls who arrived at the barn in their tailored riding habits. Much like the DQs at Cherry Hill Farm, their grooms prepared their horses, and at the end of their rides, the girls handed them back to the grooms. Chauffeurs or governesses picked them up right after their lessons. They never hung out at the barn or played with their horses. God forbid they get dirt under their manicures or on their expensive clothes.

Even though Kate knew she'd probably never own a fancy horse, she wouldn't trade places with those poor little rich girls for anything. They'd never build the kind of bond with their horses that only came from spending hours in the stable with them.

Kate knew the princesses considered her a second-class citizen. She'd heard whispers about her thrift-shop riding clothes and second-hand equipment. And although the princesses and DQs smiled politely at her because that's what they'd been taught to do, they made it obvious they felt superior.

But that didn't bother Kate. For all the trappings of wealth and fancy horses, she had the two things they wanted more than anything in the world—the horses loved her, and she could ride.

# TWELVE

*Chris*

Chris called Ben and told him he planned to arrive at Cherry Hill the next day between five and six o'clock. He'd confirmed that the feed store would drop off what he'd need in the morning.

Ben told Chris he'd asked Audrey and Kate to meet him, take him to the barn, and help him get settled.

By five, the girls sat munching apples at the upper fork of the drive leading to the quarantine barn.

Audrey grilled Kate. "How did this Chris sound? Like a nutcase? Did Ben say anything about her? I'm picturing a hoarder with thirty cats. Or a peace and love flower child from the sixties who lives in a commune."

Kate waited until she finished chewing. "Ben didn't say anything, and we've only been in touch by e-mail. But I can tell what kind of person she is by her forum post. She doesn't tolerate any kind of animal abuse. Chris is taking on these horses at her own expense—vet bills and all.

She doesn't just talk the talk. She walks the walk. Most people say, 'How terrible!' but don't do anything. Chris didn't walk away. You're such a cynic, Audrey."

At that moment, the sound of an engine distracted the girls from their speculation.

Kate's ears perked up. "Oh, listen. Here comes a truck and trailer now. I wonder if Chris hired a commercial shipper to bring them over. It never occurred to me she might not own a rig. We should have offered to get the horses for her."

Both girls leapt to their feet as a silver truck hauling a 4-Star trailer lumbered toward them. They waved their arms like two people stranded on a deserted island. The driver stopped when he got to the girls and rolled down the window.

"Hi there! Looks like I found the place. How do I get to the quarantine barn?"

Audrey pointed to her chest and then flicked her thumb toward Kate. "Hi, I'm Audrey. This is Kate. Keep going to your left. Once you get over the hill you'll see the barn. It's not far. Wait! We'll go with you and show you. Where's Chris? Is she behind you in her car?"

With a lopsided smile, the driver tipped his hat back with his thumb to reveal crystal blue eyes. He drawled, "No, ma'am. She's not."

The driver's answer puzzled the girls. It seemed out of character for Chris to hire a driver to transport the horses and not follow them. They wondered if there'd been a problem. Was Chris going to dump the horses on them and not show up?

Audrey's eyes narrowed as she regarded the hot-as-hell driver. "Is everything okay? Did she have car trouble? We thought she'd come with the horses."

Seeing the confusion on her face, the driver smiled to reveal a dimple on one cheek. "Oh. Sorry for the misunderstanding. I'm Chris. Chris Barton."

Kate's face registered shock. "But...but...you're a man!"

Chris' grin morphed into laughter. "I hope so. My folks will be glad to hear that! I'll be damned. You mean all this time you thought I was a woman?"

Kate's face and ears turned three shades of red. "Well, I thought most of the people on the DressageChat forum were women."

"Well, sorry to disappoint you," said Chris with a grin. "Hop in. You can show me where to go."

With Kate in the lead so she could get to the door first, the girls skittered around the front of the truck to the passenger side. Kate held the door for Audrey so her roommate would have to climb in ahead of her. She was too mortified to sit next to Chris.

Kate clung to the door, wrapped in a shroud of embarrassment while Audrey peppered Chris with questions. "Did they load okay? How did they travel? Ben said the owner practically gave them to you. What's up with that?"

Chris laughed at Audrey's machine gun-like questions. "The mare and three-year-old didn't want any part of the trailer. So I led the gelding on first through the side ramp and backed him into one of the stalls. He's a little spooky, but I coaxed him in with carrots. Once he was on, the other two loaded okay. I didn't hear a peep out of them the whole trip. They're too weak to put up much of a fuss about anything. It took me less than an hour to get here so at least they didn't have to deal with a long ride."

Audrey's nostrils flared. "What kind of moron allows something like this to happen?"

Chris let out a puff of air. "When you see their condition, you'll wonder why she didn't pay me to take them. Actually, she practically did. I only paid a dollar for all three of them to make it legal. They're emaciated. You can count every rib. The sun washed their color out, and they're covered in scabs."

Audrey snorted and slapped her arms across her chest. "How despicable."

He added, "By the way, please thank Ben for calling Dr. Roberts. That's great that he can come out tonight. I hear he's terrific. He'll have his hands full with these three. They need some serious nursing."

"Well, Kate and I can help out when you're not around. Right, Kate?"

"Um, yes. Of course." Audrey's offer to pitch in surprised Kate. But as she peeked at Chris out of the corner of her eye, she understood the reason for Audrey's sudden interest in helping.

With his dirty blonde hair and sparkling eyes, Chris had the same rugged good looks and seductive voice of

Chris Hemsworth, the actor from the movie *Thor*. Kate continued to study him from beneath lowered eyelids as he eased the trailer up the driveway.

While he drove, Audrey pressed Chris for more information about himself. "So, what do you do for work? If you own a rig like this, I imagine you do pretty well for yourself."

Chris laughed at Audrey's forwardness. "I'm actually just a writer for the *Herald*. I freelance and mostly do features—human interest stuff. Right now, I'm working on a piece about a local self-taught classical pianist. He's a fascinating guy, and I love that I can work from anyplace at any time. As long as I get my pieces in by Wednesday each week, my editor is happy."

"Oh, that sounds cool. It's so nice that you get to pick your own subjects. I'd love to be able to write, but I'm afraid I don't have much talent in that area."

Chris gave Audrey a side eye. "Don't be so sure about that. Even though I studied journalism in college, my first articles were pretty terrible because they were so dry. I learned to make them more interesting just by doing it over and over again every week. And, of course, reading features in the big papers. I get The New York Times and some others."

"Hmmm. Maybe. But I think I'll stick to training horses for the time being and leave the writing to people like you. Oh. Here we are. I hope the horses are comfortable here."

When they arrived at the quarantine barn, Chris

stopped the truck and leaned muscular forearms on the steering wheel. He stared at the tidy building with its ad-joining paddocks. "It's perfect. I don't how to thank you."

Kate said quietly, "Don't thank us. Thank Ben."

Flinging his door open, Chris stepped down, his boots crunching on the gravel. "Let's get these guys out of the trailer and settled into their new home. I hope they han-dled the ride okay. I drove like a snail so they could keep their balance."

The girls jumped out of the truck and followed Chris to the back of the trailer. He put the ramp down, and they all stared at the horses. Horror and anger overtook Kate. The young horse looked mildly curious about his surroundings, but the older horses just hung their heads and ignored them.

Kate shook her head. "How could anyone let animals get into this condition?"

"It's appalling, but the owner isn't in much better shape herself," Chris said. "She's so depressed about her divorce that she can't take care of herself, let alone ani-mals. I'm just sorry that it had gotten to this point before I got involved."

Kate said, "At least you did something. And it's a huge something. Most people don't bother."

Chris tossed three lead ropes to the girls. "Here you go. You're probably right. It's so sad."

They hooked the ropes to the horses' halters before removing the butt bar. Chris unfastened the youngster first. Since he seemed the brightest, he assumed he'd be the most eager to get off. Chris backed him down the ramp and handed him to Audrey. She led him off to the side and waited for the others before heading to the barn.

Chris brought the gelding down next. The big bay minced down the ramp as if walking on ice and made it without incident. Chris handed him off to Kate and returned for the mare.

As she staggered off the trailer, her knees buckled, and she almost fell. Chris stopped on the ramp until she could balance herself. He crooned, "Easy, girl. You wait here a moment. I'll help you down when you're ready."

He stroked her neck and whispered to her until she looked like she had all four legs underneath her body. Then he guided her the rest of the way down, step by step.

Chris explained, "She's in the worst shape, for sure."

Kate reached over from where she was holding the gelding and patted the mare to comfort her. "It's okay, sweet girl. We'll take care of you. You'll love your new home."

They led the horses into the boxes, where Kate and Audrey had filled the twelve-by-fourteen stalls with fragrant shavings. All three horses headed for the buckets and gulped down water. After drinking, they circled the stalls, and then rolled in the fresh bedding. The mare didn't want to get back up.

Chris furrowed his brow. "Let's get her back up for now," he said. "I think it might be bad for her to lie down for too long. We'll have to see what Dr. Roberts says. He might decide to let her rest any way she wants. But for now, let's help her up."

It took all three of them to encourage the mare to stand. Once up, she moved over to the bucket and sipped a bit more water.

"That's a good sign. I'm sure they're all dehydrated. The owner told me she thought they'd be fine because there was a stream running along the back of the field. But I checked it out. It had dried up to just a trickle. She didn't even realize it. I'm surprised they survived with so little water. I'm sure Dr. Roberts will give them fluids. They hadn't had grain for months. They've been living off whatever they can forage in the pasture. Slim pickings, for sure. Probably the safest thing to do is to give them some wet hay until Dr. Roberts gets here."

Audrey asked, "What are their names? Do they have papers? From what Kate said, it sounded like they're well-bred."

Chris cocked his head. "You know what? I don't know. And I didn't ask the owner. I just wanted to get them away from her. I've been calling the older horses 'the mare' and 'the gelding' and the youngster 'kid.' Want to name them?"

"Let's wait and see what suits them once we know them better."

The trio stood shoulder-to-shoulder in silence listening to the munching of hay. Soon they heard a truck rumbling up the driveway.

Kate's head popped up like a dog hearing an unfamiliar noise. "That must be Dr. Roberts. Yay!" She headed out to greet the vet with Audrey and Chris hot on her heels.

The vet parked his truck, checked his cell phone, and then climbed down out of the silver dually for his last farm call of the day.

A smile cracked Dr. Roberts' face. "Hi, everyone. I see the horses arrived okay."

Kate said, "Yes, but they're in bad shape. Thank you so much for coming out so late in the day. Dr. Roberts, this is Chris Barton. He rescued the horses."

The vet walked toward Chris, shot his arm out, and clasped his hand. "Pleasure to meet you, Chris. You're doing a wonderful thing."

Chris looked at the man whose salt-and-pepper hair and weathered skin belied his youthful energy and said, "It's nice to meet you too. When you see them, you'll know why I didn't have a choice. I'm most worried about the mare."

"I wish I could say I haven't seen neglect cases before, but it's far too common. Often, the abuse isn't deliberate. It's from ignorance and not understanding the needs of horses. One of the most common things I see is people putting too many horses out on poor pasture. They end up eating each other's manure, and besides being malnourished, they get infested with worms. That sets them up for all kinds of problems."

Dr. Roberts took his time examining the horses. "I'm going to draw blood and do a complete panel to check their general health. Based on their dull coats and pot bellies, I assume they're loaded with worms, so I'd like to take care of that as soon as they can tolerate the treatment."

The vet pinched a fold of skin on each horse's neck. When the skin stayed tented and didn't smooth right back down, he said, "They're severely dehydrated. I'm more concerned about that at the moment than the malnutrition, so I'll give them some intravenous fluids. I'll hang some bags of lactated Ringer's solution so we can get fluids and electrolytes into them. Can anyone stay here tonight to monitor them? Someone needs to make sure the tubing doesn't kink and also change the bags. I want to get at least twenty liters into them overnight."

"I'd planned on staying anyhow," Chris said. "I have a cot in the back of the trailer. I'll set it up in the aisle so I can keep an eye on all of them."

Dr. Roberts nodded and said, "Great. Give then some wet hay tonight. And tomorrow let's start them with some small, soupy bran mashes twice a day. If all goes well, we'll add a little grain to the mashes next week."

While he talked, the vet picked at a scab on the older gelding's body. "It looks like they've got some rain rot. I'll leave you some Betadine scrub for it. When they're up to it, pull off the scabs and clean the wounds with the Betadine. You'll probably have to do that for the next couple of weeks. When you can turn them out, the sun will also help dry out the sores. Any questions?"

Chris spoke for the group. "That seems clear to me. When will you have the results of the blood work?"

"I'll have them by tomorrow and will call you right away. Kate, I have the barn number and your cell. Chris, can you give me your cell number?"

"It's 555-7137."

"Okay," said the vet. "They appear stable right now. Call me if you see any changes in their condition. Good luck. I hope you have a quiet night."

As Dr. Roberts drove away, Kate's fear about being alone bubbled up. She turned toward Chris and asked, "Will you be okay by yourself tonight?"

Chris said, "I'll be fine. I'm a great camper. And I wouldn't have it any other way."

Kate dropped her gaze and said, "Okay. I'll bring you some food later. It won't be fancy, but you won't starve. There's a toilet and sink in the tack room there on the right. Here's my cell number in case you need any help with them."

Kate and Audrey took one last look at the horses and then said goodbye to Chris as they headed down the hill to their apartment.

# THIRTEEN

*Kate*

As the girls walked home, Kate spoke first. "Those poor horses. I hate seeing animals suffer like that. I don't see how they could have survived much longer if Chris hadn't come along."

Audrey said, "I know. I get so angry. People who abuse animals need a taste of their own medicine. Get this! I heard on the news the other day about some nut from Virginia who buried his seven-month-old puppy in a hole in the backyard. He covered the hole with boards so there wasn't much light or air. He didn't give the pup any food or water for days."

Kate shook her head in disbelief. "Omigod! That's terrible. He should be put in jail for animal abuse! What happened to the puppy?"

"A neighbor got suspicious when she heard whining. She called the Humane Society, and they rescued him. When they asked the man why he did it, he said he was teaching him not to dig holes. Can you imagine? Like a puppy could ever figure out the connection between digging holes and being buried alive. Someone should bury that guy in a hole without food or water."

A tear trickled down Kate's cheek. "I don't get it. People should have to have a license to own animals." She squeezed her eyes shut to block out the image of the puppy. "And not to change the subject or anything, but I'm mortified that I thought Chris was a woman. I just assumed he was since most of the people on the forum are women. I'm so embarrassed."

Audrey's eyes twinkled, "He'll get over it. I thought it was funny. He's quite the eye candy, though, don't ya think? Why don't you do something about it?"

"I suppose. I hadn't noticed," Kate lied. "I was thinking about the horses. Besides, I've got enough on my plate without complicating my life with men."

"Oh, get real. You're not that busy. There's always time for romance. Spice up your life a little. I wonder if he's married." Before Kate could react, Audrey went on. "Nah. I doubt he's married. If he were, he would've said something about calling his wife to tell her he'd be staying here tonight. Besides, I didn't see a ring. Not that that means anything. When you come back with food tonight, find out everything you can about him. How can someone that yummy, not to mention nice, be unattached? Hmmm. He's probably gay."

Kate raised her voice. "Audrey! Stop trying to play matchmaker. I'm telling you I'm much too busy, and anyway, I'm not interested."

Her feisty friend shook her head. "C'mon, Katie-girl. It's about time you got a life. And I think that one just drove into our driveway with three starving horses. If you're not gonna do something about it, I might just have to step up to the plate."

Kate was surprised by the wave of jealousy that flooded through her. She admitted that claiming her life was too busy for romance was just an excuse to avoid getting involved in a relationship. The thought of getting close to a man terrified her. She'd never shared her history with anyone except Wheeler. But her mind betrayed her by frequently replaying the horror of the rape that had traumatized her since her teens.

As they neared the main stables, Kate's mind drifted back to the moment that changed her life.

As a devoted fifteen-year-old barn rat, at the end of each day, she'd sneak up to the hayloft to wait for her mother to pick her up. She loved the solitude of the loft. It was her special place to daydream and relax after chores.

One evening, she was so lost in her dreams she didn't hear footsteps coming up the steps. Startled out of her reverie, she scrambled to her feet at the sight of one of the racehorse grooms looming over her.

Jimmy Smith groomed for the horses who were at the stable for lay-up from various injuries or to rest between races. Since those horses lived in a different barn at the far end of the property, Kate seldom saw the grooms except in passing. She knew their names, and they acknowledged each other with a wave. But that was the extent of their interaction.

When he saw her, Jimmy leered at Kate. He slurred, "Whassa matter? Are you too good to say hello to me?"

Kate stammered, "Uh, uh...I thought I was alone."

"Nah. That's not it. I've seen you around before. I bet you think you're better than everyone and won't lower yourself to talk to the likes of me."

Kate backed away from Jimmy, but he continued to stalk her until he pinned her against the wall. As he leaned in toward her, she turned her head to avoid his rancid breath.

Turning her head away seemed to infuriate him. She knew it wouldn't do her any good to scream because no one was around. She tried to placate him but before she could get the first words out, calloused fingers grabbed her throat.

Kate struggled as Jimmy pounded her head against the wall. She gasped for air as he held her neck with one meaty hand and tore at her clothes with the other. He pawed and groped while continuing to ram her head against the wall.

Her ears rang. It surprised and confused her when she saw stars. She knew she had to fight. So, she mustered every ounce of strength and slammed her knee into Jimmy's groin.

He bellowed with rage. Through a semiconscious haze, she recognized the sound of his heavy belt buckle coming apart and then felt a searing pain between her legs before passing out.

As Jimmy hammered into her again and again, he hissed in her ear, "If you tell anyone about this, I'll kill ya."

# FOURTEEN

*Alyssa*

A cultured voice snapped Kate from her reverie about how lucky she was to be working at Cherry Hill.

"Good morning. You must be the new girl. I see you've met one of my horses."

Although startled, Kate finished picking dirt and grass from Celebrity's hoof. From her upside-down position, she got a glimpse of a pair of tall, black Der Dau boots and periwinkle Pikeur breeches—both top-of-the-line.

In response to the greeting, she straightened up and peeked at the fine-featured face staring at her. With an effort to overcome her shyness, she extended her hand and said, "Hi, I'm Kate. You must be Alyssa. Pleased to meet you. I'm excited to be taking care of Celebrity and Chancellor. I hear they're amazing."

The woman, who looked like a model straight from the pages of Vogue, greeted Kate with a Farrah Fawcettlike smile, only hers didn't quite reach her eyes. She glanced at Kate's extended hand, hesitated a moment, and shook it with the ends of her fingertips, as if to avoid contamination.

"Yes, of course they are. Daddy always makes sure I have the best horses. I shouldn't have to waste my time on anything that's not up to my ability." Alyssa gave Kate a warning look and said, "Has Audrey filled you in on their special needs? Especially my new horse, Chancellor? He hasn't been here long, but he's quite the hothouse flower. I'll give you a list of what he needs above and beyond normal barn care. And don't worry about expenses. Money isn't an issue, so don't buy stuff at the Dollar Store. Charge whatever you need to the farm, and I'll settle up with Ben later." Furrowing her brow, Alyssa went on, "He has all kinds of allergies, so examine every inch of his body each day. Never use a saddle pad more than once without washing it. Dried sweat is the kiss of death. He's allergic to harsh detergents, too, so the only soap you can use to wash pads, sheets, and leg wraps is something that is dye free, fragrance free and hypoallergenic. Also, once you've cleaned his bridle and girth with a damp cloth and warm water, use glycerin. Then wipe all that soap off with a dry cloth. If you skip that step, he loses his hair where the leather touches his skin."

Kate grabbed her notebook and jotted down Alyssa's instructions.

"Plus, they told me in Europe that he gets welts if you even touch him with the whip. If you see any marks, use white vinegar on them right away. You can even apply DMSO gel but be sure you don't use it when we show. Are you paying attention, Kate? If you make a mistake, you'll cost me a lot in vet bills and lost training time."

Kate stroked Celebrity's neck and stared at the girl. This DQ assumed she'd screw up before she'd even started.

Alyssa rambled on, "Also be careful when both horses get their shots. Give only two shots at a time over several weeks, or they might get stiff or even spike a fever."

Even though Alyssa had scolded her before she'd done anything wrong, it comforted Kate to learn about the horses' needs. She focused on grooming Celebrity and said, "Oh, I'll be careful. I'd hate for either of them to have problems."

"Okay. And wrap Celebrity's hind legs in standing bandages at night. Now that we're doing all the advanced work from the Grand Prix, he gets stocked up overnight because he's taking so much more weight on his hind legs."

"It must be like doing deep knee bends for him."

Alyssa bragged. "Well, it's a good thing, in case you didn't know, because it shows I'm working him correctly. Make sure you add this to your notebook so you don't forget anything."

"No problem," Kate said. "Thanks to Audrey's input, I've already started a journal for both horses, including a record of dates for shoeing, shots, floating teeth, clipping, and any special needs. I hear you'll be competing

Celebrity soon. When are you showing next?"

"We're going to the Mystic show in Connecticut. I'll compete him there. I'll bring Chancellor along to give him a road trip and see how he acts away from home, but he won't show."

Kate nodded. "That sounds like a good idea. That way you'll know what to expect when you show for real."

Alyssa looked at Kate like she was a dummy. "Well, duh. That's the plan. But for sure we'll debut at the Green Mountain Horse Show in Vermont the middle of June so he can get his feet wet. Both horses will go to Birchwood in July, and Devon in September. Birchwood and Devon are qualifiers for the USEF Training List. You do know what that is, don't you?"

Without hesitation, Kate said, "Yes. You get to ride with top European trainers. That's so thrilling. And from what I've heard about your horses, the odds of making that list are good."

"Good? Better than good. We're shoo-ins. Besides, it has little to do with odds. To make that list, you need talent and a cool head under pressure. I'm not short on either."

Kate smiled to herself. She knew that talent and a cool head sometimes weren't enough. You also needed luck, politics, chemistry with the right horse, hard work, and the stars and the moon aligning so both horse and rider peaked at the same time.

Only a handful of riders experienced all of the pieces falling into place on the one day it counted. If your entire reason for riding was to make a team, you could expect to be disappointed. Only a few lucky horses and riders earned that honor. Sure, making a team would be the icing on the cake, but fortunately for her, loving the horses and the training process were enough for Kate.

Alyssa rambled on. "Chancellor is new to the Grand Prix this year, but my plan is to get the powers-that-be at the team to add him to that training list. Celebrity is already on the list because we did well last year. He placed third in the Horse of the Year standings with the U.S. Dressage Federation, and I earned my gold medal. People at the stable talked about it for weeks. I'm sure you read about it in *Dressage Today* magazine. Ben got a lot of recognition because of us. I'm his top student."

Kate thought it was sad that the girl seemed to think she had to give her entire resume at their first meeting. The two were polar opposites. Kate wondered if she and Alyssa would eventually clash with each other. Would they be able to work well together as a team? No one made it in this sport by herself. Horse, rider, trainer, groom, vet, farrier, and a host of other support people all rode down the centerline together.

"Anyhow, as I'm sure Audrey told you, my two guys are the most valuable horses in the barn. The last girl who took care of Celebrity was an idiot. Thank goodness she left. She probably ended up getting a job mucking stalls at some hack stable. She didn't belong here. I had to monitor her every day to make sure she didn't screw up. She stressed me out completely. I pay a lot of money to be here and I expect top-notch care without having to supervise my groom all the time."

Kate picked up a jelly currycomb and massaged Celebrity's neck. He showed his ecstasy by stretching his neck forward and wiggling his upper lip back and forth. Kate laughed at his antics. She kept her eyes on the horse, and said, "No worries, Alyssa. I'll treat them like they were my own."

Needing the last word, Alyssa snapped, "Fine. Make sure he's ready by 8:40. I expect to be putting my foot in the iron by 8:45. I like to walk him at least fifteen minutes before my lesson, and I don't enjoy hurrying because you made me late. Don't tighten his girth completely. You can help me with it after I've walked him around a few minutes. And bring some bottled water with you. I'll need it when I take a break during my lesson."

Alyssa stomped into Ben Ellis's office like a spoiled child. "Honestly, Ben. Where do you find these people? What's her name again? Kit? Kim? She's as bland as milk on toast. The whole time I was talking to her, the little mouse didn't make eye contact. She acted like I was going to hit her or something. And she looks like a refugee. I bet she buys her clothes from the thrift shop. She's an embarrassment to the stables. She better take care of my horses better than she takes care of herself or she won't last long here. I don't want to be humiliated at shows.

Her appearance reflects on both me and my horses. She better clean up her act or she'll be taking care of someone else's horses."

Ben raised weary eyes from the lesson schedule he was working on and warned Alyssa with a look. He spoke as if to a child. "As you well know, her name is Kate. Back off, Alyssa. You better not start one of your one-woman campaigns to drive out another one of my working students."

"Louise left of her own accord. She was a dimwit."

"I really don't need to explain myself to you, but I've interviewed Kate thoroughly. Jim Bailey from Bailey Stables and Beth Bradley from Johnson & Wales recommended her highly. They sent me videos of her riding a bunch of different horses. She's very gifted, one of many reasons I've accepted her into the program. She works hard and loves the animals. Give her some time to settle into the routine."

Jealousy bubbled up inside Alyssa. She choked down a flip remark and said, "Well, all I care about is that nothing and no one interferes with my riding and competing Celebrity and Chancellor. As far as I'm concerned, she's on probation."

Ben raised his voice dismissively. "I'm sure you'll approve of her work. Give her a chance before condemning her. I'm serious, Alyssa. Don't intimidate her with your queen-bee attitude. I've seen you operate, and I won't allow it to happen again. Now, I need to finish this schedule, so go get ready for your lesson."

Needing to get the last word, Alyssa declared, "By the way, I didn't drive that simpleton Louise out. She was a lazy slob and didn't want to work."

Before Ben could respond, Alyssa tossed her long blonde hair over one shoulder and marched out the door without bothering to close it behind her.

# FIFTEEN

*Kate*

Kate didn't see Ben that day until she brought Celebrity to the indoor arena for Alyssa's lesson. He strode into the ring and approached her with a big smile and an extended hand.

"Good morning, Kate. We're so happy you're here. Was your trip okay? Did you find everything you need? Don't be shy about asking anyone for help while you learn your way around."

Kate gaped at Ben. Now that her interview nervousness had abated, she could get a good look at the man, who was a living legend. He was in his early forties, with dark hair and strong features, and a body made wiry and strong from years of working with horses.

She tried not to show him how much he intimidated her. "Thank you so much, Ben. I'm thrilled to be here. Wheeler and Peter drove me over his weekend. Jason gave me the tour, and Audrey helped me settle in. The farm is incredible!"

"I'm glad you like it. We're proud of the work we do here. By the way, as I mentioned in your interview, I scheduled you to ride Jolicoeur in the group lesson. Joe is a reliable schoolmaster who enjoys his job. He's the type of horse who picks up his briefcase and goes to work every day with enthusiasm. You'll find that at seventeen, he's a little stiff in the beginning. But once he warms up, he's great fun."

"I'm sure he'll teach me a lot. Do I need to know anything special about him?"

"Just plan on giving him at least fifteen minutes to walk before you start your trot warm-up. He needs that time to..."

At that moment Alyssa stormed into the arena and cut Ben off mid-sentence. "There you are, you moron! I told you to meet me at the outdoor arena because I like to walk around outside before my lesson."

"Alyssa, we're talking here," said Ben in a stern voice. But despite Ben's reaction, Kate felt her cheeks get hot. Here it was her first day, and she'd already screwed up. She slumped her shoulders to try to make herself smaller in front of Ben.

Alyssa snatched the reins from Kate and led Celebrity over to the mounting block. "Never mind. Just pay more attention next time. Wait here while I walk around and then help me tighten the girth."

In her mind, Kate heard the unspoken word "loser" at the end of Alyssa's tirade. She agreed with her. She deserved nothing less for her mistake. She was a loser. She'd never be good enough. When she died, she expected her epitaph to read, "She failed."

# SIXTEEN

*Kate*

Dan Roberts arrived to find Chris and Kate struggling to hoist the mare up on her feet.

"She's been trying to go down for the last half hour," Kate told the vet. "What should we do?"

"You've done the right thing," Dr. Roberts said. "It's okay for her to lie down to rest, but as you know, it's not good for horses to stay down too long. Their systems can't work very well that way. They need to make and pass gas. In her case, unfortunately, I'm afraid it's not going to matter. I'm sorry about this, but her tests show she's in kidney failure. She wants to lie down because she's exhausted."

Kate and Chris relaxed their hold on the mare, and she collapsed with a groan. They sat in the shavings beside her, murmuring in comforting tones while stroking her neck.

Kate crooned, "We're with you, girl. You're not alone."

Even in the middle of a crisis, Chris was calm. He asked Dr. Roberts, "Should we put her down? If she's not going to make it, I don't want her to suffer."

Before the vet could answer, the mare gasped, and her breathing become more ragged. Her sides heaved and her muscles twitched. Roberts looked at her through clinical eyes and said, "Yes, that's probably the best thing. It's a painful decision, but it makes the most sense. I'll be right back."

The vet got what he needed from his truck to put her out of her misery. But before he returned, the mare gave one last shuddery breath and her heart stopped.

Kate and Chris looked on in disbelief. They sat in the shavings in stunned silence, next to the dead mare. A kaleidoscope of emotions overwhelmed Kate—mostly helplessness and sorrow. Kate turned toward Chris with tear-filled eyes.

Chris opened his arms and Kate let him surround her in his embrace. He wrapped his arms around her like a cocoon as sobs wracked her body. She was grief-stricken, and furious at the woman who was responsible for the mare's needless death.

Chris said nothing and simply rocked her back and forth like a parent soothing a child. After a while, Kate was aware of her head pressing against his solid chest and of his comforting warmth. Even after she'd cried herself out, she allowed herself to stay within the shelter of his arms. And despite her rage and grief, she experienced the flicker of another emotion. She felt safe. It was a foreign feeling and a welcome one.

After Kate quieted down, Chris leaned back and gazed into her eyes. She surprised herself by not looking away. She'd never held direct eye contact with him for more than a few seconds. She wasn't sure what she felt. Sadness? Longing? Desire? He leaned in closer and she thought he was going to kiss her. But instead, he gently pushed her hair back from her face and stood up, giving her his hand to help her up.

Later that day, the grounds crew buried the mare. Kate knew when it was happening because Greg, the farm's caretaker, drove the backhoe up to the backfield. She stayed away to avoid being engulfed by her heart-wrenching sadness. For so many years she'd survived by numbing herself to emotions––especially emotions that, in her mind, hinted of weakness.

As a teenager, she'd resolved to leave the vulnerable part of herself behind in that hayloft with her assailant. She'd made a vow that no one and nothing would ever hurt her again. The flood of feelings that washed over her made her angry.

Her reaction to Chris made her mad, too. She'd constructed a wall around her heart. Was that barrier simply a house of cards that would collapse in the slightest breeze?

It was true she enjoyed the blossoming camaraderie

of helping Chris with the horses. But she was mortified that she'd fallen into his arms like a swooning damsel. The fact that she enjoyed the feeling horrified her even more. She liked his muscular arms enveloping her. She even liked the little thrill that rippled through her stomach when she suspected he might kiss her.

*Oh, c'mon, Kate. Be honest. You didn't just like it. You loved it, and you wanted more.*

She did love it, but the emotions also terrified her. The barricade she'd erected around her heart, brick by brick, had served her well over the years. But in Chris's arms, those walls had begun to crack.

*No. Stay aloof. Keep your distance. Avoid dangerous feelings. Too much pain possible. Vulnerability is a trap. Stay strong. That way you can't get hurt.*

Decision made. She shoved the mutinous thoughts behind the safety of her emotional fortress and distracted herself by focusing fiercely on her chores. How would it be when she and Chris ran into each other again? She'd play it cool, and that would be that. He'd get the message.

# SEVENTEEN

*Ben*

Still feeling sad about the death of the mare, Kate forced herself to shift gears and prepare Jolicoeur for her first lesson.

From her high school French, Kate thought his name meant something like "pretty heart." If it did, he sure lived up to it. She loved working around this kind and polite horse.

Once she'd groomed and tacked Joe up, she led him to the mounting block in the indoor school. He waited patiently for her to mount and adjust her irons.

When she asked the chestnut gelding to walk off, he startled her by propelling himself forward with rear wheel drive. Jason chortled as he rode by on Denali.

"Whoa! Fasten your seatbelt, Sweet Pea. He has a big walk, doesn't he?"

Kate's eyes widened as she worked to regain her balance. "I guess! Wow! He's so cool."

It didn't take Kate long to adjust to Joe's strides. She'd learned to adapt to a lot of different mounts over the years from catch riding other people's horses. Soon she reveled in the way Joe carried her along like a surfer riding a wave.

Ben came into the ring, sat on the mounting block and watched his riders. He let them walk on a loose rein for about ten minutes and then started the lesson. He loved these students' hunger to learn and their love of the horses.

Most of his other students loved their horses, too. But some had other motives for riding. Some of them, like Alyssa, seemed to consider the horses a status symbol. Others, like Wheeler, rode because he enjoyed the social life as much as anything else. Still others used riding and competing to build their self-esteem.

Ben found this last group of riders the hardest to coach because they were so fragile. If they had a good lesson or did well at a show, they were happy. If they had a bad ride, depression set in. Ben wanted to teach them to value themselves either way rather than finding their self-worth in ribbons, awards, or praise. If they loved the horses and the training process, he tried to convey to them, that would be enough.

Standing up, Ben said, "Okay, guys. Let's begin our session in the usual way. Kate, we start with walk, rising trot, and canter in a long-and-low frame so the horses can stretch. After the warm-up, do some circles, loops, serpentines, and small lengthenings and shortenings.

I'll decide what to work on after that, depending on the warm-up."

Ben sized his students up quickly. "Good, Jason, except slow Denali's trot tempo down. We know he's an eager beaver and likes to run. But when he runs, he's not in good balance. Use your back and outside rein so he doesn't get so quick.

"Melissa, shorten your reins so your hands are more forward. Right now, it looks like you're pulling back. Our Kammie is a lazy girl, and you're making it hard for her to go freely forward with your hands in that position. Your hands should receive power from her hind legs rather than steal power from them. Pretend you have a basketball in front of your stomach that stops you from bringing your hands toward your body when you give rein aids.

"Nice, Kate. Bring your right shoulder back. Imagine you want to touch the point of Joe's right hip with your right hand. That'll open up the right side of your chest and bring your shoulder back so you don't sit against the bend.

"Audrey, always check that Remmy is in front of your driving aids. He's great at fooling people. I know it seems like he's moving forward because he covers a lot of ground. But if he's really thinking forward, you'll be able to whisper with your aids and he'll 'shout' his response—not the other way around. Don't forget that one of your jobs is to make him easy for John to ride. I know you can make him look like he's motoring along on his own, but if he isn't in front of light driving aids, John is going to struggle to get him going forward."

As the riders continued warming up, Ben made precise yet positive corrections. Kate couldn't stop grinning. The thought that this warm-up indicated what was to come made her giddy with anticipation.

Ben said, "Okay, guys. That looks good. Take a break and then start some leg-yields. I want to check out the lateral work."

Even with four horses in the ring, Ben saw everything. "Melissa, that transition from canter to walk was too abrupt. Do it again."

Melissa's mouth fell open. "Whaaat? How did you see that? I was behind you. I swear you have eyes in the back of your head!"

Ben smiled at the waif-like woman. "No trick. I heard Kammie hit the ground too sharply. Now, do it again. Prepare better and think about drifting to the walk like a feather."

As Jason rode by, Ben said, "Keep Denali's neck straight in the leg-yields. If you bend his neck to the right, his left shoulder pops out and he won't cross his legs enough.... That's better, Jason. Now sit to the left in the direction of the movement so you stay balanced above him. If you lean to the right, you'll make it hard for him to move to the left. Imagine a seam that runs from the middle of the back of the saddle to the middle of the front of the saddle. Now pretend you're going to dismount. Put your weight down into your left iron without leaning forward and slide your seat over to the left. That motion gets your seat bones equidistant from the center 'seam' of the saddle. Then you'll be sitting in the middle of the horse rather than falling to the right and getting left behind the movement. That's right. Much better.

"Kate, the leg-yields look fine. Do a lengthening to freshen Joe's trot. Then after a break, start shoulder-in to shift his balance back toward his hind legs and collect him. Go to the left first."

After their walk break, Kate asked Joe to pick up the trot again. She bent him in the corner and then brought his front legs away from the wall toward the middle of the arena. She continued to keep his hind legs moving parallel to the wall so he ended up traveling on two-tracks in shoulder-in.

"Good, Kate, but use your inner leg on the girth for more engagement of his inside hind leg. If you move it back, he won't be able to bend around it. Then the shoulder-in turns into a leg yield because you've pushed his hindquarters out at an angle to the wall rather than keeping them parallel to the track."

Kate did her best to carry out Ben's instructions. She closed her inside calf on the girth, and Joe responded by bending the joints of his inside hind leg. Knowing Ben's emphasis on visualization, she imagined Joe's hindquarters lowering and his forehand elevating like an airplane taking off. As Joe's balance changed, his front end got lighter and freer, and he danced down the long side of the ring.

"That's better!" A smile split Ben's face. "Feel the difference? Do the same thing to the right and then let him rest for a few minutes."

After riding the shoulder-in to the right, Kate broke to the walk and gave Joe a loose rein so he could stretch out his long neck. "Good boy, Joe! You're such a star."

While Joe relaxed, Kate watched Melissa, Audrey, and Jason school Kammie, Remmy, and Denali. She also noticed a small group of people, including Wheeler and Peter, sitting on chairs that were set up in one corner of the indoor ring.

Others watched the lesson from the lounge, but it was too dark in there for Kate to make out specific people. She assumed they were checking her out. Her insecurity swelled like a tidal wave. She wondered what they thought of her and decided they probably thought she didn't ride well enough to deserve a position in Ben's stable. Did they feel sorry for Joe because he had to put up with her? She knew they were judging her, and that she'd never measure up.

Kate came back to the present when Ben said, "Okay, Kate. Pick up the reins and start some canter work. Do some rubber-band exercises. Alternate six strides of a canter lengthening with six shorter strides. Do that several times until you feel the power of an extension start to boil over at two-hundred and eleven degrees in the shorter strides and the uphill balance of a speed boat slicing through the water in the longer strides."

Kate loved Ben's images. She shortened the reins and

giggled when she felt the big chestnut's eagerness. Joe had enjoyed his walk break, but she felt his readiness to go back to work. It was a glorious sensation. She thought about how much she loved the horses that were volunteers. They were always willing to give you more than you asked for.

The riders continued to school their horses for another half hour. Satisfied with the session, Ben sent them on a hack around the grounds so their horses could relax and cool out. They decided to leave through the back door of the arena so they didn't have to dismount to go outside. If they'd chosen to leave by the side door, they'd have to get off in order to lead their horses down the barn aisle.

As they headed toward the large field, Kate patted Joe's neck. "Wow, wow, wow! I'm so excited. Ben is so positive and encouraging. Is this the honeymoon phase, or is he always like that?"

Audrey said, "I've been riding with him for over three years, and he's always supportive and kind. I've never seen anyone who knows classical principles better than him. You couldn't be anywhere better if you want to learn how to ride and train with empathy and correct technique."

"Yeah," Jason added. "Hang out in the arena this afternoon as much as you can and watch the lessons. Soak up everything. It doesn't matter whether Ben is teaching a beginner or coaching a Grand Prix rider—he gives the same focus and attention to detail to everyone. Some barns would horrify you. People pay through the nose to ride with the 'greats' and get little or no help. I've even seen trainers on their phones selling horses while they're supposed to be giving lessons. I guess it boils down to ethics and pride in what you do."

Kate shook her head and said, "I know. I saw it first-hand when I interviewed to be a working student. Why don't the riders leave and train with someone else?"

"Who knows?" Jason shrugged. "Maybe they enjoy the prestige of saying they ride with someone famous even if they only get crumbs. To some people, it's more important to be able to brag at a cocktail party that they ride with so-and-so than it is to actually learn how to ride. They delude themselves that if they ride with top trainers, they must be future stars. A lot of the time it's all about image."

The horses seemed to enjoy their leisurely hack around the field as the girls and Jason continued to discuss the dynamics between trainers and their students. Kate didn't understand why anyone would put up with verbal abuse—much less pay for it. If you took someone's money, you owed them a service. She didn't know which was worse, not providing that service or the yelling and scolding she'd seen at Carlos de la Vega's Windsong Stables. The other students accepted that treatment as a given, but that part of the horse world infuriated Kate.

# EIGHTEEN

## *Kate*

When they finished their hack, Kate brought Joe to the wash stall to take off his tack and give him a shower.

Wheeler and Peter rushed up to her. Peter gushed, "Great job, Honey!"

Wheeler added, "How do you do that on a horse you've never ridden? I'm so jealous. I'm the worst catch rider. It takes me at least a week to get comfortable with a new horse. But you got on Joe and rode him like you've been partners for years."

"It's not me, guys." Kate protested. "Joe is so well-trained that all you have to do is imagine what you want, and he does it."

Wheeler shook his head. "Ya know, my little love chop. One of these days you'll learn how to take a compliment. It's insulting to argue with someone who says something nice to you. You don't sound humble. It sounds like you have no respect for their opinion."

Kate looked horrified. "Oh, no, Wheeler. You know I didn't mean it like that. It's that Ben and Joe deserve all the credit. Ben trained that horse so even a cretin could ride him."

Wheeler grabbed the sides of his head and pulled his hair straight out. "Kate. You're not a cretin. Stop it! You're giving me a headache!"

"Okay. Okay. I promise I'll work on taking compliments better. But I get so uncomfortable. I always think people are just being polite. Or they have some kind of hidden agenda."

Peter moved closer to Kate and said quietly, "You know, hon. I learned a long time ago that the inside of you is looking at the outside of everyone else. Everyone feels the same way. So, the insecure child in you looks at the rest of the world and assumes everyone else has it together. You think you're the only one who's a mess. Well, guess what? All those people who seem so poised and self-assured are looking at you wondering how you're so confident while they're so screwed up."

Wheeler added, "Anyhow, whether or not you want to hear it, you impressed everyone. That includes the buzzards that were hiding in the viewing room. And I could tell the way you rode Joe thrilled Ben. That old horse danced around the arena like Nureyev."

Kate scraped the excess water from Joe's body and asked, "Who was in the viewing room? I couldn't really see who was there."

"Alyssa was there," Wheeler said. "God forbid she'd come into the arena with the rest of us. I'm sure she didn't want you, a mere working student, to think she had any interest in your riding."

"I'm not sure who the others were. Lots of people wandered in and out, but I did see John Davis. He's the guy who owns Remmy. Even though Audrey was riding his horse, he was glued to your lesson the whole time instead of watching them. John only started riding about ten years ago. You know how frustrating that can be. It's hard to develop an independent seat if you don't start as a kid."

Wheeler looked skyward and mused, "Remember all the crazy games we used to play, like sitting sidesaddle and then doing backwards somersaults off our horses? Or standing on the saddle and then walking and trotting to see who'd fall off last?"

Kate giggled at the memory. "I sure do! I even remember running up and mounting from behind like the Lone Ranger. We were nuts!"

"John is so lucky to have Remmy," Wheeler added. "The man has a lousy seat, but he does pretty well. Remmy is a saint and tolerates John bumping around on him. I think it's a waste for him to have such a nice horse, but that's what money can buy."

Peter laughed. "Too bad all that money can't buy a good seat too! I'd be first in line! I'm sure you'll meet him at some point. He likes to hang around most of the day on the weekends. We don't see him too much during the week because he travels a lot for business. He's a high-powered investment broker. He's a nice enough guy when he's here, but I hear he's ruthless when it comes to deals. Luckily, we never see that side of him."

After putting Joe back in his stall, Kate headed to the tack room to clean his bridle and saddle. She filled a bucket with warm water and wiped the sweat off the leather. As she reviewed her ride on Joe, Audrey and a distinguished looking man came into the tack room.

"Great lesson, huh?" Audrey's eyes sparkled. "Joe looked fabulous! Katie, this is John Davis. He owns Reminisce, the horse I was riding. He saw your lesson and wanted to meet you."

Kate grabbed a towel, dried her hands, and extended her fingers toward the tall, silver-haired man. "Hello, Mr. Davis. It's nice to meet you."

John's hand swallowed Kate's delicate one. "Please, call me John. We're not formal here at the stable, are we Audrey? Kate, I'm impressed with your riding. I've been here for years and seen many people ride Joe. But I have to say that I've never seen him move like that."

Kate squirmed. She felt the heat crawl up her face and tried to shift the focus away from herself. "Thank you, but really, it's all Joe. Ben has trained him so well that he practically goes on autopilot."

"You're much too modest. I've seen other people ride

Joe. He's always obedient, but he rarely dances like that. I'd give my eyeteeth to ride like you. But because of my work, I guess I'm destined to be a weekend warrior. I understand the dedication and commitment required to do what you guys do. And at my age and with my schedule, it won't happen. I feel badly for Reminisce though. He's such a great horse, and he's stuck with me thumping around on his back. Oh, well. I'm happy he puts up with me and lets me learn on him."

Always the cheerleader, Audrey patted John's arm. "Oh, John. Remmy more than puts up with you. I think he enjoys being a teacher as much as anything else. Just hang in there and before you know it, Remmy will dance for you the way Joe danced for Kate today."

# NINETEEN

*Kate*

As she puttered around the galley kitchen in their apartment, Audrey blurted, "I want to know how you did that."

Kate glanced up from her *Dressage Today* magazine. "Did what?"

Audrey planted her hands on her hips. "Look. I've ridden Joe. When we warm up, he feels like rigor mortis has set in. He loves his job, but he's not a ballet dancer. When you ride him, he looks like Baryshnikov. Spill it. What's your secret?"

"He probably feels stiff to you because your seat is so sensitive." Kate said. "He felt tight to me, too, when we started. But I didn't have any expectations of how he should feel so I just let him do whatever he normally does. I guess if I have a 'secret,' it's Ben's book. I've devoured it and really taken his philosophy to heart. I bet I could quote entire passages from it."

An uncharacteristically quiet Audrey stared at the floor.

Kate narrowed her eyes at her roommate. "Don't tell me you've been here this long and haven't read Ben's book? He shows you how to use visualization and self-talk to improve your riding. You must know that from your lessons."

"Yeah. But I think I'm a 'seat-of-the-pants' kind of rider. I ride mostly by feel."

Kate's eyes lit up. "Well, you're cutting off your nose to spite your face. Here's what Ben believes. He thinks that not only do animals react to the pictures we hold in our mind's eye, but also when we visualize what we want, our muscles fire correctly. When you imagine a skill like riding a shoulder-in, your muscles engage as if you're physically giving the right signals. That's so cool for us since we're always trying to give invisible aids. I mean one of our goals with dressage is to make it look like we're sitting there doing nothing, and the horse is doing all the work."

"Yeah. Doing nothing." Audrey rolled her eyes. "I love it when people who don't ride ask why I get tired after schooling a few horses a day. They don't consider riding a sport because they think the horse does all the work. I try to explain how much body control and core strength it takes just to sit like we do, but they don't get it."

Kate warmed to the subject. "I know. I get that from non-riders, too. Anyhow, here's what I've learned from Ben's book. I give normal cues for movements with my seat, legs, and hands. But I also hold a picture in my mind of what I want my horse to do. If I want an extended trot, I visualize my horse coiling the spring of his hind legs and then propelling himself up over the ground like an airplane taking off."

Audrey pursed her lips and said, "And that's your secret?"

"Oh, yes. Once I started playing with visualization, my riding changed so much. I think the horses love it. They act like I'm speaking to them in their own language. The best part is that I can use a fraction of the strength that I used to use when I only gave physical cues. The horses know exactly what I want so they don't get confused. You know what I mean. Take the aids for canter departs. They're similar to the aids for trot half-passes. So, I could be trotting along and ask for a half-pass, but my horse isn't sure if I want him to half-pass in the trot or to canter. So, he chooses to canter. He's not being disobedient. He just has to play multiple choice because I'm not clear enough. And in this case, he made the wrong choice. It's my fault—not his."

"I know!" Audrey's curls bounced as she shook her head. "I had that happen to me at a show once. So, I changed how I taught my horses to canter. Instead of holding my outside leg back until they cantered, I taught my horses to canter when they felt a quick wiper-like action of my outside leg. That way they felt a difference in the aid for canter and an aid for half-pass."

"That's a great start. Now you can make your aids even

more effective by visualizing the movement you want. I'm not saying it's easy for me, either. That's why I've latched onto Ben's approach. It keeps me out of my own head. If I don't drown out the chatter in my mind, my internal dialogue sounds something like. '*Stop pulling on the reins, you idiot. How can you expect him to go forward when you're hanging on his mouth?*' Or, '*If you weren't so crooked, he wouldn't have such a hard time going sideways to the right.*' Or, '*Stop riding him with his head and neck so low! How do you expect him to keep his hind legs going when you have a stranglehold on his front end?*'"

It was a big step for Kate to admit her shortcomings to Audrey. She usually hid her self-doubt. But sharing her anxiety with her new friend made her feel like someone had lifted a concrete block off her chest. The last thing she needed was expectations about her riding. She put enough pressure on herself without help from anyone else.

Audrey looked at Kate and then gazed at the floor. "I'm embarrassed to say I'm not much of a reader. I have skimmed sections of Ben's book because I felt obligated to do it. But I haven't committed it to memory or practiced like you have. Promise me you won't tell Ben. Anyhow, I know athletes in other sports use mental rehearsal to improve their skills. It makes sense that it'd help us, too."

"That's right," Kate said. "It boils down to that old saying. 'Practice doesn't make perfect. Perfect practice makes perfect.' And the only place you can practice perfectly is in your imagination."

Audrey narrowed her eyes at Kate. "But I guess I missed that other part of using visualization to communicate with animals. It's just a little too woo-woo for me. I'm a meat-and-potatoes kind of girl."

"Well, it's your loss." Kate laughed. "Besides, it's fun."

"Okay, let's say for argument's sake, that I worked on this visualization stuff. How would I start?"

"It's sort of up to you. Decide what's easiest for you to do." Kate cocked her head. "When I ride, sometimes I imagine the whole horse moving the way I want. Other times I 'see' just one part of his body. If I have a horse that's tense, I focus on his eye staying soft and calm. If I'm doing a half pass and I want to go more sideways, I mentally zoom in on his legs and see them crossing high up by his knees and hocks. But whatever I focus on, I make the image vivid by filling in details."

"Okay. That sounds easy enough. Tell me specifically what you did with Joe today."

Kate beamed at her friend. "First, I pictured his big white star, his floppy ears, and the way his mane splits in half with some of it falling on the right side of his neck and the other half falling to the left. I also use my five senses. This part is really important. I feel a light contact with his mouth. I hear the regular rhythm of the trot. I smell the fly spray. I taste the sweat dripping down from underneath my helmet. I see his hindquarters lower and his front end elevate. Give it a try, Audrey. It's so cool to ride more with your mind and less with your body.

It also blocks any negative chatter that pops up because you can only think about one thing at a time. Once it becomes a habit, you'll love it."

"All right. All right. I'll give it a try." Audrey held her arms up in surrender. But the real reason she'd experiment with this weird stuff was because she'd be damned if she let anyone get a leg up on her, riding-wise.

# TWENTY

*John*

John's work took him out of town during the week. But he enjoyed riding on the weekends or watching Kate school Remmy for him. Ben had assigned Kate to take over the ride on Remmy because Audrey had her hands full with the other horses.

On one particular Saturday, John told Kate he wanted to study her schooling session instead of riding himself. Kate rode Remmy in the outdoor arena while John watched from the shade of the gazebo.

Kate began their warm-up by walking around the outside of the ring on a loose rein for ten minutes. Then they entered the arena and walked for another five minutes. Next, she picked up rising trot and rode circles, serpentines, lengthenings, and leg-yields so he could relax and stretch his muscles. She followed the trot work with some canter to loosen him up. When they started to canter, Remmy shook his head like he wanted to buck and play. Kate laughed with delight.

John beamed at his horse. "He looks supple and loose today."

"Yes. And he feels so festive, too! I love it when he shakes his head and shows me he's happy and playful."

John watched the pair intently. He'd become familiar with how Kate warmed up his horse to prepare for the more advanced work. She always made sure Remmy was ready for the collected movements they'd do later in the ride. To collect him, Kate would shift his center of gravity toward his hind legs with half-halts so he carried more of his weight on his hindquarters and less on his front end.

Collection worked the hindquarters like deep knee bends so horses had to build strength gradually. Kate knew how much effort the collected work took, so she always finished the session before Remmy got too tired. She avoided crossing the line between doing just enough work to help him get stronger but not so much that he strained himself. Too many riders learned about that line the hard way and ended up either injuring or souring their horses.

As a relative novice, John liked doing the fancy tricks like pirouettes, piaffe, passage, and flying lead changes. When he asked Kate why she spent so much time doing basic exercises, Kate explained that a horse needed to stretch, warm up, and build a solid foundation just the way a ballerina needed to warm up at the barre and focus on fundamentals before the demands of the dance. As four-legged dancers, Kate told him, her horses needed the same warm-up and basic work before being asked to do collected work.

After warming up, Kate started the more advanced movements like shoulder-in, haunches-in and half-passes. Remmy performed the movements well, and Kate felt his weight shift back toward his hindquarters. To reward him, Kate stood up in her stirrups so her weight wasn't on his back and galloped Remmy around the ring while patting him on his neck.

After celebrating with their gallop, they walked until Remmy caught his breath. During the next phase of work, they did piaffe and passage. John loved these movements. They mimicked a stallion, showing off for his mares. Kate started with piaffe, a trot on the spot.

From the piaffe, Kate asked Remmy to propel himself into a lofty cadenced trot called "passage." John loved watching them passage because it looked like they were flying.

He also marveled at how Kate sat on Remmy. They looked like a centaur—two creatures sharing one body. Kate seemed to do nothing and Remmy did everything by himself. It didn't seem like work at all. It looked like play. At that moment, John made a decision about his horse's future.

At ten years old, Remmy was at a crucial time in his life as a competitive dressage horse. He had a fabulous mind, and Ben had told John that his gaits were as good as any of the top horses in the country. Should Remmy remain John's school horse or should he fulfill his poten-tial as an international prospect?

John thought the timing might work when the next Olympics came around in three years. By then Kate would have had enough experience with Remmy to so-lidify their partnership, and the two of them could make a bid for the Olympic team. It might be a crazy dream, but it would be an exciting adventure.

Giving up riding his horse would be tough. But he knew Ben would let him ride Kammie or Jolicoeur. Rid-ing was just a hobby for him, anyhow. He'd continue to learn on a schoolmaster while giving Kate and Remmy this opportunity. Kate could never afford an internation-al horse, and Remmy was in his prime.

With his decision made, John watched the rest of the schooling session with a Cheshire-cat grin on his face. It would be fun to be an owner. God knew the sport needed sponsors. Too often, gifted riders remained un-knowns because they didn't have money. He liked the thought of being part of a team, supporting his horse, and helping a deserving young rider.

John's strong suit, however, was not selflessness. He was also motivated by being able to get closer to Kate. Not only was she gorgeous, but also she seemed like ev-erything he was looking for in a life partner: humble, graceful, and self-effacing. He'd make himself indis-pensable to her and show her how to express her grat-itude. Oh, yes. He had big plans for his Eliza Doolittle and their future together. But he'd have to proceed cautiously. She was obviously a timid creature, and he didn't want to scare her off.

John looked up to see Kate and Remmy floating through some canter zigzags where they cantered sideways to the left in a half-pass for a few strides, did a flying change, and half-passed sideways to the right. He marveled at their fluidity. They finished the session with flying changes every other stride and then one-tempi flying changes every stride. John enjoyed watching the one-tempi's the most because Remmy looked like a child skipping across the arena.

When they finished, Kate went back to rising trot and let Remmy cool down by asking him to stretch his neck again. And just as he'd done in the beginning, Remmy shook his head like he wanted to buck and play.

When they broke to the walk, Kate threw her head back and laughed. "I love that! He's proud of himself. And he's just as fresh at the end of the work as he was at the beginning. That's always a good sign. It means he's happy and still full of energy."

John nodded in agreement and said, "That was a great session, Kate. It's obvious how much stronger he's getting with the work you've been doing. I couldn't be happier. Can we talk for a minute?"

Kate brought Remmy near the gazebo but kept him walking in a circle so his muscles cooled down slowly. Wearing his business face, John asked, "Can we get together later today? I need to make some calls for the rest of the afternoon, but I want to discuss something with you. If I come back later, can we meet in the lounge?"

"Oh. Sure. I can get there by five. Will that give you enough time to make your calls? Or you can text me when you're ready."

"That should be fine. I'll see you in the lounge. That was a great session. I have to admit I enjoy watching you school Reminisce almost as much as I enjoy riding him."

⌒ ◦

Punctual to the minute, John entered the lounge at five sharp to see Kate drumming her fingers on the armrest of the leather sofa.

John sat down across from her. He leaned toward her with furrowed eyebrows and rested his elbows on his knees. "Why so anxious? I don't bite."

"I'm sorry, John. My imagination ran away with me all afternoon. I assume you're going to ask someone else to ride Remmy. I don't blame you. Lots of people have a ton more experience than I do."

John sat back in his chair, his mouth gaping. "What are you talking about? I told you today how happy I am with his training. In fact, I tell you that every time I see you. When are you going to believe me?"

Kate stared at her feet as if they held the answer but said nothing.

"Never mind. That's not the issue," John said. "My concern is that your working student duties keep you very busy here. I don't know how much you can put on your plate." With a smile, John continued, "What are your thoughts about taking Reminisce on as a long-term project? You do an amazing job with him. You can ride him instead of Joe in your lessons. We could show in Wellington this winter. You have a fair bit of competition experience under your belt here in New England, but Wellington is a whole different ballgame. Riders come from all over the world to compete there. What a great way to get your feet wet."

Kate gawked at John. "Seriously? That was kind of the last thing I was expecting you to say."

"Then once you guys are more experienced, we can go to some selection trials," John said, as if he hadn't noticed what she said. "I'm realistic. I don't expect us to win this year or even next year. But from what I can see, it'd be reasonable to compete in the qualifiers by your third season. When you make the semifinals as part of the top horses and riders in the country, we'd go to the final selections. This journey would be quite an adventure. What do you think?"

Kate's mouth fell open, but words failed her.

"So, I take it from your silence that it's a lousy idea?" John asked, with a mischievous grin.

When Kate found her voice, the questions tumbled out like marbles rolling every which way. "Omigod! Omigod! Do you mean it? Are you sure? Won't you miss riding him? Can I do him justice? Don't you want to think it over a little more?"

John said, "Yes, I mean it. And I don't need to think

it over. I've learned to trust my instincts. This plan is the best thing for all of us. Reminisce is such a talented horse, and he has the mind to cope with the pressure of intense competition. It would be a shame to waste his talent. You two have the most incredible rapport. I'd have a lot of fun watching your partnership develop. Of course, I'll miss riding him. But I'd get a bigger thrill seeing him reach his potential and maybe even make a team. He obviously won't do it with me aboard. I can't think of anyone else I'd rather have ride him."

Kate forced herself to look professional rather than like a giddy little kid. "I'd love to ride and compete Remmy, John. Just let me check with Ben to see if it would be okay."

John winked. "Don't you worry about Ben. I'll handle him. I'm sure he and I will agree. He'll want what's best for both you and Reminisce, so I'm positive he'll be on board."

"What can I say except thank you, thank you! Never in my wildest dreams did I ever imagine I'd have an opportunity like this on such an incredible horse. But what about you? I can only guess what it's like to give up riding your own horse."

"No worries. It's my pleasure. I'm excited too. From now on, we're Team Gage."

Despite her shyness, Kate catapulted up off the couch and closed the distance between them in three steps. She threw her arms around John. He returned the hug and the two of them stayed suspended in time for a minute. While enveloped in John's embrace, Kate mused how she'd missed having a father when she was growing up. And she knew that if she'd had a dad in her life, he'd be just like John—kind, supportive, and understanding.

# TWENTY-ONE

*Kate*

Within a week of John's decision to turn Remmy over to Kate, packages started arriving at the stable. Audrey and Melissa carried boxes that were almost bigger than they were up to the apartment. Audrey kicked the door until Kate answered it.

The banging on the door surprised Kate. Almost everyone let themselves in. "Who's there?" She asked suspiciously.

Audrey said, "Let us in, for God's sake. We're about to keel over."

When Kate opened the door, she laughed at the sight of the huge boxes with legs.

Melissa added, "The UPS man just delivered them. There are more downstairs. Hey! He's kinda cute. Are you holding out on us?"

Kate ignored Melissa and examined the shipping labels. "Wow! They're from Dover Saddlery and the

Dressage Connection."

As Kate started to open a box, Audrey said, "Hey! Don't get too comfortable, Missy. There are more boxes downstairs. Melissa and I aren't your pack mules, you know."

"What? More boxes? Who are they for?"

Audrey gave Kate a sarcastic look. "You, Blister Butt."

Kate was almost speechless, "But who sent them?"

"Well, we won't know for sure until we open them," said Melissa, "but my guess would be John."

The three girls scampered downstairs in a tangle of legs to get the remaining boxes.

Kate said, "This is unbelievable. John must have gone on a shopping spree for Remmy. How exciting! He didn't say anything to me about it. Merry Christmas in the spring, Remmy!"

They tore into the packages like little kids. Audrey opened a big one first and held up a pair of black Schumacher breeches. She looked at Kate with steely eyes and said, "It's more like Merry Christmas, Kate! This whole box is filled with breeches."

Audrey continued to paw through the box as Melissa and Kate tossed packing materials into the air.

Melissa said, "Wow! These are amazing colors. What size are they? 28 long. They'll fit you perfectly."

A dumbfounded Kate said, "I have to call John. This is unbelievable. Did you tell him my size, Audrey?"

"Not me. He must have talked to one of the boys or looked in your cubby in the tack room. Let's check out the other boxes before you call him."

Audrey tore into a package. "Holy crap! There are five pairs of white show breeches. Try on a pair, Kate. Let's see how they look."

Kate grabbed a pair of white breeches. She pulled off her cheap schooling tights and slipped on the exquisite breeches with the buttery leather seat. "Omigod! They're wonderful. Do you like them?"

Melissa said, "They're perfect! Spin around. They look like they were made for you. Hmm. I wonder what else he sent."

In the other boxes, Kate found almost everything she'd need for schooling and showing—Reitsport stock ties, vintage stock pins, Kyra K gloves, competition shirts, Balkenhol spurs, Fleck whips, and a midnight blue Charles Owen helmet with its seams sparkling with bling.

When the three girls finally finished digging through the boxes, they sat on the floor buried in a mountain of bubble wrap, Styrofoam packing peanuts, and clothing. Kate motored through the heap of packing materials on her hands and knees until she found her phone under a pile of schooling shirts.

She dialed John's number and boogied around the room while waiting for him to answer. On the fourth ring, he picked up.

Trying to keep her voice neutral, she said, "Hi, John. This is Kate. I'm kind of at a loss for words at the moment."

John laughed. "I take it UPS brought you a little surprise."

Not being able to contain herself a moment longer, she squealed, "Little? John, this is too much! I can't accept it."

"Oh, yes, you can, young lady. We're Team Gage. You'll be riding and showing my horse. I want you to look professional. By the way, I hope you don't have any plans for your day off next Monday."

"I don't. Why?"

John said, "We'll be spending most of the day on the road. I made an appointment with Charlie Grenier at Derby Tack. He'll measure you for custom-made boots. Would you like Cavallos, Konigs, or Der Dau? I'm not up on all the latest fashions and best brands, but I'm sure you are. If not, ask Ben what he recommends. Money isn't an issue, so don't skimp on anything. Charlie will also fit you for a new custom-made tailcoat. He can tell us about anything else you and Reminisce might need. I want you outfitted perfectly from head to toe when you canter down the centerline. Plan on a road trip when we need something special. Besides with all that time on the road, we'll have a chance to get to know each other better."

Kate squealed like a puppy. "I'm speechless. Somebody pinch me!"

John laughed. "It's a lot of fun for me to do this."

"Well, words seem inadequate, but all I can say is thank you so much!"

"I'm out of town on business all this week. But I'll pick you up at seven in the morning next Monday, and we'll head down to Lincoln for our appointment with Charlie."

"I'll be ready. See you then. Have a great week. I'll take good care of Remmy. And, John, thank you again. No one has ever done anything like this for me. It's like a fairy tale."

"You're welcome, my dear," John said. "You deserve everything and more. See you soon."

Kate hung up the phone and turned to the other girls. She looked flabbergasted.

Melissa asked, "So spill. What did he say?"

"Not only did he order all this stuff, but he's taking me to Derby Tack next Monday to get a custom-made tailcoat, boots, and anything else I might need."

Audrey gaped. "Holy Cinda-fuckin-rella! I'm thrilled for you. And...I don't mean to be Debbie Downer or anything but watch your step. Don't become indebted to him."

"Oh, Audrey. You're so suspicious! John doesn't have hidden agendas. He just doesn't want me to embarrass him in public."

"Just keep it professional. I've seen what happens when sugar daddies get rejected. It's not a pretty sight," Audrey warned.

Kate's hackles went up. "John is not a sugar daddy. Besides, I'm interested in Remmy, not John."

"Okay. Okay. Calm down, Blister Butt. But don't say

I didn't warn you if he gets manipulative. He's got the power. One wrong move, and he could yank that horse away from you. I've seen sponsors take horses away from riders if they don't get perfect results in the show ring or they gain five pounds or they decide the grass is greener with a different rider. It's a lot of pressure, and you never know where you stand."

"Audrey, you're such a cynic. I have faith in John. The whole thing was his idea. He'd never do anything like that."

Audrey shrugged. "No, Kate. I'm a realist. I've seen it happen more times than I'd like to remember. But I hope for your sake that I'm wrong."

# TWENTY-TWO
## *Kate*

K ate left the arena at the Mystic Dressage Show to the roar of the crowd's approval. Her face was flushed as much from exertion as from the exhilaration of the ride. She gave Reminisce a big pat and said, "Good Boy, Remmy! You're such a star!"

Once she was outside the roped off competition area, she dismounted and loosened Remmy's girth while praising him the entire time. He gave her an impatient nudge as if to say, "Well, that's fine, but where are my carrots?"

Kate laughed at her demanding horse. "I know. I know. First things first. Treats first. Compliments later."

Shifting from foot to foot, John waited by the in-gate. As Kate got closer, he made a beeline for her and scooped her up in a bear hug.

"Sweetheart, you were brilliant! Good boy, Reminisce! I'm so proud of you both. I held my breath the entire ride."

He patted Remmy's neck while firing off a round of questions. "How did he feel? He looked so light and responsive. Are you happy with your ride? Was the footing okay? Was it deep in the corners? Did the people moving around on the metal bleachers bother you?"

Kate laughed at John's barrage of questions. She knew he rode every stride of the test with her from the stands. Sitting on the sidelines could be more nerve-racking than riding. She put her index finger beside her cheek and said, "Great! Thrilled. Fine. Not at all." She giggled. "Did I answer all your questions?"

"For the moment, yes. Take our boy back to the stables. I'm going back to catch the rest of the rides. It's early. But so far, no one has come close to a test like that. I bet the scores are amazing!" He punched the air with one fist and said, "Go Team Gage!"

As Kate left the area around Mystic's main ring, friends and fans swallowed her up.

"Good job, Katherine! That was just lovely."

"The picture of elegance!"

"Fantastic!"

"Wow! Amazing ride!"

"How did Remmy feel? He sure didn't look like a green FEI horse."

Kate smiled and nodded to the well-wishers as she wove her way through the crowd. She didn't dare stop or slow down. She wanted to get Remmy back to the stables and give him a shower to help him cool out. Several enthusiastic admirers followed her the whole way.

Everyone wanted to associate with the stars. For some, mingling with the riders and horses was as close as they'd ever get to the big arena.

When they entered the stabling area, a security guard stopped the wannabes. Only riders, grooms, trainers, owners, and family members could get to the barns. The guard's job was to ensure the safety of the horses. Unfortunately, at this level of competition, sabotage ran rampant. As shows became more important and the stakes got higher, so did the threat of harm.

Kate knew that just last month at the Fox Ridge competition, Paul Depuis arrived at the showgrounds to give his horse breakfast only to discover a residue of white granules at the bottom of the feed tub. He brought the bucket to the technical delegate. Even though Paul had nothing to do with it, the TD disqualified him from competition because the powder turned out to be acepromazine, a tranquilizer.

Riders eyed each other suspiciously. They beefed up safety measures. Grooms slept on cots in front of their horses' stalls. Eventually, security discovered that the culprit was a disgruntled spectator who had a grudge against Paul. He wanted Paul suspended from showing, so he'd sprinkled the tranquilizer in the horse's feed tub.

Kate moved with purpose and smiled at the guard as she entered the stabling area. Protection of the horses aside, it was a relief for her to find sanctuary away from the groupies.

To get sponsorship for their events, riders needed favorable public perception. But they also needed private time so they could concentrate on doing their jobs without answering a lot of questions or needing to babysit fans and friends. The restricted stabling area became a haven for competitors where they could focus on their rides or relax without having to deal with the public.

Inside the stabling area, Kate and Remmy made their way back to the stall among a barrage of questions and comments from other competitors who'd missed her ride.

"How was your test, Kate?"

"Was the footing deep?"

"Did Remmy mind the people sitting on the hill?"

"Did the clapping bother him?"

"How was his piaffe?"

Kate kept moving but responded politely to the onslaught of questions. When they arrived at Remmy's stall, she took his bridle off and put on his halter so he'd be free to indulge in some well-deserved treats. He munched on a carrot as Kate prepared to bathe him.

As she added liniment to a bucket of warm water, she heard footsteps running up behind her. She turned and Audrey almost knocked her over as she threw her arms around her. "Oh, Kate. You were wonderful. Remmy looked fantastic! How did he feel?"

"He was awesome—so light and responsive. But I made a lot of pilot errors." Kate shook her head. As usual, she beat herself up about her own riding. "I don't know why I didn't prepare better for the pirouettes. And

I almost forgot to do the extension on the diagonal!"

"You looked great to me. Those are green rider mistakes. Once you have more mileage in the ring, you'll stop riding the pattern of the test and be able to focus on yourself and Remmy instead. It's normal to memorize the pattern. In the beginning, you think, 'First we do extended trot. Next we do half-pass. Then we halt and back up at C.' Eventually you'll ride the test on autopilot. Then you can make adjustments for Remmy and yourself as the ride unfolds. You can't multi-task like that now, but it'll come with experience."

Kate smiled at Audrey. "Thanks for the pep talk. Even with all of Ben's great coaching, sometimes I'm my own worst enemy. I appreciate you supporting me. You're the best cheerleader ever. Hey! When do you and Joe go?"

"Oh, God! Not until 3:20. I hate waiting all day."

"You'll be fine. Tell you what. After I put Remmy away, let's have some breakfast at the concession area. I couldn't eat before I rode, but I'm starving now."

Audrey rubbed her stomach and said, "Sounds like a plan to me. I can always eat. It'll help pass the time too."

"Okay. I need about forty-five minutes to finish up with Remmy, so you can either wait here or come back later."

Just as Audrey was about to answer, the announcer's voice came over the loudspeaker. Kate held up her hand to shush Audrey.

"We have the scores for number 289, Reminisce and Katherine Gage. Judge at C—74.8%. Judge at M—73.2%.

Judge at H–73.9%. Judge at E—74.6%. Judge at B—75.4% for a total percentage of 74.4%, which currently puts them well into the lead."

Kate threw her arms around Remmy's neck and gave him an enormous hug. She heard the crowd shout their approval all the way from the stands. "You did it, Remmy!"

Audrey hugged her friend. "You both deserved every point, Kate. You put in a super ride."

"I don't know about that. I think beginner's luck had a lot to do with it. Remmy was phenomenal, but you and I know that the judges don't always agree with us."

"Ya got that right. Usually, they don't even agree among themselves," Audrey laughed. "Sometimes it's because they have different vantage points because of where they're sitting. But other times, you'd think they're judging a different ride. Did you see that Colonel Preston had Louise Whitehall twelve points higher than any of the other judges? Unbelievable! Her horse was so overbent that his chin was on his chest the whole time. At least all your scores were close. Anyhow, I'll go back and check on Joe. Then I'll be ready for breakfast."

Kate and Audrey found an empty table at the far end of the concession area. Just as they were sitting down, Cara scurried over. "Oh, Kate. What a fantastic ride! I'm so thrilled for you. No one rides as elegantly as you do. You have this way of dressing up every horse you sit on. I bet you made the judges' day. I doubt they'll see anything that amazing for the rest of the show."

"Thanks, Cara. Remmy was such a good boy. I'm really proud of him."

Cara leaned in and whispered conspiratorially, "Well, that's fine. But you and I both know you could sit on a donkey and still have a test like that. I'm not saying that Remmy isn't incredible. But I think you could ride anything and take everyone's breath away. If I didn't adore you so much, I'd be jealous."

"Well, lucky for me I don't have to ride a donkey," Kate said, laughing at the picture in her mind. "But thanks again anyhow, Cara."

Cara lingered by their table. But when the girls didn't invite her to sit down, she wandered off, mumbling about having to catch up with someone.

Audrey rolled her eyes. "She must be on her way to find someone else to suck up to. Thank God she left. I could feel myself going into sugar shock. How can anyone be that sickeningly sweet constantly? Doesn't she realize people see through her schtick? No one is that syrupy all the time. She probably goes home and kicks her dog."

"Oh, I don't mind Cara," Kate said. "She's harmless enough. I do feel sorry for her, though. She doesn't realize that her gushing backfires. Most people think she's fake, so they avoid her. She doesn't have any close friends. But at least she's not mean like Alyssa."

Audrey's eyes burned like wildfire, "Yeah. Don't get me started on my favorite DQ. What a bitch! Did anyone tell you what she did at the first show of the season? You weren't at Ben's yet so you might not know about this."

Kate grinned at her gossipy roommate and said, "No, I don't know. But I'm sure you'll tell me."

Audrey didn't skip a beat. "Well, you know how she tries to convince herself and everyone else that she's the best rider in the country? If she really felt that way, she wouldn't have to resort to psychological warfare. Right?"

Kate rolled her eyes and asked, "So what did she do this time?"

Audrey charged on. "Two things actually. First, she rode around in the warm-up area with a whip in each hand. Then, she rode right up beside Jack Connors. His horse, Bonaventure, is really hot. When she got near them, she whacked her own horse with one of the whips and smacked Bonny 'by accident.' The poor horse panicked and freaked out. Jack couldn't get him to calm down and had to scratch from his class." Audrey lifted a corner of her upper lip in a sneer. "Alyssa apologized and rode off to harass someone else. She's brilliant at doing things like that. I wonder if she really thinks she's fooling anyone."

Building a head of steam, Audrey said, "And if that's not enough, she rode by Ron Kingsford while he was giving his horse a walk break. She said, 'Hi, Ron. Nice to see you. Gee. I saw some of your canter work, and it looked terrific. But your boy looked a little sore behind in the trot. Is he okay?' Then she trotted away with no explanation." Audrey stuck her index finger down her throat. "She left poor Ron with his mouth hanging open, probably trying to figure out if his horse was lame. She's a master manipulator. Why do you think she does stuff like that?"

Kate shook her head. "Beats me. Maybe she thinks it's all part of being the ultimate competitor—you know, waging a mental battle as well as riding a good test."

"She's a competitor all right," Audrey said. "But I agree with Jason that she should compete race cars or bicycles or anything without feelings. You know as well as I do that she doesn't care about her horses. I'm sure if she had to choose between competing a horse that was in pain or scratching out of a class, she wouldn't even consider the horse. I feel sorry for Chance and Celebrity."

Audrey glanced at her watch. "Hey! Grab your coffee, and let's run over to the warm-up area. That asshole Michael Gifford is about to ride Bentley. At the last show, Bentley went on strike and refused to piaffe. He planted all four legs and grew roots to China. Michael turned five shades of purple. It serves him right for torturing that horse. He's always brutalizing Bentley with the whip or digging those big pizza-cutter spurs into him to get him to piaffe. That poor horse must think that piaffe is 'fear on the spot' instead of trot on the spot. When Michael can't carry a whip in the test, Bentley pays him back big time. I'd like to rip that horse away from him. He doesn't deserve him—or any other horse, for that matter."

The Intermediaire II went on for the better part of the day. By the end of the class, Kate and Remmy remained in the lead. Alyssa and Celebrity came in second with the rest of the top riders placing close behind them.

The riders lined up by the in-gate to prepare for the awards ceremony. Everyone gathered together except for Alyssa. She didn't seem to be in a hurry. Spectators rustled in the stands impatient to see the stars of the class and cheer for their personal favorites.

"Where's Alyssa? They're getting ready to start." Kate asked Ellie Marshall who was in line behind her. Ellie and her horse Menno had placed third.

"Here she comes," Ellie said as she backed her horse up to make room for Alyssa to get behind Kate and in front of her.

Alyssa, however, hadn't bothered to check the scoreboard and marched to the front of the line.

When Alyssa entered the ring, Kate assumed it was time to start and walked Remmy in, too. She picked up an easy trot and passed Alyssa to take their rightful place in the lead. No sooner had Kate gone by when Alyssa asked Celebrity for a bigger trot to overtake her groom.

Alyssa's jockeying for position confused Kate. But she urged Remmy on and passed Alyssa again. When Alyssa realized what was happening, she trotted faster to catch up with Kate. The two of them ended up trotting side-by-side in a bizarre pas de deux. When it finally dawned on Alyssa what was happening, she snarled at Kate, "You mean you won?"

Kate stammered, "Uh, well, um. I guess so. They must have liked my trot work."

As they trotted side by side, Alyssa sneered, "Your trot work sucked. In fact, your whole test stunk! Even a moron could see all your beginner mistakes."

The six riders finally found their places and lined up beside each other to get their ribbons. Alyssa leaned toward Kate as if to shake her hand and congratulate her. Instead, she asked under her breath, "Who did you sleep with to pull that one off? Or maybe you had John pull some strings for you. No way you could beat me otherwise."

Kate withdrew her hand as if she'd touched a hot stove and instead raised it to wave to the crowd, who cheered their approval. The tension between the two women was palpable, though the spectators didn't seem to notice.

After getting their ribbons, Kate and Remmy led off at the canter on a lap of honor around the outside of the arena. The others followed single file in the order of their placing in the class. The crowd cheered for each of their favorites. Only a few sharp eyes spotted Alyssa taking the ribbon from Celebrity's bridle and tossing it at the judges' feet as she cantered past.

# TWENTY-THREE

*Alyssa*

In the name of training, Alyssa tortured her horses on a daily basis. Dr. Jekyll and Mr. Hyde had nothing on Alyssa. And the defenseless animals regularly endured Mr. Hyde.

But Alyssa knew she had to be discreet about the beatings she gave them. She claimed that none of her horses would go forward for her. And in her frustration, she resorted to beating them with her whip and poking bloody holes in their sides with sharp spurs. Then she'd make sure her groom covered their bodies with coolers after work so people couldn't see what she'd done. Since using a cooler after work was common, the other grooms at her last farm didn't wise up to her right away. When the owner found out, he gave her one day to pack her things and get off the property.

Alyssa scrambled to find a place for her horses and finally ended up at Cherry Hill. She told Ben that her horses were incompatible with the trainer at Essex Farm. Alyssa was many things, but she wasn't a fool. She knew a paying boarder who also took a lot of lessons had power. Few training facilities could afford to pass up that chunk of income.

Regardless of the leverage she had from bringing a lot of money to Cherry Hill, Alyssa knew she had to control her temper when she moved to Ben's barn. She couldn't afford to get kicked out of another facility. That might be the final straw for her father, who considered horses a ridiculous self-indulgence and a waste of money.

Alyssa's mother had started her with both riding and ballet lessons when she was ten. Mrs. Smithson considered those pursuits appropriate for a budding socialite. And when her mother died from pancreatic cancer five years later, her father had continued the lessons.

Donald Smithson had always financially supported his daughter in her current hobby. But he guessed that the spoiled girl's passion for horses would fade quickly, like the rest of her whims. He found it easier to indulge Alyssa than to parent her. He knew she'd get bored sooner rather than later. Or maybe she'd realize she didn't have the talent to make it to the top and would move on to the next thing.

That's what had happened during her stint with acting. Because her father gave a generous donation to the Actor's Loft, the prestigious school had accepted her. She'd dreamt of being a star and winning a Golden Globe or an Oscar. Maybe then her father would be proud of her. She did her best at the school, but eventually she realized that even her father's influence wouldn't be enough to help her get her foot in the door for actual jobs. So she quit.

Alyssa suspected that if her dad heard the real story behind why she'd switched barns, he'd balk at continuing to supply her with one expensive horse after another. He accepted her story that she switched to Cherry Hill because she wanted to work with Ben Ellis. He knew little about the horse world except for what his daughter told him. She claimed she needed international quality horses and a top trainer like Ben if she ever hoped to make a team.

In a never-ending search for her father's love and approval, Alyssa hoped making a team and riding for the United States would make him proud of her. She just needed the right horses and trainer.

It never occurred to Alyssa that her last three horses didn't have a problem. Instead, she blamed her Dutch dealer for finding only lazy horses for her. If he didn't get her the right horse soon, she'd fire him and get someone else.

Agents were a dime a dozen—especially European agents who viewed wealthy Americans as idiots. Those agents happily helped Americans buy their garbage even if it meant selling them lame or unsuitable horses.

Alyssa fumed about Chancellor. He was her laziest horse yet. Since her father had spent more than $650,000 in Holland for him, she felt he should do his job—no questions asked.

She always started off their schooling session walking around on a loose rein, crooning to him. But as soon as they started trotting, she became possessed.

She'd kick and hit him with the whip until he was galloping around the arena. Then she'd wheel him onto small circles, screaming like a banshee, "Go forward, you stupid piece of shit! Go! Go! Go!"

The longer she rode him and the harder she beat him, the more Chancellor shut down. And the more he shut down; the angrier Alyssa got. It seemed bizarre to anyone who knew her that the girl who patted and spoke sweetly to Chance in the barn turned into a raving maniac when she rode him. But by the time she finished riding, she was exhausted, and the tantrum was a memory.

# TWENTY-FOUR

*Kate*

Alyssa's treatment of poor, sweet Chance horrified Kate. She discussed it with Audrey and Jason, and the three agreed that good riders didn't blame their horses. Instead, they asked themselves if they caused the problem.

Kate explained her feelings to her friends. "Top riders ask introspective questions. You know what I mean. Am I sitting crookedly so the horse can't cross as well in a left half-pass as he can in a right half-pass? Am I using too much inside rein and overbending the neck to the inside so the horse does crooked flying changes? Are my reins so long putting my hands too close to my body that they stop the hind legs rather than creating a receiving and recycling action?"

"Yeah. And good riders also know that their riding mirrors what's going on in their lives that day," Jason added. "So, if they're in a bad mood, they don't school their horses. They go for a trail ride instead."

Audrey tilted her head. "You're absolutely right. So why do you think Alyssa is so angry? My guess is that it has something to do with her relationship with her father. She talks about him all the time, but he never comes to watch her ride. She's always looking for his approval. I once overheard her tell Cara after she won a class at the Spring Fling Horse Show that maybe now her dad would be proud of her. It sounds like he doesn't give her what she needs emotionally. Of course, I have no way of knowing that. I'm just guessing. And if she weren't so obnoxious and mean to everyone, including the horses, I'd almost feel sorry for her."

"I know. It's pretty sad." Jason shook his head. "But I wish she'd take up skiing or volleyball instead of horses. If she's so driven to make a team, she should compete in something that doesn't involve an animal. I haven't spoken to Louise, but I bet she left because Alyssa was so abusive."

"She should get some professional help so she can work through her issues. But who am I to talk?" Kate shrugged her shoulders. "I should probably see someone, too. I don't know how to help her or her horses. But it breaks my heart to see the defeated look in their eyes when she brings them in after work."

One day Alyssa was particularly frustrated. She hadn't calmed down as she usually did by the time she brought

Chancellor back to the barn. Instead, she snapped at Kate, "What's wrong with this horse? He's the laziest piece of crap I've ever ridden. If he doesn't get his act together soon, he's headed down the road. Throw a cooler on him so no one can see the spur marks on his sides. I don't want anyone to know how dishonest he is."

Alyssa tossed the reins at Kate and stomped off toward the tack room, where she kept her street clothes. She rarely spent time with her horses after their torture sessions. Today was no exception. She wasn't interested in building trust and connection. She only cared about riding at Grand Prix and getting the scores she needed to get long-listed for the equestrian team.

Kate soothed the dejected horse. "It's okay, boy. Here's a carrot. I'm sure you tried hard. You're fine now. I'll give you a nice shower, and then we'll graze in the big field. I promise I'll do something about that monster, even if it means I lose my job."

Kate was in a quandary. She had no control over the situation, and it was an unspoken rule that you didn't rat out others. In the past, she consoled herself that the poor horses only had to endure Alyssa's torture for an hour—although sometimes their sessions lasted up to two hours. On those days Kate wanted to march out to the ring and rip Alyssa off her horse. Maybe it wasn't Kate's place to tell Ben what she witnessed daily, but she had to protect the horses. So, she talked to Audrey about it. Since Audrey was the barn manager, it made sense for her to be the one to tell Ben.

In the meantime, the best she could do was soothe and fuss over her charges. She spent many a restless night worrying about the horses that had captured her heart.

Kate led Chance into the wash stall. She adjusted the temperature of the water and began to rinse him off. It horrified her to see the welts on his hindquarters where Alyssa had beaten him with the whip.

The girls and Jason knew that Ben didn't see Alyssa's abusing her horses because, if it wasn't a lesson day, Alyssa rode in the back ring. Kate was sure that if he'd ever seen what Alyssa did when she wasn't supervised, he'd put a stop it. But the girl was no fool. She knew why her last barn made her leave and kept a lid on her temper when Ben was around.

During her two private lessons each week, she played the role of an obedient student. It amazed Kate that Alyssa had enough control over herself to behave in lessons. If she could do that under supervision, why couldn't she do it when she rode by herself?

Kate had already figured out why Chance didn't like to go forward for Alyssa. She watched her lessons and saw that she had a "stopping seat." Her stiff hips didn't follow Chance's natural movement. As she kicked, dug in her spurs or whacked him with the whip, she gave conflicting signals. Her driving aids said, "Go forward," but her dead seat prevented him from moving freely.

Alyssa also had rigid elbows. She didn't offer an elastic contact with Chance's mouth. She locked her elbows by her waist, and her arms didn't follow the natural forward-and-back motion of his head and neck in walk and canter.

Between her stopping seat and stiff elbows, it was like stepping on the gas pedal while the emergency brake was engaged. Poor Chance and the other horses that had come before him couldn't go forward when they were blocked by her seat and arms.

Kate saw Ben try everything in his bag of tricks during Alyssa's lessons to get her to loosen her hips and elbows and go with the movement of her horse. But Alyssa wouldn't take responsibility for what was going on. She told everyone that the horses were the problem. They were just plain lazy. She'd make half-hearted attempts to open and close her hips and elbows when Ben reminded her, but she'd soon go back to her old ways.

# TWENTY-FIVE

*Ben*

In her next lesson, Alyssa whined, "You see how he keeps switching leads or trotting with his hind legs in the canter pirouettes?"

"It's not him, Alyssa. It's you," Ben said. "You need to keep moving your seat in the rhythm of the canter and follow with your arms. Your arms are an extension of the reins. They belong to your horse. Otherwise, you stop him, and he can't keep cantering."

A frustrated Alyssa came to the walk and threw her hands in the air. "Here. You ride him. I'm telling you it's not me. It's him. He has no work ethic. How am I ever going to get through my tests at a show if he keeps doing that to me?"

"Bring him here, and I'll see what's going on."

"He's all yours," Alyssa said as she hopped off and led Chance over to Ben. "He sucks back. It's a miracle I can do as much as I can with him. Luckily for me, I'm a strong rider. I can make him look like he's going on his own even when he isn't."

"How many times have I explained that strength isn't the answer? He's discouraged from going forward because you're blocking him with your seat and arms. The stronger you are, the duller he gets."

Ben mounted Chance and walked him around on a loose rein while he established two ground rules. The first rule was that Chance was to go energetically forward on his own with no urging from his rider. Once Chance was asked to walk, trot, or canter at a certain speed, it was his job, not his rider's, to maintain that speed all by himself.

To do this, when Chance slowed down, Ben gave him a couple of bumps with the flat of his calves to activate the walk. Once Chance was marching along, he let his legs drape on the horse's sides like wet towels.

Ben never kicked him with his spurs the way Alyssa did. In Ben's mind, spurs weren't for making aids stronger. They were used to refine the aids. The moment Chance slowed down, he bumped him again, and then returned to quiet legs.

Chance learned the new rule quickly. If he maintained his own energy, Ben wouldn't thump him with his legs. He'd get rewarded, and life would be peaceful.

The moment he cheated and used less power, Ben would correct him by bumping with his legs. Once Chance figured out this lesson in the walk, Ben gave him the same lesson in trot and canter.

Next he taught him rule number two. Given that a horse can feel a fly on his side, Ben insisted that Chance react to feather-light aids.

He asked for a transition from walk to trot by closing his calves lightly. He wanted a surge from behind into the trot as if Chance were a car with powerful rear-wheel drive.

When Chance reacted lethargically, once again he sent him forward by bumping him with both legs. Unfortunately, that's all most riders did. They corrected their horses for not going forward from light aids. But they left out the most critical part of putting a horse in front of the driving aids. That part involved retesting with light aids and expecting a surge from behind. Without the retest, he'd be training Chance to ignore light aids and react only when he got a big correction.

After Ben chased him forward, he went back to the walk. Then he retested Chance's reaction to light aids by asking for the walk to trot transition again. Chance surged forward, and Ben laughed as he almost got left behind the movement.

He patted him and chuckled, "Good boy! That's exactly what I'm looking for. Here's the rule. I whisper with my aids, and you shout your response. Not the other way around."

After testing Chance again with transitions from gait to gait and lengthenings and shortenings of strides, Ben was satisfied that the horse understood the new rules. He thought about how wonderful it would for this generous horse to feel aids as light as a mosquito bite instead of nagging, spurring, driving with the legs or whacks from the whip.

Ben glanced at Alyssa's pinched face. He had no way of knowing for sure, but from her expression, he assumed she thought he was just wasting time. She probably just wanted him to get on with it and fix the pirouettes.

But Ben knew he had to explain the ground rules to Chance before he could get to the "fancy stuff."

When he was satisfied that Chance understood the new rules, he let him walk on a loose rein to relax and catch his breath. He praised him for being a smart boy. Then Ben picked up the reins and put him through all the movements in the Grand Prix—half-passes, tempi changes, canter pirouettes, piaffe, and passage.

Alyssa's mouth fell open. It looked like Ben was doing nothing, and Chance did everything by himself.

As she watched from the barn along with Jason and Audrey, Kate said in awe. "Omigod! The man is a genius."

Jason agreed. "That's why you're here, my little love chop. To learn how to ride like that."

Audrey piped up, "I can't wait to see Alyssa's reaction when she gets back on."

After asking Chance to do all the movements from the Grand Prix, Ben walked him on a loose rein. He made a big fuss over the big chestnut as he headed back over to Alyssa.

"Now it's your turn. Remember that first he has to take responsibility for his own energy. Secondly, he has to respond to light aids. He's worked hard today, so just ride him for a few minutes to see how he reacts to the new rules."

Alyssa got on Chance and rode around with a big grin on her face as Chance motored along on his own eagerly waiting for her signal to go sideways, do a flying change or an extension.

Alyssa beamed at Ben. "I'm ecstatic about how he's going, but do you really think it's because of your 'rules'? Maybe he's moving better because your long legs are stronger than mine and your tall upper body gives you more leverage to drive him forward."

"Trust me," Ben shook his head. "It has nothing to do with strength or leverage. It's about training your horse to go on his own and react to light aids. Once we change your thinking, you'll be amazed at how much easier and more fun your horses are to ride."

# TWENTY-SIX

*Ben*

Kate begged Audrey to talk to Ben about Alyssa's abusive treatment of her horses. She agreed, and at the end of the day, the staff approached Ben in his office. Even though Audrey planned to do most of the talking, she brought Kate and Jason with her. She knew that eventually, they might have to have a similar conversation. So it would be a good idea for them to sit in on the meeting.

Audrey tapped on the door. Since it was ajar, the three of them entered before waiting for an answer. They walked in to see Ben staring at a spreadsheet and running his fingers through his hair.

"Oh, sorry, Ben. We didn't mean to interrupt. We thought it was okay to come in since the door was open."

"No, no. It's fine. I need a break from what I'm doing."

Ben had been trying to figure out how to balance what was going out with what it cost him to keep the farm afloat. He had a lot of options. But he wasn't particularly thrilled with any of them. He could sell some of the school horses. But that would be a hardship for many of his loyal students. He could take in more boarders. But then he'd probably end up having to deal with more DQs. Or he could raise rates on board, training, or lessons. Unfortunately, that would price him out of some riders' range. He could even buy young horses and sell them after some schooling—but that was always risky, given the time involved and the difficulties with pre-purchase exams.

Audrey said, "Okay. Thanks. Tell me if we can do anything to help. In the meantime, we want to talk to you about Alyssa's horses—particularly Chancellor."

"Sure. He's a wonderful horse. I enjoyed working him today. I just need to teach Alyssa how to ride him without blocking him and to train him to be in front of her driving aids. She's a smart girl. She'll get it eventually. I just hope Chance doesn't get too discouraged while she's learning."

"Ben. I'm afraid it's a lot more complicated than that. I hate to be the one to rat someone out, but you're busy in the arena all day. You don't get to see what goes on in the back ring or how her horses come back to the barn demoralized and covered in welts almost every day."

"What? Seriously? Alyssa seems uneducated, but I didn't think she was abusive."

"Well, that's why the owner of her last barn kicked her out. She's one angry girl and takes it out on the horses when no one's around. She doesn't consider Kate important since she's her groom, so she doesn't hide anything from her. But Kate sees her abuse every day."

"Is that true, Kate?"

Kate looked at the ground and nodded her head but said nothing.

"I appreciate you guys telling me. I can't be everywhere at once. Coming here must have been hard for you, but I need you guys to be my eyes and ears. Thank you. I'll take care of it. From now on she'll have to ride in the arena even if I'm giving a lesson. That way I can monitor her, and things won't get out of hand. I'll tell her it's because I want to give her extra attention. She'll love that."

# TWENTY-SEVEN

## *Kate*

The Green Mountain Horse Association competition in South Woodstock, Vermont, was one of the most popular shows in New England. The Cherry Hill group planned to bring four horses and students: Alyssa and Chance, Cara with Artisan, Mark and Quotation, and Luke with Denali.

Kate and Audrey accompanied them as grooms. Kate took care of Chance and Artie. Audrey looked after the school horses, Quotation and Denali.

Ben thought having two grooms for four horses would be more than enough, and he needed Jason, who usually took care of Quotation and Denali, to stay home and hold down the fort. Jason didn't mind staying home, though he'd miss being in the thick of things and hearing all the latest gossip. But part of the deal was that he'd get the following weekend off. And Jason had plans for that weekend. While the Cherry Hill students were duking it out to get qualifying scores, as well as scores for their United States Dressage Federation medals, Jason and his buddies, Kenneth and Stephen, planned to do some scoring of their own in Provincetown.

The Wednesday evening before the show, Kate, Audrey, and Jason loaded up the six-horse van. They wanted everything packed and ready to go so they could start the three-hour drive to South Woodstock by eight the next morning. That way, the girls would have plenty of time to set up the stalls and tack room before the competitors arrived for a late-afternoon schooling session with Ben.

After packing hay, grain, shavings, supplements, water buckets, feed tubs, sheets, longeing equipment, grooming equipment, saddles, washing supplies, tack-cleaning supplies, and other essentials, they loaded the final items—the tack trunks, which held the riders' personal items.

Cara, Luke, and Mark packed small tack trunks that were easy for two people to lift and load. But Alyssa insisted they bring her six-foot tall upright tack trunk.

The group couldn't imagine what she'd possibly need that would require bringing the enormous trunk. It easily held equipment for three horses.

Audrey's face morphed into a scowl. "Jeez. This is a local three-day show. You'd think she was packing for a three-month trip. Can you believe she insists on bringing a television to review rides, a barbecue grill, coffee maker, and a table and chairs so she can relax in style? Apparently, Alyssa feels that if she has to rough it, she's going to do it with panache. Spoiled rotten, that one."

Kate, Audrey, and Jason heaved and groaned as Jason pulled and the girls pushed the enormous tack truck up the ramp.

"What could Alyssa possibly have in here that's so important?" a breathless Jason asked. "It's like she has her own mobile tack store. I can't believe that every time we leave the farm even for a two-day clinic, she has to shlep—excuse me, *we* have to shlep—this enormous thing around. Not to mention her other 'essentials,' like her mini-refrigerator."

Once they loaded Alyssa's trunk, the three friends collapsed on the van's ramp to catch their breath.

"I have no idea why she feels she needs all this stuff. She does have her quirks, but I guess it calms her down to feel she's prepared for anything. Or maybe she just needs her creature comforts," Kate replied.

"I think it's because she feels she's more important than anyone else." Jason smirked. "And she loves seeing people slave for her. That's what comes from being born with a silver spoon in your mouth. But I knew you'd stick up for her even though you don't like her."

"I never said I didn't like her," Kate protested. "Besides, don't you think that's part of our job? We're their support system and cheerleaders as much as anything else. If you guys aren't in the barn, I keep an eye on all the riders to make sure they have what they need."

Jason blew her a kiss. "I see, my little Girl Scout. You're just working on your next merit badge."

Catching Jason's kiss in her raised fist, Kate said, "That's right, Smart Ass."

Audrey popped up from the ramp like a slice of toast. "Well, I don't know about you guys, but I'm going to cruise through the barn one last time to make sure everything looks good until night check. Then it's adult beverage time for me. Anyone up for a glass of wine? I think I even have some cheese, crackers, and cold pizza left over from the other night."

"Sounds like a plan to me, Sweet Pea. Let's see if Wheeler and Peter are still around. Maybe they'll join us."

Jason got up with a groan as Kate nodded in agreement. She looked forward to spending time with her friends.

The group headed to the barn, eager to finish up for the day so they could enjoy a glass of wine and snacks. They ran into Wheeler and Peter on the way and invited them along. The boys rarely turned down a good time and looked forward to being with their friends.

⌣ ·

After morning chores on Thursday, Jason, Kate, and Audrey loaded the horses in the van. Audrey tossed some drinks and snacks into the cab, and then hoisted herself into the driver's seat. Kate climbed into the passenger seat, and the two girls started the drive to the Green Mountain showgrounds.

They arrived without incident, located their stalls, bedded them, and hung buckets while the horses stood in the van, eating hay.

Their stalls faced the brook that meandered behind the shed rows. No other show in New England boasted such an idyllic and picturesque setting than this much-loved facility nestled in the Green Mountains of Vermont.

Once they set up the stalls, they took the horses off the van and settled them into their temporary homes. Then they unloaded the hay, equipment, feed, supplies, and trunks, and organized the tack stall.

By three in the afternoon, Kate and Audrey were sweaty, exhausted, and hungry. They were about to grab something to eat at the concession stand when Ben, Cara, Mark, Alyssa, and Luke arrived.

"So much for food," Audrey lamented. "We better get the horses groomed. Ben will be ready for them soon. The day before a show, he usually just does a light session and then sends the group for a hack around the showgrounds."

The riders greeted the girls and then wandered around to their horses' stalls. Once they'd located them, they went into the tack room to find their equipment.

Alyssa laughed. "Look. It's like magic! I click my heels together, and my stuff just appears."

Kate and Audrey exchanged looks. Audrey whispered, "Gag me. See? That's exactly what Jason means by Alyssa needing to feel important. What a diva!"

"I think she was just trying to be funny. You have a little chip on your shoulder about her," Kate said. "It's not her fault she comes from money. Maybe you should stop looking for reasons to be pissed off at her."

Audrey's face pinched into a scowl. "Well, after almost four hours of setting up, I'm not in the mood for her brand of humor. But I get your point. I'll try not to be such a bitch. It's just that I get so annoyed by these people who sashay into the barn in the latest fashion and won't get their hands dirty. The rest of us know that horsemanship is as much about care on the ground as it is about riding. Anyhow, let's get to work. Ben wants us to start with Chance and Denali. Once we get Alyssa and Luke on, we can groom and tack up Artie and Quotation."

The light schooling session went well. Ben wanted the horses to loosen up and relax in what would become an electric atmosphere the following day. To that end they just warmed up at the walk, trot, and canter. And then the riders asked their horses some basic questions. *Will you go forward when I give a light driving aid? Will you come on the bit when I ask for connection? Will you go sideways from a light aid?*

Satisfied that the horses were attentive and obedient, Ben sent them on a hack around the grounds so they could familiarize themselves with the surroundings. Chance was a bit suspicious of walking through the brook and going across the wooden bridge, but Denali's nonchalance comforted him. Chance simply put his nose on Denali's tail and followed closely behind.

Thursday night, Kate and Audrey set their alarm for four in the morning so they could get to the show by five. They needed to groom and braid the horses and be ready for Alyssa's ride at 8:30 a.m. The others didn't compete until late morning, so everyone would have a chance to watch Alyssa and Chance do their first Grand Prix together.

The rest of the Cherry Hill crew arrived around seven. Everyone was in good spirits and excited about the start of competition.

They checked the whiteboard outside of the tack room to confirm what time they were to meet Ben at the warm-up area. They also checked to make sure that their ride times were the same as the times that had been mailed to them the week before the show.

Alyssa approached Chance on the cross-ties while Kate was braiding him.

"Good morning, Alyssa! What a gorgeous day for competing, eh?"

"Yes. It's perfect!" Alyssa patted Chance on the neck and said, "You're going to be a good boy today, right?"

During the time Kate had been taking care of Celebrity and Chance, she felt that Alyssa was beginning to trust her. Maybe their relationship would evolve into friendship at some point. She knew Alyssa didn't have any close friends. Maybe she'd enjoy the shift in their relationship, even though Kate knew Alyssa had always made it a policy not to fraternize with the "help," and Kate herself was cautious about making new friends.

As Alyssa continued to pat Chance, she confided to Kate, "I'm actually really nervous. This will be our first Grand Prix together. The scores are going to be so important. We need to get the judges to sit up and take notice. I know they've never seen Chancellor before, and it takes time for them to develop some confidence in our partnership. But I want them to come away thinking that they've just seen the next Verdades and Laura Graves."

Kate smiled weakly at Alyssa. In her heart she knew that Alyssa and Chance didn't have an ounce of the love and communication that Laura and "Diddy" had for each other. Alyssa rode solely for her own glory.

But Kate knew part of her job was to support her riders and help them with their show nerves. So instead she said, "You guys are gonna be great. Chance knows his job. Just breathe and pretend you're riding in a lesson at home instead of in front of judges. I'm going to tack him up now so you can head over to meet Ben at the warm-up arena. I'll see you there as soon as I put his grooming stuff away."

Were her encouraging words heard? Kate wasn't sure. Alyssa seemed more interested in checking out the shine on her tall black boots.

When the rider before Alyssa entered the ring for her test, Ben told her to head over to Kate for last-minute preparations, which included removing Chance's bandages, giving Alyssa her shadbelly coat and a sip of water, and wiping down her boots.

The Cherry Hill entourage followed en masse to the competition arena, where Alyssa waited for the rider before her to finish. While Ben gave her some last-minute instructions, the group headed to the white post-and-rail fence enclosing the arena and found a good spot for viewing.

Even though it was early, lots of people showed up to see Alyssa's new horse. It was fun for the girls to chat briefly with friends and trainers they hadn't seen for a while.

Then Audrey whispered to Kate, "Sleaze alert! Dietrich Krause is coming our way."

"Hello, ladies. Audrey! You're looking quite exquisite this morning, my love. You must introduce me to your charming friend."

Audrey looked like she was going to retch as she introduced Kate to Dietrich. "Dietrich. This is Katherine Gage. She started working for Ben a couple of months ago."

Dietrich took Kate's hand and kissed the back of it. "Such a pleasure to meet you, my dear. I look forward to seeing a lot of you." He gave her what he thought was his sexiest smile.

Kate politely answered, "Thank you. Nice to meet you."

At that point, the girls turned their full attention back to Alyssa, giving Dietrich a not-so-subtle signal to move on.

"Aargh!" Audrey groaned, "He's so gross, but he thinks he's God's gift to women."

"Yeah. I kind of got that impression."

"Want to hear a good story? At the New England Dressage Association show last fall, he walked around with a big bulge in his breeches. Apparently, he had stuffed a sock in the crotch!"

"Seriously? How could you possibly know that?"

"I got it on good authority from Jason. He's friends with one of Dietrich's grooms. Just mind yourself. I'm sure he sees you as fresh meat and probably will try to make a move on you at some point. Some people actually find him charming. He makes me want to puke."

"No worries. He made my skin crawl, too. Oh, look! Alyssa's going around the outside of the ring. Doesn't Chance look beautiful?"

"He sure does. He's glistening like a new penny, and his braids are gorgeous. You did a good job preparing him."

"Thanks! I just love that horse to death. I'm so nervous. I hope he goes forward for her. This test is hard enough, but as we know, when you get to that last centerline you have a very tired horse. And he still has to do all that passage and piaffe."

The beginning of the test looked great. Alyssa was still coasting on the work Ben had done at home. But it didn't take long for Chance to figure out that he was getting blocked again by Alyssa's rigid seat and arms. To the educated eye, it was apparent that Chance was falling increasingly behind Alyssa's aids.

"Oh, dear." Kate furrowed her brow. "I think she's going to be in trouble when she gets to the first piaffe."

Sure enough, instead of trotting in place, Chance just shuffled his feet around while Alyssa kicked and spurred to get him to go. The second piaffe was even more of a disaster. Chance rooted his feet to the ground and threatened to back up. In desperation, Alyssa frantically bounced up and down in the saddle in an effort to get him to move.

By then, Dietrich had stopped watching them. As he walked by the girls, he said with mock sympathy, "That's really a shame. He looks like he could be a nice horse. But it's not going to happen with her. I must say she looks like a monkey bouncing around on a football. For their piaffe, I'd give the horse a one, and Alyssa a nine. She does quite an active piaffe all by herself, bumping around in her saddle." And he continued on his way, chuckling at his cleverness.

"Idiot." Audrey muttered.

"Oh dear. This test is getting more and more painful to watch," Kate said. "Chance has got her number, and there's nothing she can do about it."

Alyssa had figured out the same thing, and rather than face further embarrassment and a low score, she turned down the centerline to halt, salute, and excuse herself from finishing the test.

Kate met a tightlipped Alyssa at the in-gate. She noticed a lone tear trickling down the girl's cheek. Kate walked along beside them but didn't say anything because she didn't want Alyssa to have a public meltdown.

But Alyssa seemed calm. By the time they got back to the shed row, she dismounted, patted Chance, and said, "I'm going to scratch from the rest of the show. Obviously, he's not feeling well. Maybe his back is sore—probably from the work Ben did with him the other day. When I finish at the show office, I'm going to ask the vet to take a look at him."

Kate sighed in relief. "That sounds like a good plan. Let me just put him on the cross-ties, and I'll go get some stuff together to give him a shower."

As Kate walked to the tack room, Alyssa whispered to her horse, "You don't fool me for one second, you pig. There's nothing wrong with you. You're just a stubborn, lazy piece of shit with no work ethic. But you just wait until we get home. I'm going to fix your wagon once and for all."

# TWENTY-EIGHT

*Kate*

By the end of the day on Saturday, Mark and Quotation were in the running for the High Score at Third Level, Cara and Artie had a good shot at winning the FEI High Score trophy, and Luke was thrilled with Denali's performance at Training and First Level.

So, it was with high spirits that the Cherry Hill group arrived at the competitors' celebration at nearby Zuleika Farm. Wheeler and Peter had driven up from Massachusetts the day before to watch the classes and come to the party. They showed up fashionably late, with Chris in tow.

The party was just as Kate had anticipated. It was held at the mansion that had once belonged to actor Charles Bronson and his horse-loving actress wife, Jill Ireland. Equifare, the best in the business, catered the event. A band played under the tent set up behind the mansion, and the guests—riders, coaches and judges alike—did their utmost to outdo each other with their glamorous outfits. Audrey loved the competitors' party. It provided the perfect opportunity to show off and share gossip.

Wheeler flagged down a passing waiter who balanced a tray of champagne flutes. He handed glasses to Kate, Audrey, Peter, and Chris, and kept one for himself. "Yummy. What did I tell you? Great party, huh? We wouldn't have missed it. By the way, Kate, did I tell you that you look absolutely breathtaking?" He grabbed her by the hand and twirled her around.

Kate shook her head. "No, I don't. I look like a scarecrow." She felt like a little kid who'd dressed up in her mother's clothes. And, in fact, Maria had lent her an exquisite cocktail dress. Kate had that old feeling, as if at any moment she'd be discovered as a party crasher and get kicked out.

To turn attention away from herself, she said, "But you, kind sir, look dashing. Just don't go overboard with that champagne. I'm glad you guys are staying over tonight and not driving home."

Kate glanced around the crowded room. "It's really fun to see all these people I've only ever read about. Look. That's Adrienne Lyle! And there's Kasey Perry-Glass! They're my idols. They are such beautiful riders and seem like nice people. I've heard that some of the top riders are really nasty."

At that moment Cara breezed by, clinging to the arm of a tall, imposing man. She stopped so she could show off her date. With a saccharine-laced voice she said, "Kate, don't you look nice! What a darling little dress!

Wherever did you get it?"

Kate's face turned red, but before she could open her mouth, Wheeler rescued her. "Oh, we hit the Savoir Faire trailer yesterday and just about cleaned Sally out. It's Kate's favorite boutique, isn't it, hon?"

Before Kate could answer, Cara turned to her escort and announced, "Everyone! This is Antonio Baines. Tony owns Mulberry Farm in Danville, Connecticut. Tony, this is Katherine Gage and Audrey Rhodes. Katherine is a working student at Cherry Hill Farm. She takes care of Artisan for me, and I don't know what I'd do without her. Audrey manages the barn and makes sure everything runs like clockwork. And this handsome couple is Wheeler Grant and Peter White. They board at the farm and always keep us in stitches. And this is our newest addition, Chris Barton. He has two horses at the barn that he rescued from a horrible situation. I don't expect you to remember everyone's name yet, but I just wanted you to meet my dear friends."

They all shook hands and exchanged greetings while Cara droned on. The group listened politely as she filled them in on every boring detail of her day at the show. Cara sighed and added that, even though she knew management had turned themselves inside out, they had really dropped the ball this year when it came to the stabling and the footing.

Finally, Audrey couldn't take Cara's syrupy façade anymore and interrupted her monologue by blurting out, "I think the stabling and footing are fine. I haven't heard any complaints." Then to change the subject, Audrey asked, "Hey! Did you guys hear what happened to Julie Clark?"

"I was wondering why we hadn't seen her yet. Where is she?" Wheeler asked.

Audrey went on. "Well, she was on her way here by way of Interstate 91. I hate that road anyhow. It's always in terrible shape or under construction. Anyhow, she was in the traveling lane, and the next thing she knew, her trailer went by her in the passing lane! Apparently, the hitch broke. After the trailer passed her, it rolled across the other lanes and flipped over on its side in the median."

"Oh my God!" Peter cried out as the color drained from his face. "I've had a recurring dream like that for years. Julie just lived my nightmare. Is she okay? How is Perseus?"

"Julie's okay, thank God. Of course, she's really shook up," Audrey explained. "Percy's bruised and cut up pretty badly, but he's alive. He's at the vet clinic right now. I don't know how bad his injuries are, but I imagine he's going to be out of it for quite a while."

Peter looked beyond distressed at the news. "That's terrible. Julie's worked so hard to get where she is. She's had Percy since he was a three-year-old and has done all the schooling pretty much by herself. And now to have such rotten luck when they're so close to making the training list. I just hope he's going to be okay."

Word spread fast, and soon the people eager to hear about Julie swallowed up Wheeler, Peter, Chris, Audrey, and Kate. Talk of Julie's accident dominated the evening. The riders had mixed feelings. On the one hand, the accident upset most everyone. Riders on the circuit liked Julie and admired her for her kind training methods. That respect was rare among horse people who generally were a critical, insecure, and competitive lot.

On the other hand, they felt unspoken relief that the tragedy had happened to someone else. You never knew what the next day would bring in the horse world.

Audrey often said the whole sport was a crapshoot. You're doing well, and then you get bucked off a young horse and end up out of commission for months with a broken leg. Or you doggedly climb toward your riding goal over months and years. Then one day you turn around to find your horse needs colic surgery or is lame from a torn suspensory ligament. Dressage certainly tested your resilience. The old saying, "It's not how many times you fall. It's how many times you get back up and keep moving forward" must've been coined for dressage riders.

Eventually, Kate grew weary of the party scene and wandered out to the veranda that overlooked the lush gardens. It was a crystal-clear night that held the promise of perfect weather for the next day's competition. Kate took a deep breath. She savored the silence and crisp air after the din of so many voices and the close quarters inside the tent. She felt peaceful and truly privileged to be part of this world.

Her thoughts drifted toward the next day's show routine. As she went over the schedule in her mind, a voice directly behind her startled her.

"Some night, huh?" she turned to see Dietrich Krause standing behind her with a drink in hand. Judging by the way he swayed, it probably wasn't his first one.

Kate looked at him warily and said, "Yes. It's just gorgeous. I love being in Vermont. This is a magical farm. I feel like I've been carried back in time.

Dietrich moved closer, slipped an arm around her waist, and buried his nose in her hair, taking in her fragrance. "I feel that way too. It's like we've been transported back to a very romantic era."

Kate stiffened and jumped away from his grasp. "Dietrich, please! What do you think you're doing?"

"What you mean, what am I doing? I'm just taking you up on your invitation. You wouldn't be wearing that dress if you weren't looking for attention." And, then, to soothe his bruised ego, he said, "You know, Katherine, I've heard stories about you. I bet you don't know what everyone calls you. They've dubbed you the Ice Queen, and, if you ask me, it's a well-deserved title."

She backed farther away from him and said, "Well, I didn't ask you. And there's nothing wrong with me, Dietrich. You're the one with the problem. Just leave me alone, will you?"

Too late, Kate realized that Dietrich interpreted her

stepping back as an invitation for him to step closer to her.

"Come on, Katherine. Loosen up. We could have such a great time. I can't believe you'd turn me down. Maybe you have something going on with Ben Ellis. Or maybe you're into women."

Kate looked at Dietrich with undisguised contempt. She remembered their conversation earlier that afternoon at the stables. He had courted her with his soft, melodic voice and fatherly concern. Dietrich told her she was a sweet girl and a talented rider but was entirely too trusting for her own good. He had gone on to say that her mentor, Ben, and her so-called friends used her. They were after her money or after her body. She'd laughed so hard at that.

According to Dietrich, he was the only one who didn't have ulterior motives. He was also one of a handful of trainers who was into dressage for pure art. And he intimated that if she stuck with him, he'd take good care of her and put in a good word for her with the equestrian team.

Kate's anger bubbled over as she now glared at Dietrich. "And maybe you're so busy tripping over your own ego that you just don't get it that not every woman you meet wants to fall into bed with you."

Kate turned to escape, but before heading back to the safety of the crowd, said frostily, "I'm so sorry, Dietrich, but I have to go now. Enjoy the party."

Although she'd had a good time earlier, Kate now regretted coming to the party at all. Audrey had insisted she come because she couldn't stand it that Kate worked so hard and had no social life. But Kate had made a vow a long time ago that her personal life would never distract her from her goals. At least that's what she'd told herself. In her heart, though, she knew the real reason. And although she tried valiantly, she knew it was impossible to bury the past. The horror of that long-ago attack always found its way to the surface to haunt her.

Kate remembered that first week after the rape as if it were yesterday. She could barely function. She told her mother she was sick and stayed home from school. Each day, she stood under the scalding spray of the shower for what seemed like hours. She wrapped the hot water around her like a protective cocoon. But no amount of hot water could wash Jimmy's filth from her soul. When the water turned cold, she stepped from the shower and looked in the mirror to study the angry purple bruises on her throat. She could hide the bruises with turtleneck sweaters or scarves, and soon they would be gone. But she wondered how long it would take before she'd stop being tormented by the invisible bruises of violation.

As she'd stared numbly at her reflection, she'd vowed never to be vulnerable to anyone or anything ever again.

Kate returned to the safety of the tent, where she locked eyes with Chris, who sat alone at one of the dinner tables. She was pale and her eyes had the stunned look of a deer in headlights. Chris jumped up and hurried over to her.

"Are you okay, Kate? You look ill."

Kate rallied, and tried to distract him. "Jeez. Thanks a lot, Chris. I'm fine. I just wanted to explore the grounds a bit. It's so beautiful here."

Chris didn't press her any further. Instead, he took her hand and said, "C'mon. Let's dance."

"Oh. No. I couldn't. I'm a terrible dancer. I think I have two left feet."

"No worries. I'm a terrific leader. You just follow me, and we'll be fine."

He led her onto the dance floor, took her in his arms, and started to sway slowly side to side. It didn't take long for Kate to relax in the warmth of Chris' embrace and stay softly connected to him. They danced for several songs, and contentment replaced the disgust Kate had felt at Dietrich's attempt to seduce her.

After three dances, Chris looked at Kate, his blue eyes somehow both merry and serious, and said, "We're a perfect fit, you know. This is where you belong. And I plan to spend as long as it takes for you to feel the same way about me as I do about you."

Kate was taken aback but didn't say anything. She'd had no idea Chris felt anything but friendship for her. He'd never actually said or done anything to make her think otherwise.

Finally, she nodded her head and allowed herself to entertain the thought that their relationship might develop beyond friendship. She knew in her heart that this was a solid man—a man that she could trust. She laid her head on his shoulder and savored the feeling of being wanted and safe.

As they danced, Kate thought about the old horseman's remedy for all wounds—tincture of time. And Kate knew Chris would give her the time she needed—time to nurture her acceptance of herself and what she realized might just be deepening feelings for this man.

# TWENTY-NINE

*Kate*

On the Tuesday after the Green Mountain show, Kate waited for Alyssa to show up to school Chance. As Kate prepared him, Alyssa arrived in a cloud of Chanel No. 5.

"Well, he's had three days to rest so I'm sure he's fine by now. I'm not going to work him today anyhow. I'm just going to longe him and go for a hack. Don't you think that's a good plan, just in case he's still a little uncomfortable?"

Kate nodded, but she knew there was nothing physically wrong with Chance. He was simply discouraged from being asked to go forward while his rider had the hand brake on. She quietly finished getting him ready, and after giving him a cookie and a pat, she handed him over to Alyssa.

Alyssa led Chance out the back of the barn toward the round pen. Kate followed and watched the beginning of the session.

The first thing Alyssa did was attach the side-reins to the bit. She didn't even give Chance a minute to walk around to loosen up without the side-reins. Instead, she immediately sent him out on the circle in the walk. Chance had barely started walking, and Alyssa shouted, "March!" as she hauled off and smacked him on his hindquarters with the lash of the longe whip. She startled him, and he broke into a canter.

Alyssa let him canter a few strides, and then yanked on the longe line to bring him back to the walk. Then she yelled again. "March!" Chance became a bit more active this time, but she still walloped him and chased him into the canter again. Alyssa punished him over and over until a frightened Chance walked briskly on his own.

Alyssa was trying to mimic what Ben did when he rode Chance, but she used the whip as a punishment rather than to teach him anything. Chance marched now, but it was more from fear of getting beaten than from his understanding that he should walk actively and energetically on his own.

Once Alyssa was satisfied with his energy in the walk, she started the same process for the walk-to-trot transitions.

By that time, Kate left the scene of the crime. She needed to get Fantastique ready for Jackie who was due to arrive soon. As she prepared Fanny, tears streamed down her cheeks.

When Jackie arrived. She looked at Kate with concern and asked, "Are you okay?"

Kate wiped her runny nose on her sleeve and said past the lump in her throat, "Yes, I'm fine. It's just terrible allergies. Thanks for asking. Fantastique is almost ready for you. She's so wonderful. She sure lives up to her name."

"I know. I thank my lucky stars every day for having such a wonderful horse. I'm going to go get my boots, helmet, and gloves, and I'll be back soon. Let me know if you need anything."

As Jackie turned to leave, Kate's thoughts returned to Alyssa. She agonized over what to do about the girl's treatment of her horses. She considered talking to her herself but wasn't sure Alyssa would even listen. After all, she was only a groom. But maybe it was worth a try. It certainly would be better than running to Ben to rat her out again. Still, Kate knew that it might come down to getting him involved. She wondered if he'd kick Alyssa out of the barn when he learned that she was continuing to abuse her horses.

Audrey looked over at her friend, sitting on the couch in baggy sweats with an "I'm in for the night" vibe.

"C'mon, Kate. Come out to dinner with us. You've been here for two months and except for the competitors' party at Green Mountain, you've been a total hermit. You need a social life."

"I'm fine, Audrey. I have a lot of work to do and then I'm going to bed early."

"Yeah, right. A lot of work. I know what you're doing. As soon as I leave you'll pull out your computer and get on one of those chat rooms so you can eavesdrop on a lot of dressage hens who don't have a life. I swear. I think some of them must have slept in the alley near the Spanish Riding School in Austria, and they think that gives them the right to advise other people on how to train horses. You couldn't get me in those chat rooms if you paid me."

Kate shrugged. "They're fun. I get to read about ideas from people from all over. A couple of weeks ago someone wrote in because her horse had chronic bit sores. No matter what kind of bit she used, the corners of her horse's mouth cracked and bled. It was a great brainstorming session. Tons of people wrote in, including several veterinarians. It turns out her mare had a metal allergy. She switched bits, and her horse's mouth has been fine ever since."

"That's all well and good. But I want you to know, Katherine Gage, that you're not fooling me a single bit. You like these chat rooms and message boards because you don't have to actually interact with people in the real world. You need a break from the horses once in a while. And PJ's is such a fun place. Great food, fun people, and terrific music. Pleeeease reconsider."

"Not tonight, Audrey. Next time. I promise."

"Okay. You win, Blister Butt. Enjoy your sewing circle."

As soon as Audrey left, Kate went to her room and grabbed her laptop. She hit the bookmark that would get her into one of her favorite forums, DressageChat.com.

Audrey was right. Kate loved the anonymity of the forums. They gave her a chance to network with people yet maintain a safe distance. For the most part, she lurked on several sites—reading the questions and replies but rarely taking an active part. If she wanted to ask a question or make a comment, she used the name "Barnrat" to conceal her identity.

She clicked on a question about a long-standing controversial training technique called "rollkur." Rollkur was a term used to describe an extreme position of the horse's head and neck where his neck was curled in tightly and his chin almost touched his chest. The question was posed by KarenH. Karen wrote:

> *Does anyone out there agree that putting a horse's chin on his chest is just plain horse abuse?*

There were lots of responses, and Kate worked her way through the answers. Everyone was passionate about her own viewpoint.

> **DQWannabee:** *How can it be abuse? Some of the top riders in the world use this technique, and they're winning medals. There are many roads to Rome. Maybe this is just another way to get the same result.*

> **Sitthetrot:** *I'm sorry but, for me, the means don't justify the end. How can it be okay? In the first place, the horse can't even see where he's going. Sec-*

*ondly, he must be in incredible pain to have his neck cranked in so tightly. It's cruel.*

*KarenH: I totally agree with Sitthetrot. I read somewhere that vets have done studies that actually show the damage that's done to the neck from being held in such an unnatural position.*

*Evergreen: If it's so bad, how come some of the top horses in the world stay strong and sound well into their twenties?*

*Seabisquit68: That's a great question. I think some of you are blowing this out of proportion. It's a tool, not a method. The very best riders change the position of the horse's head and neck frequently. They don't ride around for an hour in that position.*

*CareyL: I think you're right, DQWannabee. The best riders know how to use the technique without causing their horses harm.*

*XHaltSalute: Yeah, but that's the scary thing. You get a bunch of amateurs who try to imitate what the high-profile riders do, and they don't have the skill to do it correctly.*

*DressageLvr: That's true. I actually heard that an amateur from Canada didn't know how to get her horse's head in that position so she tied it down with a nylon boat rope!*

**Piaffe75:** Well, I hate to sound like a purist (not really), but it's not classical, and it's not dressage. I think in Europe they even call it "dressage perverse."

**Newbie:** Isn't it just another version of long-and-low so the horse is really round over his topline?

**MarshaP:** It's not long-and-low. A true long-and-low position strengthens and supples the horse's back. Rollkur is just plain short and tight in the neck. My trainer would have a fit if I rode my horse like that.

**Extendedtrot:** The fact is that a lot of riders who use this technique win. How can you argue with success? If you knew that schooling that way would help you make a team and win a medal, wouldn't you be tempted to try it?

**Nightrider:** No. It's like runners or cyclists using steroids. They win. But at what cost?

**Chestnuts4ever:** That's part of the problem. Some judges reward the riders who school their horses like that. What message does that send? The judges need to be more honest. If those riders were losing, they'd have to find a different way.

The discussion went on for pages, and Kate lurked in the forum for about an hour. She wanted to read more of the responses, but it was her evening to do night check.

She shut off her computer, her mind buzzing with the pros and cons of rollkur. Kate decided that, for her, the jury was still out. Was rollkur really so awful? Many of the riders who used the technique had happy, healthy horses who led long, useful lives. But in the hands of less-talented riders, rollkur could be a disaster. Ben adamantly refused to school his horses like that. She planned to ask him about it.

She couldn't imagine sacrificing the comfort of her horses for personal glory. But she considered whether the lure of a medal would tempt her to compromise her principles. On the one hand, she knew she wouldn't allow it. She loved the horses too much. But on the other hand, she wondered if she was being naïve. Audrey probably would've thought she was. Did most of the top riders put their horses' well-being on the back burner for the glory of an Olympic medal? Or were those top riders just so gifted that they could use rollkur without causing harm to their horses?

Before she headed down to the stable for night check, Kate brought her computer back to her small bedroom and placed it on top of her desk. Her desktop was neat, orderly, and a little bit bare, like the rest of the room, which was stark and utilitarian—desk, chair, bed, and dresser. That was about it. She'd never bothered to decorate it with photographs or posters. Except for Wheeler, she didn't really have any friends from her past, so the few pictures she had on her dresser were of horses she'd ridden and loved.

# THIRTY

*Kate*

Over the next couple of months, Kate and Remmy formed an amazing partnership. Remmy seemed to turn himself inside out to please her. She was gentle and spoke to him in a way he could understand—through crystal clear mental pictures and consistent signals.

Kate suspected that John confused Remmy because he couldn't hold a clear picture in his mind of what he wanted him to do. Between work and riding, John's thoughts were always on overdrive, with bits and pieces of different images floating around in his head at the same time.

When Kate watched him ride, it was apparent to her that John couldn't concentrate on one thing. Just about the time he focused on one picture, such as riding a shoulder-in, he'd ask Kate an unrelated question that showed his mind was elsewhere. Because his signals were muddy, Remmy often had to guess what the man wanted. When he guessed wrong, he was corrected with a sharp smack from the dressage whip. Remmy showed his frustration by swishing his tail and pinning his ears, but never stopped trying. That's just the kind of horse he was.

Kate felt that Remmy was happier when she rode him. He even recognized the sound of her footsteps as she came down the barn aisle. As soon as he heard the light but purposeful rhythm of her steps, he'd head to the front of his stall like a loyal dog waiting for the first glimpse of his beloved owner returning home. He'd fix his eyes and ears on the end of the aisle, and as soon as he saw her, he'd toss his head and nicker enthusiastically. He was happy to see her, and just as excited that she probably had something yummy for him to eat.

Kate laughed at his shameless begging for treats. "Hey, sweet boy. I bet I know what you want." She went into the stall and let Remmy search her pockets for horse cookies. "You certainly have me well trained, don't you?" She pulled out a treat and handed it to Remmy.

After finishing his cookie, Remmy started nuzzling Kate's hair while Kate hugged and kissed his neck.

"Eeewwwwwww! Now you've got slobber all over your hair!"

Kate turned to see Audrey approaching her with a saddle over her right arm and a bridle nestled in the crook of her left arm.

Audrey scrunched up her face as if she were going to throw up. "How can you let him drool on your hair like that? He was probably just groveling around in his manure."

"He was not. Besides, I like it. That's how he kisses me and shows he loves me."

"Yeah, right! Loves cookies, you mean. But I assume you save those kisses for Chris, right?" Audrey teased.

Kate answered a bit too hastily. "Knock it off, Audrey. Chris and I are just friends."

"Terrible waste, Katie." Audrey kept walking and tossed over her shoulder. "It's obvious the guy has a thing for you. Why don't you put him out of his misery?"

*A thing for me? What is she talking about?*

Sure, they worked together well with the horses. Both of the rescued horses had filled out, and their coats gleamed with good health. But did Chris really have feelings for her beyond caring for the horses?

The two of them had only had physical contact three times—the first night when she brought Chris dinner, the day the mare died, and when they danced at the Green Mountain competitors' party. Chris hinted that he wanted to be more than friends. More than hinted, really. But she'd said nothing in response, and since that time, he'd kept his distance, and their relationship had remained platonic.

They rarely discussed anything personal and most of the time only talked about the horses. Their most recent discussion centered around giving them names. They didn't want to keep calling them the gelding and the youngster. After much discussion, they agreed that since the horses had fought their way back from the brink of death, they should, therefore, name them appropriately.

They dubbed the older horse Triumphant and called him Tee for short. They called the youngster Victorious and called him Victor.

As Kate mused about Chris and the horses, she felt an arm slip around her shoulders. Instinctively, she stiffened. Once she realized it was John, however, she relaxed. John had become such an important part of her life. Yes, she was grateful that he was her sponsor. But he had also become her mentor—much as she imagined her own father would've been if he had stuck around long enough to be part of her life.

"Hi, Sweetheart. How's our boy?"

She smiled at the man she considered a surrogate parent. "He's great. Begging for cookies, as always."

"And, how are you? Nervous about the Devon show?"

Kate lifted one shoulder and said, "A little, I guess. Mostly excited. It's like a dream. When I arrive in the warm-up area at shows, I can hardly believe that I'm surrounded by the biggest names in American dressage. Most of them are very gracious, but I feel like I'm sneaking into a concert without a ticket. I'm waiting to get kicked out. But everyone treats me like it's normal for me to be there. That just blows me away."

"You do belong there, Kate. You ride as well as any one of them and you know it. The only thing they have over you is experience in the Grand Prix ring. And we're taking care of that right now. You have a gift. How can I get you to believe in yourself the way you believe in Reminisce?"

Kate eyed the floor and shook her head. "I don't know,

John. But for now, it's enough that I believe in Remmy one hundred percent, and that you believe in both of us."

John gave her a squeeze. "Well, you know I'm here for you. You don't have to put up a brave front for me. You can tell me if you're afraid or worried or concerned about anything. You can lean on me. When you share your fears, you lighten the load."

"I know that, John. And I appreciate it so much. Having you, Ben, Wheeler, Peter, Chris, Jason, and Audrey for moral support makes all the difference in the world. When I canter down the centerline to start a test, I feel like I'm bringing all of you with me. It's a wonderful feeling to have a support team."

John grew animated. "Yes! Team Gage! That's what we'll call our little group. Now get our star ready for your training session with Ben, and I'll go grab my pom-poms so I can cheer you on!"

# THIRTY-ONE

*Chris*

After several weeks, Chris started longeing Tee. He thought letting him trot and canter for ten or fifteen minutes at the end of a thirty-five-foot longe line without the weight of a rider on his back would be a good way to start to get him in better condition.

Chris knew he had to be careful about how long he longed Tee. It could be a strain for him to go around in circles for too long. He'd been longeing him briefly for about ten days and now planned to get on him for a few minutes each day. By the following week, he'd start walking him around the fields to build him up even more.

Chris waited for Kate to join him during her lunch break. He wanted her there when he first got on in case he needed help. After all, Tee hadn't been ridden in over a year.

He had some suspicions that in his former life Tee was a handful. To be fair, the owner hadn't said anything specifically about his behavior, but Chris wondered if he had some skeletons in his closet. But at the time of the rescue, Chris's only concern was saving the horses' lives. Riding them was the furthest thing from his mind.

But now, as he was preparing to ride Tee for the first time, he remembered the owner saying that she hadn't shown him because he was a bit strong for her. That caused Chris's internal caution lights to flash. He'd been around horses long enough to read between the lines. He knew if you didn't ask the right questions, no one was going to volunteer information—particularly negative information.

He chuckled to himself when he thought of how people described sale horses. If their ads said things like "enough quality for a professional," it meant that the horse probably bucked, bolted, reared, or all three. On the other hand, "perfect for an amateur" meant you needed a cattle prod to get the horse going. "Needs a competent rider" meant that the horse was so insecure that he'd spook, wheel and run for the next county at the sight of anything that looked strange.

In Tee's case, "strong" could mean anything from a benign "leans on your hands" to a life-threatening "bolts blindly out of control." He wouldn't know for sure until he started riding him.

Kate showed up at the quarantine barn at noon to help

with Tee. Chris had just finished longeing him. Chris wanted to be ready to start as soon as she arrived so he didn't take up her entire lunch break.

For a few minutes, Kate admired the big bay trotting on the longe. "He's really starting to look good," she said. "He's put on weight and his topline muscles have started to develop. It's hard to believe that not too long ago he looked like a starvation case. Now that he's so much stronger, I can see what a pretty trot he has. He has a nice hind leg that reaches under his body, and he swings along so fluidly. I remember the first time you longed him. I think you trotted him for less than two minutes, and he barely jogged around."

"I know. His canter is pretty amazing too. He bounds over the ground like he's wearing Nikes," Chris agreed. "I'm excited to start him under saddle and see what he knows. I just have to keep reminding myself that he's still pretty weak and to take it slowly.  Are you ready to help me? I don't know how he's going to react to me getting on, so my plan is to treat him like a young horse just starting under saddle."

"That sounds like a good idea. Do you want me to lead you around after you get on?" Kate asked.

"Yeah," Chris nodded. "But first, I just want to lie across the saddle and belly him like he's never been ridden. I want to see how he reacts to that. Can you bring the mounting block over here?"

Kate picked up the blue plastic mounting block that looked like a three-step staircase. Climbing on the block would give Chris an extra twenty-two inches of height so he wouldn't have to mount Tee from the ground. She brought the block over and set it down on the left side of the horse.

Chris said, "I know I'm being overly cautious, but since I don't know what he's going to do when I get on, I'd rather do it this way."

"I absolutely agree," Kate said. "You can't unring the bell. Better to steer clear of problems than have to deal with a mess you could've avoided. I'm with you on the conservative approach. We're not in any rush. Remember that old saying? Act like you have all day, and it'll take fifteen minutes. Act like you have fifteen minutes and you'll need all day."

"Ain't that the truth!" Chris laughed.

Kate removed the side-reins and took the longe whip from Chris. Holding on to the longe line, she stood at Tee's head and spoke softly to the gelding. She stroked his neck as Chris stepped onto the mounting block.

On the mounting block, Chris was tall enough to reach over Tee's back and touch him on the other side of his body. He patted his shoulders and hindquarters on both sides and slapped the saddle with the palm of his hand to make sure the noise didn't bother him. Throughout this procedure, he kept an eye on Tee's eyes and ears for signs of anxiety. When he was satisfied that the horse was calm, he lay across the saddle with his belly so Tee could feel his weight on his back.

"He seems totally unconcerned," Kate murmured.

Chris agreed. "Okay. This time I'm going to swing my leg over and get on."

Kate continued to croon to Tee as Chris mounted. The big horse was completely unperturbed by the procedure.

"He seems fine. Go ahead and lead me forward a few steps."

Kate did as Chris asked. They walked and halted several times. Both of them patted and spoke to Tee throughout the process.

"All right, Kate. Now, gradually let some of the longe line out until we're circling around you. I'll ask him to walk and halt from my aids, and we'll see how it goes."

Tee was the perfect gentleman. He responded to Chris's aids obediently. "I think he's adjusted to my signals, so let's just have a short trot in each direction, and then we'll call it a day."

Chris lightly pressed his calves against Tee's sides, and the bay trotted off with a happy shake of his head.

Kate said, "It's great that he feels a little fresh. But I'm also very glad he's being polite and not getting too exuberant."

"You're not the only one," Chris joked. "He's a big boy, and it's a long way to the ground. I'd rather not buy any real estate today, thank you very much."

They trotted a couple of circles to the left, and then Chris stopped so Kate could change Tee's direction. Then they did the same thing to the right.

When they finished, both Chris and Kate were ecstatic. Chris dismounted and patted Tee enthusiastically.

"What a good boy you are!" To Kate he said, "Can we do this for the next few days? I want to increase the work gradually so I don't make him sore. Hopefully, in a few days, I can wean us off the longe line. But I'd still like you here as my security blanket and possible emergency brake until he and I get to know each other better."

Kate was happy that she could help Chris and that he trusted her. In that moment, she realized that she was beginning to trust him more, too. He never made any inappropriate moves toward her. Like her, he only wanted to rehabilitate Victor and Triumphant.

"I can be here every day at lunchtime," she said. "Does that work for you?"

His eyes lit up. "Absolutely. I have a feeling we have a very cool horse here. I can't wait to see what happens when he gets strong enough to do some real work."

Kate beamed at the word "we." She loved that Chris included her in his project. Even though it was her choice, she was a loner. She carried the pain of the old trauma with her every hour of every day. She insulated herself from others by wearing her shame like an overcoat. It screamed at her. It was your fault. You deserved it. She said these things to herself until she sometimes felt totally worthless. Except when she was with the horses. The horses accepted her unconditionally, and it amazed her that Chris seemed to also. Of course, he didn't know her awful secret.

Chris gave Tee a treat, waved at Kate, and headed for

the barn. Kate smiled and walked back to the main barn with a light heart and the word "we" echoing in her mind.

# THIRTY-TWO

*John*

John loved sponsoring Kate. He knew he represented the father figure she'd missed most of her life—enthusiastic, supportive, and kind. He loved that Kate relied on him as a sounding board for her decisions about Remmy's training and care as well as her advisor for many of her personal issues.

John also enjoyed the fact that Kate and Remmy gave him a ticket to the inner circle of the dressage world. As an owner, he was automatically invited to the competitors' parties at the big shows. He got a kick out of networking with the other owners, sitting in the VIP section at the shows, and being recognized and acknowledged by the top riders and the power players from the United States Equestrian Federation.

And, if the truth were told, he delighted in playing Henry Higgins to Kate's Eliza Doolittle. He saw her as an enchanting project. He reveled in introducing her to the finer things in life—fashionable clothes, elegant restaurants, concerts, and sophisticated parties. As he watched her blossom and become more self-assured, he took pleasure in the idea that he alone was responsible for molding this exquisite creature.

Soon after a local show in Holyoke, John and Kate had dinner together to outline their plans for the Devon show in Pennsylvania in September and the winter circuit in Wellington, Florida. They sat in a corner booth in a cozy little restaurant called Wiggins Tavern in Northampton, sipping the Chardonnay that John had ordered. He usually decided what they'd eat and drink. John knew that left to her own devices Kate would probably order a cheeseburger and a coke.

While Kate studied the menu, John watched her and thought how lovely she was–strikingly beautiful yet unaware of her looks. If anything, she was just the opposite. Her feelings toward herself often appeared to cross the line from humility to self-loathing. Kate's insecurity baffled John, but he thought it might have something to do with her father leaving the family when she was so young. She didn't offer any explanation, and he didn't ask. Yet he thought it was amazing that she could love the horses unconditionally yet struggle to muster a grain of self-love. She did an admirable job of disguising her low self-esteem, he could see that. But he could also see that, once in a while, her insecurities about herself and her abilities leaked through her façade.

Kate peeked up from the menu through long, dark eyelashes and asked, "What are you going to have?"

"I'm going to go with the salmon. It's always good here. What about you?"

As usual, she had whatever he was having. "That sounds delicious. I'll have that too."

She closed her menu, and John signaled to the waiter that they were ready to order. That done, she took another sip of wine and toyed with the single candle that sat on the table between them.

John reached over and laid his hand on hers. "I'm so proud of you, Kate. You're doing an amazing job with Reminisce. People have noticed both of you, and there's a lot of buzz about making the Training List."

Even though John's touch was a fatherly gesture, the intimacy of his contact made Kate stiffen. But she left her hand where it was for a few moments and then casually withdrew it and reached for her wine in one smooth movement.

Oblivious, John continued, "Let's talk about our strategy for Florida. As you know, Ben takes a group of horses to Wellington in December and sets up Cherry Hill Farm South in one of the permanent barns at the showgrounds. Starting in February, there are three possible selection trials we could go to. We won't actually be vying for a spot in the final trials, but I think we should enter so you both get to experience that atmosphere.

Kate's jaw dropped. "You sound awfully sure we'll be

competitive in that company. Do you really think we're ready for that kind of pressure? What if I blow it, and let you down? I'd feel terrible if I disappointed you and everyone else."

"You could never disappoint me, Kate. Just do what you always do––the best you can. I'm sure that will be good enough. You and Reminisce have barely had a chance to get to know each other and look what you've already done. And now you have a few more small shows to get more comfortable with each other in the ring. Then you have Devon as another opportunity to practice at a big show against the people who'll be your future rivals. Simple as that."

John grew even more animated. "I'm not sure you realize this, but during the Florida circuit, there are also a couple of training sessions with the coach of the team, Bela Szabo. I know you rely on Ben, but if, excuse me, when you make the Training List and later on the team, you'll ride under Szabo. The sooner you build a rapport with him, the easier that transition will be."

Kate extended her palms toward John as if trying to stop a runaway train. "I don't want to work with anyone but Ben. I trust him. If we make the Training List, maybe he can come to Europe and help us there."

John tried to set Kate's mind at ease. He'd heard the rumors about the team coach. He was considered a brilliant horseman, but he often unleashed his temper on his students. It had even been rumored that he hit his students with the long whip he carried when he taught or coached.

Kate had a lot to digest, and John didn't want to over-whelm her by putting even more on her plate. He calm-ly said, "It doesn't work that way, Kate. You can still have Ben there, but when you make the team, Bela will oversee your training. That's part of being on a team. But that's a long way off. Don't worry about it now. Let's just focus on the upcoming shows. Ah, here come our salads."

They spent the rest of dinner discussing going to South Florida for the winter. Kate pushed the food around on her plate while she listened to John describe life in Wellington, known to many as "Welly World." It sounded exciting to her. But it also sounded terrifying for a small-town girl from Rhode Island who'd never been out of New England.

"I spoke to Ben yesterday," John said. "He's only going to take eight horses down this year. You, Audrey, Mateo, and Phillipe can easily handle that. Jason and Melissa are willing to hold down the fort up here, and Ben's hiring two more people to help them with the barn work. He'll bring Reminisce for you, Alyssa's Celebrity and Chancel-lor, Cara's Artisan, Chris' Triumphant, Jolicoeur for Au-drey and a couple of the young horses that need mileage in the ring."

"That's so exciting. Oh, I hope he brings the babies, Kingston and Happenstance. I think they're ready to start showing. And it'll be great for them to continue their training during the winter instead of having it off like they did last year."

John continued filling Kate in on the plans for Florida.

"Yes. That sounds like a good idea. And it would give you and Audrey another horse to ride. By the way, Ben leased a two-bedroom apartment near the showgrounds for you and Audrey. Mateo and Phillipe each have a room in Peter and Wheeler's place. Alyssa and Cara will have to find their own housing. I'm not sure if they'll want to share a place or do their own thing. I haven't heard what Chris plans to do. I own a house in the Polo Club. It's just a few minutes from the showgrounds.

"So, since you have a place in the Polo Club, I'm guessing you've been to the Wellington shows before. Are they as intimidating as I imagine?"

John's face lit up. "I suppose. But I love the atmosphere. And it's such a great experience for the horses. The Wellington competitions challenge even the most seasoned horses. It's like a three-ring circus. There are golf carts, bicycles, spectators, scooters, and vendors everywhere. The hunters and jumpers are just down the road from the dressage horses. It's a very electric atmosphere, and a lot of the horses that trailer in and out for the three or four days of a show don't handle it very well. But you'll have the advantage of stabling there, so the horses will get used to it and think it's normal. It's a great chance to experience all the chaos of multiple disciplines competing together, as well as lots of spectator activity. That's what Ben tells me you'll find at the European shows.

The butterflies in Kate's stomach bounced around like hip-hop dancers. She wasn't sure if was from excitement or fear. She warned herself not to go down a negative road mentally, but despite her resolve, she found herself asking "what if" questions. What if she let John down? What if the atmosphere at the big shows overwhelmed Remmy? What if she totally blew it because of her inexperience?

Even though Birchwood and Devon were big shows, they were practically in her backyard. But this was Wellington. Horses and riders from all over the country and even the world would be there. And who was she? An amateur from Rhode Island. Kate had dreamt about this opportunity since she was a child. But now that it was within her grasp, fear and insecurity smothered her like a blanket.

# THIRTY-THREE

*Cara*

The group from Cherry Hill Farm arrived at the Devon show two days early to settle in before they had to compete. The breed show had started the day before so the young horses who'd be shown in hand packed the showgrounds. The close quarters at the show and the mass of young horses, some who'd never been off their farms, contributed to the supercharged atmosphere.

Even though the stable area was a chaotic mess, with people hurrying to unload horses and equipment in the cramped quarters, everyone was in high spirits. After all, this was Devon, one of the most prestigious shows in the country, and the highest rated international dressage competition held outside of Europe. Devon selected its competitors carefully. It wasn't open to just anyone who wanted to compete. To limit entries to the cream of the crop, riders had to qualify at other shows earlier in the season.

While Kate and Audrey took care of business at the stables, Ben went to the show office to get the competitors' packets containing programs and numbers for the horses. By the time Ben returned, Kate and Audrey had settled the horses into their boxes. The girls set up one of the stalls as a tack room for their equipment. They arranged the trunks and equipment to make the crowded stall a practical and efficient work area. Wheeler, Cara, Audrey, and Kate would share one tack stall. The second stall was for hay, grain, shavings, and supplements, and they made a grooming area out of the third stall.

Cara giggled as she watched Alyssa's employees—Anastasia and her husband, Igor—set up her private tack room, grooming area, and sitting area. Having organized many tack rooms for her over the years, they knew exactly how their boss wanted things arranged. But even though they had been to many horse shows, the huge animals still scared them. They did their best to keep as wide a berth as possible between themselves and the throngs of arriving horses during their numerous trips to and from Alyssa's trailer to fetch her equipment. To entertain herself, Alyssa perched on a long-legged director's chair and supervised.

Anastasia and Igor set up Alyssa's grooming stall and stored her hay, grain, and shavings in Ben's feed room. They made the tack room look like a posh sitting room, complete with drapes on the walls, framed prints of scenes from the Spanish Riding School in Vienna, potted plants, cushy furniture, a coffee table and a cherry cabinet that concealed a well-stocked minibar. By the time Anastasia and Igor finished, the tack room and exterior looked like it belonged on the cover of *Better Homes & Gardens.*

When Ben returned from the show office, he gathered his group around him for a short meeting.

"Okay, gang. Here are your packets. Let's let the horses relax in their boxes, and then we'll start light sessions. I want them to get familiar with the activity on the grounds, so move them around enough to get their muscles supple and loose after the long trailer ride. I don't want to make them tired because we need them fresh for competition days. Wheeler on Baryshnikov and Alyssa on Celebrity will start at 3:00. The next group will go at 3:45. That will be Kate on Remmy and Cara on Artie. Audrey on Joe and Alyssa with Chance come at 4:30. Any questions?"

While Ben was talking, the riders flipped through their programs to find their classes. Kate found her Grand Prix class, and scanned the entries looking for her name. She leaned toward Wheeler and blurted, "Omigod! Can you believe this? I have to ride right after Steffen Peters. I'm freaking out."

Wheeler winked at her and said, "No problem. Just ride in his draft."

Kate giggled. Her friend always managed to keep her from taking herself too seriously.

Ben glanced at Kate and for her benefit as well as the entire group, he said, "Listen guys. We all know dressage is one of the few sports that men, women, professionals, and amateurs compete together on equal footing. So, you can assume that although the preliminary warm-up areas are big, they'll be pretty chaotic. Expect it, and it won't throw you. Just pass the other horses left hand to left hand like you're driving a car. And if you're taking a walk break or circling, stay well to the inside so the working horses have access to the track. When you're on deck, you'll be moved into to a different warm-up area where you'll have the ring to yourself for the last few minutes before entering the Dixon Oval to do your test. Take a few deep breaths while you go around the outside of the arena. You want to avoid transmitting tension to your horse when they see the bleachers, banners, flags, flowers, and judges' booths. But above all remember that you belong at this show. You had to qualify to get here and that makes you as worthy as anyone else."

After the brief meeting with Ben, Alyssa and Cara wandered around the showgrounds to check things out. They each had their own agenda. Alyssa wanted to see who was there and to be seen by anyone she considered important. Cara just wanted to be seen, period. She had no idea how she looked, tiptoeing through the sand in four-inch stiletto heels, skin-tight leather pants, and a nearly transparent mesh top that displayed her lacy black bra underneath.

Dietrich Krause caught sight of them heading toward the far end of the warm-up ring and changed course so he could stalk his prey. Under his breath he said, "Ah. 'DQ-ery' at its finest."

When he caught up to them, he leered at Cara and

said, "Hello, lovely ladies. So nice to see you. When did you arrive?"

Cara sidled up to Dietrich and gave him a peck on both his cheeks. She looked meaningfully at him as she purred, "Mmmm. You smell so good, Dietrich. We just got here. The horses are settling in, and then we're going to ride this afternoon. I go at 3:45. I have a huge favor to ask you. Would you come and watch Artisan, Dietrich? I'd love your opinion. You know how much I respect you."

"Of course, my dear. I'd be delighted."

The three chatted for a few minutes, each one manipulating the conversation to his or her own end. Cara pumped Dietrich for gossip. She knew rumors and scandal were the price of admission to all the interesting parties and dinners that would take place over the next few days.

For his part, Dietrich willingly supplied whatever information he wanted to circulate around the showgrounds. He raved about two of the horses he'd brought, hoping at least to influence the judges positively and at best create enough interest in them to start a bidding war.

Cara's goal was simply to let Dietrich know she was available for a good time. She was delighted to discover that they were staying at the same hotel. And she planned to make good use of that happy coincidence.

A young rider rode by them on an elegant gray horse and said, "We're here, Herr Krause."

Dietrich glanced up and said, "Excellent, Judy. Walk him on a loose rein for a few more minutes, and then do some warm-up in the trot."

He turned to Cara, "I'll see you at 3:45. I'm looking forward to watching Artisan go. I haven't seen him since Birchwood."

Cara brushed her polished fingertips against his arm and looked up at him coyly.

"Oh, I hope you're not disappointed, Dietrich. You have such a discerning eye. We've been working really hard so I hope you notice a difference. I'm very much looking forward to seeing you later."

The two women walked off and Alyssa gagged. "Really, Cara. Could you be any more obvious? What a disgusting display! You acted like a teenager with her first crush."

"You're just jealous because Dietrich is more interested in me than you."

Alyssa gave Cara a sideways glance. "Dietrich is interested in anything that breathes and has a vagina. He makes my skin crawl. Do you know that the girls in the barn call him Cyclops behind his back? His beady eyes are so close together it looks like he only has one eye. Yuck! I don't see how you can even imagine sleeping with him."

Cara giggled. "Cyclops, huh? Very appropriate. I can see it—excuse the pun. Anyhow, it doesn't bother me one bit. With the lights off, that's the last thing I'll notice. I'm not looking for a life partner, Alyssa—just a little diversion. Besides, Dietrich is very influential. It certainly won't hurt to have a little goodwill from the powers that be. Oh, look. There's George Williams.

He's so cute and nice. Let's go over and say hi."

Like predators eyeing their prey, the two DQ's descended on an unsuspecting George.

# THIRTY-FOUR

*Kate*

While Alyssa and Cara worked the crowd, Kate and Audrey headed to the warm-up ring to watch people school their horses. The warm-up area was very large, but it was still crowded with horses going every which way like bumper cars. It held an interesting mix of horses and riders of all ages and experience. Kate was intimidated, but Audrey loved the diversity and "ring-craft" with which the more experienced riders negotiated working with so many horses around them.

As they hung out on the sidelines, a wide-eyed Kate said, "I can't believe I'm going to be riding at Devon. Did you look at the program? Everyone is here. It's a who's who of the dressage world, for sure."

"Yes, it's definitely exciting. But don't psych yourself out, Blister Butt," Audrey said. The Dixon Oval looks grand and has an incredible history, but it's just another sandbox––just like the one you ride in every day at home."

Kate rolled her eyes. "Sure. I'll just ignore the grand-stands, the banners, the international panel of judges... NOT! Hey, look over there. There's Guenter Seidel on his new horse. He's the most elegant rider I think I've ever seen. Now there's a picture to hold in your mind's eye. He has a classically perfect position. Holy crap! Did you see that? That mare just rocket-launched her-self into the air, and Guenter's position never changed. Someday I want to ride like that."

"I hear what you're saying but, literally, it's a bit of a stretch for five-foot, two-inch me to visualize myself looking like Guenter," Audrey giggled. She pointed to a petite woman coaching riders at the other end of the ring. "There's my role model, Betsy Steiner."

"I know. She's lovely," Kate said. "And such a nice person, too. Oh, look. There's the team coach, Bela Szabo. He's here to help the riders on the Training List. Let's go over so we can hear what he says."

Audrey wrinkled her freckled nose. "Okay. But he's so loud we can probably stay right here and hear him. I think he shouts more to impress people rather than out of concern that his riders hear him. I can't stand the man. He's egotistical and abrasive—I think he tries to compensate for how short he is by making sure he's the center of attention. I know a lot of the riders don't get along with him. There's talk that they'd like to get rid of him and hire someone like Ben. It's common knowl-edge that Szabo is abusive to his horses. He never does it publicly so no one outside of his barn has any real proof. But I bet the people who work for him could tell you horror stories."

"Audrey! You have no way of knowing that. Don't start rumors."

"Listen, Kate. You're too naïve. Cruelty abounds in the horse world. Most trainers love their animals, but a handful see them only as vehicles for their own glory or financial gain. You can see it most at the highest levels, when winning can become more important than anything else. There are all forms of cruelty, some more subtle than others. So-called trainers make horses quiet for shows by doing things like withholding water or inserting needles in the jugular vein and draining blood out. I even heard about one professional who tied his horse's head around to a surcingle on his belly and left him like that all night. He said he was teaching his horse to bend to the right."

Kate's eyes widened. "That's horrible. If what you're saying is true, someone should ban those people from the horse world for life."

"Believe me. These are facts, not rumors. I've seen it firsthand, like when I went to the Sussex show last year. I took a shortcut to the showgrounds and saw Wilfred Geist longeing a horse. I guess he wanted the horse good and tired for his student. Anyhow, the horse slipped and fell on his side. Geist absolutely lost it. He started beating the horse with the longe whip while the poor thing was lying on the ground. I screamed at him. When he realized he had a witness, he stopped."

"Holy crap! What did you do then?"

"I ran to get the technical delegate and he reported Geist to show management. They eliminated him from the competition. USEF also filed cruelty charges against him. But the abuse goes on privately because the professionals want to keep their students happy and winning so they don't leave and go to another trainer. I think galloping ambition and greed are problems at the highest levels, but sometimes amateurs are just plain ignorant. I have a friend who does lower-level eventing. She used to work with a trainer in Nevada. There aren't a lot of professionals in her area. This trainer beats and spurs his clients' horses bloody on an ongoing basis. I asked my friend why this trainer had so many clients. She said people flock to him for two reasons: There aren't many trainers out there, and he gets results."

Kate felt sick as she listened. "Someone has to look out for these poor horses. They certainly can't defend themselves. What about the ASPCA or the Hooved Animal Humane Society?"

Audrey shrugged. "I think those organizations do what they can, but they need more funding and volunteers. And people need to speak up when they see neglect or abuse. If the organizations don't know about it, they can't do anything."

"Someone has to police those riders," Kate said. "What about the technical delegates at the shows?"

"I was lucky I found a conscientious one at Sussex,"

Audrey shrugged. "But some of them just issue warnings, and others look the other way. And just so you don't get stuck up in your ivory tower, here's a question for you. Let's say you're really close to making a team. Szabo tells you to work Remmy twice a day even though you know he's too tired. He's the coach, and you feel pressured to do what he says even though you know your horse is beyond exhausted. You rationalize working Remmy twice because you think with Szabo's experience, he must know better than you. And, of course, your lifelong dream has been to make the Team. You figure if you do what he says, you'll have a shot at it. So, what you do in that case?"

Kate's eyes sparked. "I'd never sacrifice the welfare of my horse to please someone else or for the prestige of making a team. That's a no-brainer."

"Okay. Okay. Calm down. I was speaking hypothetically." But Audrey was thinking, *When the time comes, we'll see what wins the battle between ambition and integrity.*

# THIRTY-FIVE

*Ben*

By a quarter to four, Kate and Cara entered the ring to start their warm-ups. Both Remmy and Artie looked happy and fresh. The activity at the horse shows always pumped up the horses. There weren't any collisions between the masses of horses because most of the riders knew to pass left hand to left hand. Plus, the seasoned riders had developed a sort of radar that allowed them to sense where the other horses were even though they weren't looking directly at them.

Unlike Szabo, who shouted across the ring to impress everyone with his knowledge and skill, Ben waited until his riders rode by and then spoke to them softly. He didn't use the warm-up ring to draw attention to himself or showcase his own ability. Once at a competition, as his riders knew, Ben removed his trainer's hat and donned his coach's hat. He'd told them that a horse show wasn't the place to school new work or drill movements. They'd continue training when they returned home.

As a coach, Ben's was merely a mirror for his riders. He commented in shorthand. His riders knew his system so well that one or two keywords kept them on track. He didn't need to give detailed explanations like in a lesson. Ben also gave his comments in a positive way. Unlike Szabo who would yell, "Don't pull on the inside rein!" or, "Don't sit to the right!" Ben preferred to plant the right images in his rider's minds. He gave directions in a constructive way, like, "Soften the inside rein," or, "Shift your hips left."

As Kate rode by, he said, "Make him straighter."

Kate knew he meant that Remmy's hindquarters had drifted toward the center of the ring rather than following directly behind his front legs. She straightened him by placing his shoulders in front of his hindquarters with a movement called shoulder-fore.

To Cara, Ben said, "Lower his neck." Cara knew that a high neck meant a low back. That position created a short circuit in the middle of Artie's body that prevented the power from his hindquarters from reaching his front end. So, she pressed her calves on his sides to create energy and closed her outside hand in a fist to recycle that power. That way he could lift his back and lower his neck. Those aids produced a better bridge over his back from his powerful hindquarters to his front end.

Having successfully lowered Artie's neck, Cara

smiled sweetly at Ben. He gave her a stern look and said, "Concentrate."

On Kate's next trip past Ben, he said, "Sit." Kate realized she was gripping with her legs, and as a result she pinched her butt out of the saddle. She needed to sit close to Remmy in order to give him subtle cues with her weight. So, she relaxed her knees and thighs and allowed her seat to settle deeper into the saddle.

Kate and Cara continued to work under Ben's observant eye. He gave spare and concise remarks, yet he didn't miss a stride. Ben focused completely on his riders, so he was startled when he sensed someone standing close to his left elbow.

Dietrich Krause had, as promised, come to watch Cara. Dietrich stuck his hand toward Ben and said, "Hi, Ben. How's it going?"

Ben shook Dietrich's hand. He made eye contact ever so briefly, and then looked back at his riders. It annoyed him to be interrupted while coaching, but he knew that, politically, he had to be polite. Knowing the horse world could be vindictive, he was careful not to offend Dietrich by slighting him. It was rumored that Dietrich was on the "committee" at USEF. No one really knew for sure who was on the committee or what they actually did. But everyone knew not to piss off the people who could retaliate against one of your horses or riders.

With his eyes glued on Kate and Cara, Ben said, "Just fine, Dietrich. How are you? Who did you bring here?"

"I'm great. I have some super horses in the barn now. I just got two new FEI horses in from Holland for Kathy Bigelow. They arrived too late for her to qualify to come here, but they'll be ready for the Florida circuit. Judy and Cindy are here, and they'll be doing the Grand Prix. Sandy and Marie are entered in the Prix St. Georges and Intermediare I."

"Sounds like you have your hands full."

"Yeah. But they'll be plenty of time for partying, too. That's part of the reason for coming to Devon. Wouldn't you agree?" Without waiting for Ben to answer, Dietrich babbled on. "Hey! I have a really nice young horse in my barn. Maybe you have a client looking for a top prospect. He's a six-year-old Jazz. Chestnut. Super gaits. His trot is a "10." Good size for a lady—sixteen hands and light body type. He does all the lateral work, a clean flying change in each direction, and has started half-steps. He's sensitive but not crazy. He's got a pretty hefty price tag on him because he's a Team horse, for sure. I need to get $250,000 for him. I've included your commission in that price."

Ben sighed to himself. He knew wheeling and dealing made up as much of the horse world as training. He read between the lines of Dietrich's sales pitch. The horse was from the Jazz line, which meant probably spooky. Trot for a "10"? Then his walk and canter sucked. Sixteen hands meant probably barely 15.3. Six years old and doing all the lateral work, flying changes, and half-steps? He'd been pushed too hard, too soon, and his brain was probably fried. Sensitive meant fasten your seatbelt! $250,000? Dietrich most likely picked him up for under $50,000 because he was small.

Keeping his eyes on his riders, he said to Dietrich, "Hmmm. Sounds interesting. I'll keep him in mind. I don't have anyone looking at the moment, but you never know."

And within moments, Ben purposely forgot the information about the young horse. He had no intention of getting involved with Krause in horse deals. He had his own contacts, people he'd worked with for years and trusted.

# THIRTY-SIX

*Cara*

Dietrich watched Cara ride some serpentines to help Artie bend left and right. Anyone who knew him even slightly understood he really wasn't interested in the horse. He was interested in Cara. He practically drooled like a hungry dog as his eyes roamed over her body.

Cara was delighted to see Dietrich. As she rode by, she flashed a provocative smile at him. "Hi, Dietrich. I'm so glad you came."

Ben glared at her and barked, "Focus on your horse." He was irritated at the interruption and fully aware of Dietrich's interest in Cara. Yes, Dietrich was out for a good time. Everyone knew about his carnal urges as well as his penchant for courting other professionals' students.

As Kate and Cara finish their schooling session, Audrey and Alyssa arrived for their warm-ups. Kate and

Cara thanked Ben, and then walked their horses on loose reins around the showgrounds before heading back to the barn together.

Cara gushed, "Did you see that? Dietrich Krause came to watch me. I know how busy he is. Wasn't that sweet of him?"

"Yes, I suppose so," Kate said. "But I don't think it made Ben very happy. He made it pretty obvious that he resented the interruption. You'd think Dietrich would know better than to distract Ben while he's working. But I guess he doesn't care."

Cara looked left and right and whispered, "Well, actually he came because I asked him to. I wanted a second opinion on how Artie looked. It's not that I'm unhappy with our progress, but Dietrich really knows how to get a horse and rider ready for the Team."

Kate's jaw dropped open. "And you're saying that Ben doesn't? Dietrich's talent isn't preparing a horse and rider to be successful. His real talent lies in knowing who to suck up to and which strings to pull to get a horse on the Team."

"Kate! I can't believe you said that. You sound like Audrey. Don't get me wrong. You know I love Audrey like a sister. She's a darling girl and a wonderful rider, but she's quite cynical. You're such a sweet person. I certainly hope she's not having a bad influence on you." She leaned toward Kate conspiratorially. "Anyhow, I know I can trust you so I'm going to let you in on my little secret. I asked Dietrich to come by because I'm considering working with him."

"How could you? Ben's the best. He's turned himself inside out to get you and Artie to where you are today. Where's your loyalty?"

Cara lifted one shoulder and said, "Look. I adore Ben. I'd never do anything to hurt him. But it's not his first rodeo. He knows clients come and go. I'll always be grateful to him for his help, but I've outgrown him. The truth is, his approach doesn't suit my style. He uses all that weird visualization stuff. And he's so intense. I feel like I'm in parochial school, and I'm about to get my knuckles rapped. Did you hear how he scolded me in front of Dietrich? He totally embarrassed me. Dietrich is so sweet and easygoing. He likes having a good time, and so do I."

"Well, in Ben's defense, you weren't paying attention, Cara. He told you to focus, which you should've been doing anyhow. Make sure you don't burn any bridges. Besides, how do you know Dietrich would even take you on as a student?"

Cara winked and giggled. "Oh, I'm sure he will. We're staying at the same hotel, and I'm going to invite him to have dinner with me tonight. I can be very persuasive, you know. I guarantee you that by the end of the evening, he'll welcome me into his stable and his bed with open arms."

Kate shook her head in resignation. "You're really something, Cara. You know that?"

Putting her own spin on Kate's remark, Cara said.

"Why, thank you, Honey. I think you're really something, too. That's why you're one of my favorite people in the whole world. I don't know anyone more talented or modest than you. I'm so happy to call you my friend."

Heads turned as Cara made her entrance into the hotel restaurant. She spotted Dietrich sitting at the bar and headed over to him in her gold Jimmy Choo stilettos, skin-tight black miniskirt and sparkly tank top.

"Hello, Gorgeous," she said as she extended a perfumed arm in front of Dietrich to grasp his glass. "Whatcha having?" She sniffed at the drink. "Scotch. How did you know I love scotch? It's my favorite!" She took a sip, and then licked her lips sensuously. "Yummy. Can you order one for me?"

"Of course, my dear." He signaled to the bartender to bring a drink for Cara.

Cara raised herself onto the barstool, making sure she hiked her skirt up even higher to leave Dietrich wondering if she wore anything underneath it. Before he could decide, she opened her legs provocatively before crossing them. And in that one movement, she removed all doubt from his mind. She studied Dietrich as his gaze traveled up her legs and thought, *Ah, power. Men are so easy.*

"So? What did you think of Artie today?" Cara asked as she slipped a scarlet painted toenail under his pant leg and proceeded to tantalize him by brushing it up and down his ankle.

Dietrich relished the dance as much as she did—two master manipulators jockeying for power. He considered this little vixen a worthy opponent, and over the years he'd turned this cat-and-mouse game into an art form. He thoroughly enjoyed letting the drama unfold. As an expert in psychological warfare, he leaned toward her so that his body language gave him an advantage.

"I haven't seen him since Birchwood, and I must say he does look wonderful. You two make an elegant pair." Dietrich paused dramatically, as if he had more to say but hesitated to do so.

"I hear a 'but' in there, Dietrich."

The man let several seconds drag by. "Well...you know I would never criticize another professional, so I hesitate to say anything."

*Yeah, right,* Cara thought. But she played the game. "I know, Dietrich. That's one of the things I admire about you. And normally I wouldn't press for details. But I really feel Artisan and I have hit a plateau. We're consistently getting scores in the high-60s, but I know we're both capable of doing more. I just don't know who to turn to, and you're the best in the business."

Dietrich chuckled to himself at the flattery, but he wanted Cara to believe she had the upper hand. "You're much too kind, my love. But I can tell you're sincerely concerned about the situation so I'll tell you what I think, but it must stay confidential."

To show he didn't intimidate her, Cara leaned in closer to hear what he had to say.

Dietrich inhaled her scent and plunged on. "There's no doubt that Ben is one of the best trainers around. But here's the problem. He focuses on relaxation—for both the horses and the riders. That's all well and good, but the truth is, his students' tests put the judges to sleep. They want more excitement. The judges reward tests where the horse looks like he's on the edge of being out of control. That's what they want. Barely controlled brilliance."

"Oh, Dietrich. You're a genius. I think you hit the nail on the head. That's the kind of insight you have, and it's pretty rare. But what can I do? I have to do what Ben says. But it's not fair to Artie. I owe it to him to ride to his potential. Don't you agree?"

The tension built as Dietrich stayed silent. He wanted Cara to beg him to take her and her horse on. That way she'd be obligated to him, and he'd have the upper hand.

She stared into her drink as if digging deep to come up with a solution to her dilemma. "Okay. I'm just going to say it. I know this is awkward for you, Dietrich, and I hesitate to put you in this position because you've always been so kind to me. But would you ever consider taking Artie and me on?"

Cara knew Dietrich would want her in his barn. She thought about what she could offer him in board and training fees as well as the potential for selling her one of his expensive imports. She was well aware that he made a practice of luring students to him with the promise of becoming a champion. And then once he had them in his clutches, he told them their current horse couldn't cut it, and they needed to buy another one if they ever hoped to realize their dreams. And, of course, there was the added incentive of having her share his bed at night. It was a win-win situation for him.

"I don't know, Cara. It's a delicate situation for me. I don't ever want to be accused of stealing someone else's student. In this business, all a trainer has is his reputation."

Cara questioned whether Dietrich really believed that about himself. Maybe he did. He probably needed to delude himself about his ethics so he could sleep at night. She truly wondered if he didn't know about the rumors of his lack of integrity and all the unsavory things he had supposedly done in his career.

She pushed the thought aside and smiled like an angel. "Oh, I'll make sure that Ben understands that it was my decision and that you had nothing to do with it. Listen. Why don't we take our drinks and go up to your room? That way we can discuss this privately. So many of the riders stay here, and I don't want them walking in on us."

"Excellent idea. You're a very thoughtful young lady." Dietrich swung off his seat and extended his hand to Cara to help her off the stool. As they walked out of the restaurant, Cara linked her arm through Dietrich's and pressed herself against the length of his body.

Dietrich chuckled to himself. Cara had the combination of demure and wanton down to a science.

～ ·

The Cherry Hill Farm riders had a successful Devon show. Kate and Remmy placed third in the Grand Prix with a solid 70 percent. Cara and Artisan managed a respectable 68 percent. Wheeler and Audrey blew everyone away with their results in the small tour at Prix St. Georges and Intermediare I. Alyssa did well with Celebrity although she didn't have a good test with Chance. It was dull and Chance stayed behind her leg the entire time. When they finished, she swore she'd sell him. She didn't see the point in torturing herself any further when she knew that her father would replace him.

With the major showing for the season done, the riders breathed a collective sigh of relief. They only had one small local show left, and Ben said it was optional. He just wanted to offer it to those who wanted another trip down the centerline before heading to the big shows in Wellington for the winter.

But most of them just wanted to celebrate, reflect on the show season, and give themselves and their horses time to recharge their batteries.

# THIRTY-SEVEN

*Cara*

Cara approached Ben as he sat in the gazebo, preparing to start a lesson.

"Ben, can you spare a minute before you start your lesson?"

"Sure, Cara. By the way, congratulations again on your tests at Devon. I'm very proud of you and Artie."

Cara nodded. "Well, we certainly couldn't have done it without your help."

Cara took a seat on the edge of a chair and focused on the floor of the gazebo. She'd decided to use the distraught female sympathy card for this performance and squeezed out one lonely tear.

Ben watched her easily slip in and out of various emotions. "What's wrong, Cara?"

"Oh, Ben. I've been torturing myself since the show. You know how much I love being here and training with you. We're a family. I owe everything Artisan and

I have accomplished to you and your extraordinary training."

Ben remained silent and just stared at Cara. Once she realized she couldn't bait him, she went on. Sighing heavily, she said, "I don't know quite how to tell you so I'll just come right out with it. Remember when Dietrich Krause came to watch me at the show? Well, later on he came up to me with a proposal. I didn't want to listen to him. You know how loyal I am to you. But he pretty much guaranteed me a spot on the Training List if I came to his barn to work with him. Of course, I want to stay here because you're the best, and I love it here. All my friends are here too. But I have to think of Artie and his future. If we don't get on the Training List soon, he'll be past his prime as far as making a team. Oh, Ben. What should I do?"

Cara had no doubt that Ben knew the score. People in the horse world were fickle. Many made a "career" of switching from trainer to trainer every season to find the magic key to success. They wanted quick results. They thought dressage was like instant coffee. Add water, stir, and voilà—a Grand Prix dressage horse. Cara often overheard trainers laughing at the wannabees. They made a game of guessing who they'd choose as their new guru each season, knowing they'd never "get it."

Ben didn't say anything for several moments. Cara held her breath until Ben finally said, "Cara. You need to do whatever you think is best for you and Artie. I'm sure you'll be happy in Dietrich's program. He'll teach you a lot. When do you plan on moving over there?"

Cara pulled out a lacy handkerchief from her breeches' pocket and dabbed beneath her eyes, being careful not to smudge her mascara. "He says he'll have a spot for me next week. Oh, Ben. I knew you'd understand. Will you have trouble filling the stall? I'd hate to think you'd miss out on any board or training income. No. Of course you won't have a problem. I know you have a huge waiting list. People line up at the door hoping for a chance to train with you. Well, I better go now. I've taken up enough of your time as it is."

Cara rose from the chair, took a step toward Ben, and gave him a chaste kiss on his cheek. "Thank you so much for everything, Ben. And especially your understanding of the situation. I knew you'd have our best interests at heart. I'll be sure to keep you posted on how we're doing."

One side of Ben's mouth turned up as he watched Cara leave the gazebo. "You do that. Good luck, Cara."

# THIRTY-EIGHT

*Kate*

Kate ran all the way to the quarantine barn. She arrived breathless from the excitement of her news. When she got there, she found Chris grooming Victor.

Panting, she said, "Hi, Chris."

He smiled without missing a beat in the grooming process. "Hey there, Kate. Where's the fire?"

A huge grin split Kate's face. "I just spoke with Ben. Cara is taking Artie out of the barn. She's going to train with Dietrich Krause. She's leaving in a few days."

"Ah, Cara. I met her right after I got here," Chris rolled his eyes. "She claimed she came up here to check on Victor and Triumphant. She'd show up most afternoons to fill me in on barn gossip and see if she could entice me to take her out."

Taken aback by this news, a rush of envy surged through Kate. She scolded herself for feeling jealous. *Why can't I be more forward, like Cara? On the other hand, who am I to be possessive anyhow? I don't have any claim on Chris. I've made it completely clear that our relationship is platonic.*

Kate forced herself to sound neutral as she said, "Oh. Have you been seeing her? I didn't know. Well, in that case she's already told you her news."

"Whoa! Wait a minute," Chris paused mid-brush stroke. "I didn't say I took her out. Although I must say she knows how to flatter and flirt. But I have the feeling if I let her lure me into her web, she'd leave me for dead when she was finished."

Kate scolded herself again for feeling relieved. But she wasn't going to let Chris know anything about that.

"She's a character, all right," Kate agreed. "But I think she's relatively harmless. She just has some bizarre coping skills. I guess we all do. Anyhow, she's decided to work with Dietrich Krause and hopefully get herself on the Training List. I think she and Artie would probably make the list anyhow, but she wants some insurance. The point is that when she leaves, there's an extra stall in the boarders' wing, and we already have one empty stall on the other side. Ben says you can move the horses down there if you want. It's obvious they're both healthy now."

Kate ran her hands down Victor's neck. The youngster's once-dull coat now gleamed with good health.

"Tee can go in Artie's stall and Victor can go into one of the stalls in the other wing with the school horses. It will be so great to have you in the main barn rather than being exiled up here. What do you think? Can you swing it financially?"

"Sure. Money isn't an issue right now," Chris said. "It would be great to have access to the arenas now that Tee is getting strong enough to start some real work. And it would be unbelievable to watch Ben teach and train."

For a moment Kate pondered Chris' comment that money wasn't an issue. Then she decided his finances weren't any of her business. Instead she simply said, "That's wonderful! You can move down next week. Let me know when you're ready, and I'll give you a hand."

"I really don't have that much stuff to pack, just some tack, longeing equipment, feed, supplements and grooming supplies. Want to do it Monday afternoon on your day off?"

Kate could barely contain her excitement. "You got it. I'm so happy you'll be in our barn. That way I can keep a close eye on Tee's progress." *And get to see you more, too.*

# THIRTY-NINE

*Chris*

On Monday, Chris and Kate piled his gear into the bed of his truck. They worked together in the companionable silence that had developed during the time they spent nursing the rescue horses and getting Tee started under saddle.

They planned to bring the equipment to the main barn and set everything up before moving the horses. Kate had already prepared the stalls by bedding them with fluffy pine shavings, filling two water buckets, and putting two flakes of fragrant hay in each one.

Chris led Tee and Kate led Victor to their new home. Chris worried that the horses might get upset when they separated them. They did, in fact, whinny for each other when Kate and Chris split up at the back entrance to the stable. But once out of earshot, Tee settled right down. Chris couldn't hear Victor, but he trusted Kate to keep him calm.

As soon as Tee settled into his new home and was munching on his hay, Chris hurried over to the other wing to check on Victor. He assumed Tee had seen a lot of changes during his life, including different stalls and new neighbors, but he worried about Victor. Besides his mother, the only other horse the youngster had known had been Tee. He'd probably have separation anxiety. Chris hoped he didn't get so upset that he'd work himself into a frenzy.

Chris found Kate peering intently into the stall. He asked, "How's he doing? Once you were out of sight, I couldn't hear anything."

"He's fine now. He pawed, paced in circles, and called for Tee a bit. Then he got curious about his neighbor, who happens to be Jolicoeur. They've been standing nose-to-nose, having a conversation, ever since. Knowing Joe, he's probably taking Victor under his wing by becoming the new leader of Victor's two-horse herd."

"That's a relief. I'm glad Jolicoeur has taken him under his wing, but I'd sure feel better if I could stay close by tonight. Do you think Ben would mind if I slept in the viewing room? Since it's their first night in a new home, I'd like to be able to check on them from time to time."

Knowing she'd do the same thing, Kate teased Chris, "Well, we do night check around nine o'clock. But if you're going to be a mother hen, I'm sure it'll be fine. There's plenty of room in the lounge, and the couch is really comfortable." She suddenly became shy around

Chris as she added, "Or you can stay on the couch in our apartment. Audrey won't mind. She loves company. And it might be more fun for you there."

Chris' eyes lit up. "Sounds terrific! I'm going to take you up on that. I can't believe how things have turned out. I'll always be sad I couldn't get to the mare in time, but at least Tee and Victor are thriving."

He engulfed Kate's delicate hand in his. "And I've made a wonderful friend. Plus, I get to be a fly on the wall in Ben Ellis' barn. It doesn't get much better than that."

The horses had a good night, and so did Chris, Kate, and Audrey. They sat in the living room in the apartment and talked for hours. Luckily, Jason had night check that evening, so the girls could stay and talk to Chris. But by ten o'clock they could barely keep their eyes open. So, they reluctantly said good night and went to bed.

Although he was tired, Chris couldn't sleep. He dozed fitfully on the couch, and then gave up and lay there, wide awake, until it was time to rouse Bella and go check the horses, which he did every two hours throughout the night. He moved quietly and kept the bright aisle lights off so as not to disturb the rest of the horses. Instead, he navigated by the dim light that escaped from the main foyer and seeped into the barn. He was happy to see that Tee and Victor had settled in nicely.

# FORTY

*Kate*

The next morning, Kate groomed Celebrity, bandaged his legs with white polo wraps, and put his saddle on. He stood patiently in the grooming stall while Kate picked up a broom to sweep the aisle. She'd wait for Alyssa to show up for her lesson before she put his bridle on.

While she swept, she daydreamed about having Victor and Tee in the main barn. She'd be able to watch their progress every day. In the past few weeks, she'd only seen Tee occasionally on the days she could synchronize her schedule with Chris's schooling sessions. She also admitted to herself that she was thrilled to have Chris around more often. In a short time, he'd become a good friend. She felt almost as close to him as she did to Wheeler, Peter, and Audrey. Maybe it was because they had so much in common. After all, they'd met originally because of their mutual passion for the plight of abused and neglected animals. Maybe that was it.

The sound of Alyssa's voice broke Kate out of her reverie. "So, I understand Clark Kent brought his horses into the barn. I had no idea newspaper boys made enough money to board two horses at a facility like this."

Kate scowled as she wondered how Alyssa had learned that Chris worked for a newspaper. "Apparently they do. But his income isn't any of our business. By the way, Alyssa, his name is Chris Barton."

Kate was pissed at herself for letting Alyssa bait her. Changing the subject, she said, "Celebrity is ready for you in the grooming stall. All he needs is his bridle. Do you want to put it on, or do you want me to do it?"

"Of course you should do it, dear. It is your job, after all."

Kate headed back toward the grooming stall accompanied by Alyssa's incessant babbling. "I understand he had some pretty sick horses on his hands when he arrived. Is that why Ben exiled them to the upper barn? Are you sure they're healthy now? Have you seen them lately? Did he run Coggins tests on them? They better not bring anything contagious into this barn. Can you imagine how awful it would be to have some kind of epidemic run through the stable?

Kate tried not to show her exasperation. "Do you honestly think Ben would allow sick horses in his barn? Come on, Alyssa. Give him a little more credit than that. That's why they've been up in the quarantine barn. Look. I realize you don't know Chris very well, but the last thing he'd do is put other horses at risk. The only reason he has Triumphant and Victor in the first place is because he wanted to rescue them."

Alyssa smirked. She loved the verbal battle. "Ah, I get it. Newspaper boy is a do-gooder out to save the world. Maybe he really is Clark Kent."

Kate shocked herself when she lashed out at Alyssa. "What is your problem? Can't you recognize someone doing something selfless? No, I guess that's probably a foreign concept to you."

Before Alyssa could react, Chris appeared in front of the grooming stall. "Good morning, ladies."

Part of Chris's charm was that he didn't realize the effect he had on women. In his typically affable manner, he stuck out his hand and said in his whispery voice, "Hi. I know we've never been formally introduced. I'm Chris Barton, the new kid in town. Pleased to meet you."

Alyssa flashed a brilliant smile at Chris and extended her bejeweled fingers. "Alyssa Smithson. I've seen you in passing, but we haven't really had a chance to connect. We're delighted that you're here, Chris. Please let me know if there's anything I can do to help you settle in."

Kate stared at Alyssa, dumbstruck by the complete change in the woman. In one moment, Alyssa's expression had morphed from haughty to coy. She looked like an entirely different person, one that Kate had never seen before.

"Ah, of course. Alyssa. I've heard so much about you and your wonderful horses. I know it might be a bit forward to ask, but could I sit in on some of your schooling sessions? I'd love to watch you work the horses."

Alyssa beamed at Chris. It never occurred to her that he might have heard anything negative about her. "I'd be delighted if you watched. You're welcome anytime. I normally school them with Ben twice a week in the mornings."

Chris gave a slight nod as Alyssa took the reins from Kate and led Celebrity past him. "Thank you, Alyssa. I'll look forward to it. Right now, I have to check on my horses, but I'll catch your second lesson."

"Wonderful! And I can't wait to see your boys, too. It's so exciting to have new horses in the barn. We all learn so much from each other."

Kate watched in shock as the scene between Alyssa and Chris unfolded. It didn't surprise her to hear Alyssa being a two-faced bitch about the horses being in the barn. But she was astounded to see her soft and feminine side. Jealousy bubbled up and threatened to engulf Kate. Once again, she scolded herself. *Listen, Stupid. He doesn't even know how you feel about him, since you keep that under lock and key. Besides, why would he be interested in you anyway? Compared to wealthy, sophisticated, dazzling Alyssa, you're nothing.*

# FORTY-ONE

*Chris*

Chris always made a point to ride Tee in one of the empty rings so he didn't interfere with Ben's lessons or training. The only time he schooled Tee in front of Ben was when it rained, and he had to use the indoor arena.

Even though Ben said little to Chris, he kept an eye on his progress. He was happy to see that Chris concentrated on the basics. Every day he worked on rhythm, suppleness, and building a solid connection from the horse's increasingly strong hindquarters over his back and into his hands.

After one particularly productive session, Ben approached Chris and said, "He's coming along nicely. As he gets stronger, he's looking more and more athletic. I think you have a whole lot more horse in there then you probably realize. Let me know when you're ready for an eye on the ground."

Chris' eyes widened and he said, "Are you kidding, Ben? That would be incredible if you could fit us in sometime. He still needs a lot of conditioning. It's like he's been confined to a hospital bed, and his muscles have atrophied. But I can feel him getting stronger each week. I just pretend I'm bringing him to physical therapy every day. I know myself from working out at the gym that the best way to strengthen muscles is to stress them one day, and then let them recover the next. That's the approach I'm using with Tee. Some days, I mainly work the trot. The next day, I focus on the canter. Or if I increase his entire workload one day, the following day I either hack him or give him the day off and just hand walk. Anyhow, I'd love to get some input. I've been riding most of my life but only got into dressage the last few years. I know that makes me a real novice, and I don't want to mess him up."

"From what I've seen, you're very much on the right track," Ben said. "And you're welcome to join the working-student lesson after lunch anytime. You don't have to wait until you feel he's fit enough to do an entire hour. Since you'll be in a group, you can go at your own pace and give Triumphant a break whenever he needs to rest."

"That would be terrific, Ben! If you're serious, we'll be there tomorrow. I'm happy to pay your lesson fee. Just let me know what I owe you. And...thank you!"

After Chris cooled Tee out and put him back in his stall, he searched for Kate to tell her the exciting news. He found her in the tack room, where she was working her way through a mountain of bridles hanging on the cleaning hook. It looked like a tedious chore, but Chris noticed that Kate didn't act like she minded cleaning tack any more than she objected to mucking stalls or sweeping the barn aisle.

Chris paused at the tack room door and watched Kate. Her thick hair was so black it looked almost blue. She had pulled it back carelessly into a ponytail. Wanton tendrils escaped the rubber band and framed her delicate face. Her figure-hugging breeches showed off her toned thighs.

Kate had always been warm and friendly with him, but there was still an aura about her that warned him to keep his distance. She was like a deer—elegant and graceful yet wary and ready to bolt at the slightest hint of danger.

Over time, Chris and Kate had come to rely on each other more and more. He became as much of a constant in her life as Wheeler had been throughout her childhood. When Kate took Remmy to local shows, Chris usually went along to help and drove Remmy in his own trailer. Once at the show he was happy to do everything from grooming to fetching mints to cheering her on during her rides.

Chris tried not to startle her as she cleaned the tack, but he could barely control his enthusiasm. "Kate! I have the most exciting news!"

"Oh, Chris! Hi. I was lost in my own little world, as usual. What's up?"

"I just spoke with Ben. I guess he's been keeping an eye on Tee. He told me we could join the group lesson whenever we wanted."

"Omigod! That's wonderful! He must like what he's seen. Ben doesn't take on just anyone. I'm so happy for you. When do you think you'll start?"

Chris explained, "He says we don't have to do the whole hour, so I'm going to jump right in tomorrow. I can hardly believe it. Ben Ellis supervising our training—it doesn't get any better than that!"

"Well, if anyone deserves it, Chris, you do. You brought Tee and Victor back from the brink. If you ride in the group, you'll be with Audrey, Melissa, Jason, and me. I can't wait! I'll be able to watch you when Remmy's on a break. That'll be awesome. I never get to see you work Tee as much as I'd like to."

Chris rode in the group lesson for a couple of weeks and was ecstatic about the results. Tee blossomed under Ben's guidance. As they scraped the barnacles off him, they were thrilled by what they found. They discovered a horse that at one time had been well-schooled in all the Grand Prix movements. He knew piaffe, passage, canter pirouettes, and the tempi changes, right down to flying changes every stride.

At the end of one session, Chris rode over to Ben and said, "I don't get it, Ben. Not that I'm complaining, mind you. But I've yet to discover the hole in this horse. His owner told me he could be strong, but except for the occasional loss of balance, he carries himself nicely and doesn't pull. Most of the time, all I feel is the weight of the reins in my hands."

Ben shrugged and said, "I don't know what to tell you, Chris. Maybe she doesn't have a good seat and hung on the reins to keep her own balance. Most horses are happy to lean on your hands and use them for a fifth leg if you pull on their mouths. There's no sense worrying about it. If there's a skeleton buried there, it's bound to surface eventually. In the meantime, enjoy what you have."

Alyssa cornered Chris in the wash stall while he gave Tee a shower after his lesson.

"Hi, Chris!"

"Hey, Alyssa. How's it going?"

"Very well, thank you. I had a chance to watch your session with Triumphant. He's absolutely exquisite."

"I know. I can't believe my luck," Chris said. "All I ever wanted to do was save his life. I never had any intention of riding him. And here I have this amazing horse who's had enough education somewhere along the line to learn all the Grand Prix movements."

Alyssa flashed her Julia Roberts smile. "He looks like he has a real talent for piaffe and passage. He stays right on the spot and trots in place for piaffe and does such a smooth transition into a beautifully cadenced passage. As he gets stronger, his passage will get even loftier."

"I know. It's a huge responsibility. I have a lot of work to do to catch up to what he knows. I've taken lessons on Grand Prix schoolmasters a few times, so I've felt the movements before, but only as a passenger. I've never schooled pirouettes, piaffe, passage, or flying changes myself. I feel like I'm in over my head, but I'm enjoying every second of it."

"I think I'm as passionate about dressage as you are. It's addictive, isn't it?" Alyssa looked sweetly at Chris. "Listen. I have to leave now because I have an appointment, but I'd love to talk with you about training some more." Alyssa lowered her eyes. "I've been riding the Grand Prix for a while now, and although I still have so much to learn, maybe I can give you some tips. Are you free for dinner later?"

Alyssa's forwardness took Chris back a bit, but he graciously replied, "As a matter of fact I am. I'd love to get together to discuss training. I feel like a sponge just waiting to soak up everything I can. Want to meet at the Rusty Scupper? It's a great restaurant. Fun atmosphere and good food. How's seven for you?"

"That would be fabulous. I know the Scupper. I look

forward to it." She started to walk off and then turned to flash him a brilliant smile. "Have a great day! I'll see you tonight."

As Alyssa walked away, she glimpsed Kate in Remmy's stall and gave her a sassy wink.

# FORTY-TWO

*Kate*

Two days later, Alyssa found Kate in the grooming stall, putting Celebrity's bridle on.

"Maria told me that John just called the office. She has a message for you. He's taking you out to dinner tonight to celebrate Devon. He'll pick you up at 7:30—oh, and he wants you to wear your best dress because he has a surprise for you. You know, it's none of my business, but don't you get pissed off at the way he orders you around? He's so demanding. That must be why he's such a barracuda in business. What if you already had other plans for tonight? Ridiculous, I know. But let's just pretend for argument's sake that you did. He just assumes he can snap his fingers and you'll jump—which, of course, you do."

Kate pinched her lips together and said, "You're right, Alyssa. It is none of your business." She rose to John's defense. "And John's not a barracuda. He's successful because he works hard and is very good at what he does."

Alyssa laughed at Kate's outburst. "Well, listen to you! The gutless wonder grows some backbone. I love it!"

Kate handed her the reins and said through gritted teeth, "Your horse is ready. Have a nice ride." She was annoyed at herself for letting Alyssa get under her skin because she knew that was exactly what the girl wanted to do.

Alyssa led Celebrity out of the grooming area and down the barn aisle. Without turning around, she tossed over her shoulder, "Oh, and don't forget to come out in a few minutes to help me with my girth."

Kate glared at Alyssa's back.

As Kate headed down the aisle, she ran into Audrey and told her about her run-in with Alyssa. Audrey laughed so hard her pumpkin curls danced. "Good for you! I guess I'm rubbing off on you. Can't let the bastards get you down. That's the only way to survive in this business."

Kate shrugged. "Actually, it did feel kind of good to tell her off. But I think she thought it was funny. She loves antagonizing people to see what kind of reaction she gets. I think it's a game to her."

"So, what do you think John's surprise is?"

"I can't imagine. He's already bought everything Remmy and I could possibly need for schooling and showing. He's so generous, and I just don't feel like I deserve it. These last few months have been like a dream. I keep waiting to wake up and find out none of it is real."

Audrey rolled her eyes and said, "Ya know, Miss Doom and Gloom, for someone who's so positive about the horses, you are disgustingly pessimistic. Maybe you should try some of that woo-woo visualization stuff on yourself. You know. 'See' yourself as optimistic and deserving."

A light bulb went on in Kate's mind. "Gosh, you're right. I use visualization with unbelievable results in my riding, but it never occurred to me to use it on myself. Audrey! You're a genius!"

"And you're just now realizing that?" Audrey slipped into a robotic voice, "Your mission, Miss Gage, should you decide to accept it, is to program your subconscious mind for what you want—not what you don't want. Use the stuff Ben teaches us for riding elsewhere in your life. 'See' yourself in a relationship with Chris. You know you're wild about him. Do something about it. Then 'feel' the weight of a medal around your neck as you stand on the podium at the Olympics. Then 'touch'..."

Kate interrupted. "Hang on! Hang on! One thing at a time. How about I just start with something a bit more manageable like feeling more confident when I compete against the top riders in the country. Right now, I'm terrified when I look at people like Allison Brock, Kasey Perry-Glass, Laura Graves, Steffen Peters, and Adrienne Lyle. Yikes! What a list. I can understand why every one of them deserves to make a team. But I just don't see how I belong in that company. How come you don't feel that way? You always seem to have it together."

Audrey sighed. "Hey! I have my own mental monsters. Mine are just different than yours. Okay. I'll agree that confidence is a good starting point. But you need to work on your nonexistent social life sooner rather than later. Get some balance in your life, girl!"

As Audrey bounced away, Kate thought about her funny, sweet friend. *One-track mind, that girl. One-track mind.*

Later that evening, John and Kate sat at a corner table at the Chandler House, an upscale restaurant and inn. John raised his wine glass and made a toast. "To the next shining star of the United States Equestrian Team."

Kate was embarrassed, but she touched her glass lightly to his. "I'm not a star, John. And for that matter, I'm not even a member of USEF. I had three good shows, and that's mostly because of Remmy. If I didn't have Remmy, I'd just be some nobody from Rhode Island."

John scolded her gently. "That's not true. You are somebody. And a very special somebody." He gazed into her eyes and placed his hand near hers on the table. "I can't tell you what these last few months have meant to me. My whole life used to be about work. But you've changed all that. My days are so much richer now. Kate, you mean more to me than I can ever express. Tell me you feel the same way."

Kate froze like a fawn in a car's headlights. She didn't like the direction of the conversation. She tried to steer it another way. "You're very important to me, too, John. As you know, I didn't have a father growing up. I used to look at Wheeler's dad and pretend he was my dad, too. But, of course, it wasn't the same. He was always nice to me. But when it was time to go home, my borrowed dad stayed with his real family, and I was fatherless again. You've filled that void for me, and I'll always be grateful for that."

John pretended to listen to Kate attentively, but he had another agenda. He waited until she finished her trip down memory lane, and then, once again, took charge of the conversation. "I'm happy that I've been able to give you the support you need. And I always plan to do that. But all relationships grow and change." He reached into his pocket and pulled out a midnight blue velvet case.

Kate gasped as he opened the small box. She gazed at an enormous emerald cut diamond engagement ring blinking in the candlelight. When she finally found her voice, she sputtered, "But, John. I don't understand."

"I'm telling you, Kate, that I love you and want to marry you."

Kate was flabbergasted; she had never once thought about John in that way. She considered him her mentor, sponsor, father figure, and shoulder to lean on. No way could she wrap her brain around the idea of becoming Mrs. John Davis.

She tried to let him down gently. "Oh, John. I'm so flattered. You know how important you are to me. You've changed my world. And the ring is so beautiful. But get married? I can't do that."

John generally got his way in business dealings. To him, this proposal was just another transaction. He began negotiations in earnest.

John leaned toward Kate, and said, "Of course you can. Kate, I can give you everything you ever need— international-quality horses, clothes, cars, beautiful homes. You can still train with Ben if you like, but you won't have to clean stalls or groom other people's horses. Other people will take care of your horses, and I'll take care of you."

Kate looked at her wine glass and for a moment fantasized about being taken care of and protected. She liked to work hard, but it would be nice not to worry about money. And the horses! It would be incredible to have unlimited access to top horses.

John lifted the ring out of its case and extended it toward her. "Here, Sweetheart. Let me put it on your finger. We have so much to celebrate tonight."

His words brought Kate back to reality. She didn't want to hurt John's feelings, but there was no way she going to accept this proposal.

"Really, John. I can't. This is my first time away from

home. Even when I was in college, I lived with my mom. I'm not ready to get married to anyone. I'm too young."

John winked at her. "Ah. I get it. You're worried about the age difference. Don't worry. It's not an issue. You'll find I can be very youthful when it counts."

Kate's face turned three shades of red. She put her hand on John's hand, and gently but firmly pushed it and the ring away. "I'm sorry, John. You mean the world to me, but I just can't give you more. Can't we just continue being friends?"

In a flash John's eyes grew icy, and his voice turned harsh. He leaned toward her. "No, I don't think so, Kate. We can't just be friends. I want more. And if you know anything about me, you know I always get what I want."

The sudden change in John startled Kate. She realized that this was the ruthless businessman she'd heard about but hadn't yet seen in the barn. Trying not to be intimidated, she said again, "I'm sorry, John. As much as I'd like to, I just can't give you more at this point in my life."

John's face turned to stone as he threatened, "You'll learn. You really don't have a choice, you know. Let me put it to you this way. Agree to marry me, or I'm taking Reminisce away from you. You'll lose your horse and your shot at ever making a team. Do you think it's easy for an unknown to find a sponsor? You'll probably end up shoveling shit for the rest of your life."

John's cruelty and the thought of losing her beloved Remmy horrified Kate. Her mouth fell open. "John, you can't mean that!"

"Yes, my dear. I can and I will. So, consider your answer carefully. Reminisce and I are a package deal. Take it or leave it."

John leaned back in his chair, and his expression softened. "Oh, Kate. I guess I really took you by surprise tonight. But when you've had a chance to think it over, you'll realize that this is best solution for both of us. We'll have a wonderful life together. We'll travel and dine in the finest restaurants. I'll show you parts of the world you've only seen in pictures. People will take care of your horses rather than the other way around. We'll summer up here and spend the winters in Palm Beach. You can decorate our homes any way you want. I'll treat you like a princess, Kate."

Kate stared at her hands so John couldn't see her tear-filled eyes. The voice in her head screamed "Never, never, never!" But all she said out loud was, "No, John. I'm so sorry. I'm touched and grateful, but I just can't."

John stood up so abruptly that he almost knocked his chair over. He pulled out his wallet and tossed some money on the table to cover the drinks. He hissed like a threatened reptile, "You're a fool, Katherine Gage. I've just offered you the opportunity of a lifetime, and you're too stupid to see it. I should have known better."

With that, he turned on his heels and left Kate alone at the table. She'd never seen this side of John. He'd always been kind and gracious to her, and so generous. But then again, she'd never turned down anything he'd offered—until tonight.

Kate sat alone at the table for a long time. Finally, the waiter jolted her out of her catatonic state when he asked if he could get her anything else. Not trusting herself to speak, she shook her head, got up, and walked out of the restaurant with as much dignity as she could muster.

Once outside, she dug through her purse until she found her cell phone. But who should she call? She wanted to call Wheeler, but then she remembered that he and Peter were out of town. She thought of Audrey, but it would take her a half hour to get to Chandler House. Instead, she called Chris, as she knew he lived nearby. With shaking fingers, she punched in his number. By the time he answered, she was sobbing hysterically.

Chris could barely make out her words. "Kate. Kate. Is that you? Slow down! I can't understand a word you're saying. Where are you? The Chandler House? Yes, of course I can pick you up. Don't move. I'll be there in ten minutes."

# FORTY-THREE

*Kate*

As he drove up to the Chandler House, Chris saw Kate in front of the restaurant. She huddled forlornly on the edge of a bench. As soon as he brought the car to a stop, he jumped out and ran to her. He enveloped Kate in strong arms and helped her into the car. He drove to his home, held her elbow as he escorted her inside, and settled her onto his overstuffed leather couch.

"Here. Drink this," he said, handing her a glass of whiskey. "What happened? Do you want to talk about it?"

Kate gratefully took the glass from Chris and sipped the whiskey. She nodded and gave him a weak grin. He poured himself a glass and sat beside her. It took several minutes before she could talk coherently. Finally, between sobs and hiccups, she told Chris what had happened at the restaurant.

Kate wiped the tears from her cheeks. "I was shocked by his proposal. I've always thought of John as a mentor and basically a father figure. I had no idea he felt any differently toward me. You should have seen his face. He was livid. I was actually afraid of him for a moment. I was glad we were in a public place. I can't imagine what he would have said or done if no one had been around. And the worst thing was he said he and Remmy were a package deal. He tried to blackmail me. If I don't agree to marriage, he'll take Remmy away from me!"

Kate dissolved into tears again. She'd probably lose Remmy. Things like that happened over and over in the horse world. Riders without money relied on sponsor-ship. But sponsors often used their power to threaten them. Those threats could be about anything from not winning, to losing weight, to saying the wrong thing at a press conference, to being at their beck and call any time of the day or night.

Chris opened his arms. Kate slid closer to him and found comfort in his embrace. He held her, and she started to calm down. Kate sighed. This felt like a safe place. She belonged here. She let the warmth and strength of his body surround her like a protective cov-ering. She lay her head on his chest and felt the rhythm of his heart—strong, vital, and soothing.

He pressed his lips ever so gently to the top of her head and continued to hold her. After a few minutes, Chris leaned back to see if Kate had calmed down enough to stop crying. As he did, she turned her face up to his. Their heads were inches apart. Chris brushed his lips across her mouth, and she responded by deepening the kiss.

He whispered, "Are you sure?"

She nodded. "I've never been surer of anything in my life."

Chris took her by the hand and led her to his elaborate bedroom. He laid her gently on the king-sized bed like a priceless treasure. She watched him as he lit a fire in the enormous stone fireplace. And then he came to her.

Slowly, as if they never wanted the initial moments to end, they began to undress each other. As they peeled each layer away, they delighted in the discovery of what lay beneath.

Kate shivered with desire as Chris's fingers gently glided over her body and explored her soft skin. She brushed her hand over the curly hair on his chest and giggled at how it tickled her palm. She loved the feeling of hard muscles rippling just underneath his skin. There wasn't an ounce of fat on him, and he felt as delicious as he looked. When they were completely naked, her heart and her body ached with longing.

He moved cautiously at first, but as their passion rose, they made love with an urgency born of long-denied need. Kate moaned as Chris poured every ounce of his heart, soul, and love into bringing her to a peak she'd never known she could reach. Chris was a skillful and thoughtful lover. At just the right moment, he allowed himself to join her so they climaxed together. Wave after wave pulsed through them. When it was over, they lay in a tangle of arms and legs. Chris looked into her eyes as he gently brushed a wayward strand of raven hair from her face. "You're so beautiful."

Kate's reaction surprised her. She didn't feel the need to deny his words. She believed Chris. At that moment, she did feel beautiful. He had given her a wonderful gift. She felt like a jigsaw puzzle whose pieces had started to come together to create a beautiful picture.

"I love you so much, Kate," Chris said, his right hand gently stroking her hair. "I've loved you from the first hours we spent together in the quarantine barn. I feel like we're old souls meant to be together. It just took us a while to trust each other."

Overwhelmed with love and desire, Kate said, "I think I felt the same way from the beginning, too. But I was too worried to let my walls down. I was afraid of scaring you away if I ever told you about my background. I'm damaged goods, Chris. You need to know that."

"I don't care about your past," Chris said, shaking his head. "You don't need to tell me anything. But I'm always here to listen if you want to. And as far as I'm concerned, you're not damaged. You're perfect. Everything that has happened in your life up to this moment has made you the person you are."

# FORTY-FOUR

*Chris*

Chris noticed that John didn't show up at the barn for the next couple of weeks. Kate told him that being in the dark about what John was thinking or planning made her anxious. But since John hadn't told Ben to take her off of Remmy, she kept riding him. She didn't know if he'd make good on his threat, but in the meantime, she was going to enjoy riding this extraordinary horse for as long as she could. If and when John took him away from her, she'd deal with it then.

Chris helped Kate stay grounded. She trusted him more each day. And one night she told him the story about Jimmy. He ached for her and what she'd endured. He held her closely as she poured out the story through a torrent of tears. He understood now why she'd built walls around her heart. And it moved him that she trusted him enough to let her in.

During the days, Chris and Kate spent as much of

their free time together as possible. Sometimes they'd work with Tee and Victor. Other times, they'd find a quiet spot and have lunch together. They never seemed to run out of things to say. They discussed everything from training to philosophical ideas to plans for the future.

Chris still rode in the group lesson, and he and Tee blossomed under Ben's guidance. It was at the end of one of those sessions that Ben called his riders over.

"Okay, guys. Gather 'round. Even though we're done with Devon, we still have work to do to prepare for Florida this winter. There's a small show nearby next weekend. It's optional, but I still want you to do horse show practice here. You'll warm up your horses in the ring behind the indoor. Then come to the main ring to ride your test for me. As usual, this will be a full dress rehearsal. You know the drill. Braid your horses and wear competition attire."

When Chris looked puzzled, Ben explained, "We often do dress rehearsals because we don't want any surprises at the show. You'd be amazed how many horses get tense when they're braided because they anticipate the excitement of a horse show. The same goes for the riders. As soon as they put on their shadbelly coats, the adrenaline starts pumping. Even moving from the warm-up ring to the competition arena can create anxiety.

"We do these dry runs so it's not a big deal for either horse or rider. The rehearsals desensitize the horses to show scenarios, and I'm able to see how the riders react to the added pressure. Then I can come up with a personalized strategy for each one. Some need to relax, others need to block out distractions, and others need to get pumped up. Everyone reacts differently, and it's my job to figure out what each person needs in order to maximize his or her performance. I know you're not showing Tee yet, Chris, but it'll be good practice for you to do the show anyhow."

"I'm happy to do it, Ben. But I don't have a shadbelly coat. Should I just braid Tee and leave it at that? And which test should we do?"

"I'll lend you my coat. We're about the same size so I'm sure it'll fit you. If you're going to get tense, the coat will be enough to trigger you. Let's start with the Prix St. Georges test. That'll be a good one for both of you— challenging but not overwhelming."

After the meeting with Ben, the riders dismounted, loosened their girths, and ran their stirrups up to the top of the leathers so they weren't dangling against their horses' sides. As they led their mounts out of the ring, Chris fell in beside Kate and said, "Ben really is incredible, isn't he? He's as much of a psychologist as a trainer."

"I know. And he really cares. It's certainly not just a paycheck for him," Kate said. "Plus, he's the only trainer I've ever heard of who really gets into the sports psychology of riding and competing. That's probably why his students are so successful. Ben says that at the highest level of any sport, top athletes are pretty evenly matched skill-wise. But the winner on any given day is the one who has the right mindset."

"I know! I love how he emphasizes the psychological part of competing."

"I think riders have an even tougher mountain to climb than other athletes because we also have to get our horses to the ring in the right mental state," Kate continued. "I mean, when you think about it, they have the same issues we do: nerves, lack of focus, insecurity. It's a huge task to get two athletes, one human and one equine, to peak on the same day at the right time."

Chris nodded, "I know. It's daunting. When I ran track, I only had to worry about myself. It's a whole different ballgame with an animal. What else does Ben have you do besides these dress rehearsals?"

"He has us do a lot of what he calls 'perfect practice,'" Kate said. "Ben doesn't accept the old saying that practice makes perfect. He believes that perfect practice makes perfect. And the only place you can practice perfectly is in your imagination. He believes that if you practice rotten canter departs day after day, that's what you'll get very good at doing—rotten canter departs! The heart of his program is that the subconscious mind can't tell the difference between what you really do and what you vividly imagine. If you do ten lousy half-passes when you're riding, but you do a hundred rhythmic, fluid, well-bent half-passes in your imagination, your brain thinks you've actually done ten times as many good half-passes as bad half-passes. So, you have to get better because that's what you've practiced. When we're not riding, we do a lot of visualization. At least Jason, Melissa, and I do. Audrey is a little lazy about it, but she's starting to get on board. We start three weeks before a show and visualize every stride of the perfect test in great detail."

Chris' jaw dropped open. "Wow! I definitely need to start doing 'perfect practice'! But what if it's hard to imagine the perfect 'mental movie' because your mind keeps going back to the worst-case scenario? Or maybe you've worked on 'perfect practice' in your mind, but when you actually do your test, things go wrong, like your horse picking up the wrong lead?"

Kate grinned. "In that case, you do what Ben calls 'coping rehearsal.' Go ahead and see your horse picking up the wrong lead, and then see yourself working on the problem until you have a successful resolution to it. For example, your horse picks up the wrong lead. Your breathing and heart rate stay normal. You quietly bring him back to the trot. Reestablish bend. Then ask him for the correct lead again."

Chris smiled. "I think I'll be doing a lot of coping rehearsal! What else does Ben have you do?"

"Well, not only do we use mental rehearsal for the movements like half-passes and flying changes, but we also use it to get ourselves in the right mindset. Ben has a nervous competitor like Melissa visualize going through her ride as if she's as relaxed and confident as Lisa Wilcox. Since Cara is so flighty and unfocused, he has her see herself swaddled in a blanket of concentration. Our little pit bull, Audrey, tends to get wound up and aggressive. So, whether she likes it or not, Ben has her ride in a peaceful Zen state of mind. I really think this kind of mental training is what gives Ben's riders such an edge."

"So that's why you always seem to have your head in the clouds?" Chris asked in mock surprise. "All this time you're rehearsing your rides? I'm sorry, Kate. I thought you were just ditzy."

At that, Kate punched him playfully on the arm. Chris reacted like she'd nearly knocked him to his knees from the force of the blow. The two of them beamed at each other foolishly, the electricity between them palpable.

# FORTY-FIVE

*Kate*

Kate and Chris warmed their horses up for the mock show in the outdoor arena behind the indoor school. They'd braided them, and the riders were dressed in white breeches and the shadbelly coats that were reminiscent of Fred Astaire's dancing days.

Ben let them prepare on their own in the warm-up ring. He was joined by Audrey and Melissa, who watched quietly from the sidelines. Ben had told them that even though he'd be around to help them at most of their competitions, occasionally he'd have a conflict that would keep him from being nearby. He wanted to be sure that if that happened, they'd be independent enough to warm themselves up.

After about a half-hour, Ben said, "Okay, guys. I'm heading over to the other ring to judge your tests. The order of go is the same as I told you yesterday. Kate first. Then Chris, then Audrey, then Melissa. Leave fifteen minutes between rides so I can talk to each of you after your test. Kate, you can head over now and circle the outside of the arena while I get settled in the gazebo."

Kate rode Remmy over to the main arena and trotted around it once. To check that he was paying attention, she asked for a couple of strides of extended trot and then collected the trot. In her mind's eye movie, she visualized the uphill balance of collection in the extension and the power of an extension in collection. It pleased her that he was hot off her leg and surged forward into the extension and listened to her braced back and outside rein to add his hind legs for collection. Then she broke to the walk, stretched up tall, and brought her legs slightly behind the girth. Remmy eagerly trotted in place in a classical piaffe. In her mind's eye, Kate saw his croup lowering and the resulting elevation of his forehand, saw him pick up his hind feet to the height of his fetlocks and lift his front feet to the middle of his cannon bone. She patted him enthusiastically while he was still in piaffe.

Unlike many trainers, Ben taught his riders to reward their horses during the piaffe rather than after it. Unfortunately, too many riders spurred and hit their horses with the whip to keep them going during the movement. Eventually the horses linked piaffe with punishment and dreaded doing it. But Ben had his riders praise the horses during piaffe so they'd associate the movement with something pleasurable and would eventually think of it as play rather than work. It was just another example of the thinking that made Ben so different from most trainers and coaches.

After the piaffe, Ben let Kate walk Remmy for a few moments. Then he rang the bell in the gazebo to signal that she could enter the arena to begin her test.

Their ride went seamlessly. Remmy was the epitome of controlled energy and relaxed concentration as Kate guided him from movement to movement. They showed dancing half-passes, dynamic extensions, metronome-like piaffe and passage, and buoyant canter work. As they left the arena, she looked at Ben and held her breath as she waited for his feedback.

"It just gets better and better, Kate. Every time you go through the test, it looks more polished. You and Remmy flow from one movement to the next. The only comments I have are about the right canter pirouette and the flying changes to the left. Pulse your outside rein each stride to make the right pirouette a hair smaller. On the flying changes to the left, you're using inside rein and bending his neck slightly to the left. Instead, give a quick half-halt on the right rein at the moment you ask for the change. Close your right hand like you're snatching a fly out of the air. Any questions?"

Kate exhaled. "No, Ben. I'm really happy with Remmy. He tries so hard. I'm scared that John is going to take him away from me and any ride could be our last one together."

"Well, he hasn't said anything to me," Ben replied. "In fact, no one has heard from him in weeks. He's either really busy with work or he hasn't made a decision about what to do about Remmy. I think it would be a real shame if he let his ego get in the way of something that could be really special. Try to block it out for now. When the time comes, we'll deal with whatever happens."

"Thanks, Ben. You have no idea how much I appreciate your support. And we'll work on those pirouettes and changes. Do you mind if I hang out and walk around the outside of the ring to cool him out? I'd like to watch Chris' ride. This is his first time doing a Prix St. Georges test."

"You're welcome, and I have no doubt you'll do your homework. You always do," Ben smiled. "Of course, it's fine for you to stay and watch Chris and Tee. I'm excited for him and what he's done with his horse. Oh. Here he comes now. Perfect timing."

# FORTY-SIX

*Chris*

Chris made his way over to the "competition ring" and asked Tee to pick up the trot as they went around the outside of the arena. He felt his horse puff himself up and thought, *Wow. This is going to be great. He feels like he just grew a foot.*

Ben let them trot once around the ring and then rang the bell. At the sound of the bell, Chris asked Tee to pick up the canter. As they entered the ring, Chris felt a subtle change in Tee's body. He had crossed the line from feeling pleasantly pumped up to rising panic. Chris worried that he wouldn't be able to stop him for the first salute.

Chris tried to collect the canter with half-halts as he'd been taught, but Tee had mentally left town. Chris finally had to yank on the reins to stop him. Tee shuffled around in distress, and then started to back up. Chris knew this was a serious mistake, so instead of insisting that he stay immobile for the halt he decided to go forward rather than making him more anxious by insisting that he stand still.

But when Chris asked Tee to go forward, the horse stood straight up on his hind legs. He reared so high his body was almost perpendicular to the ground. Chris flung his arms around Tee's neck so he wouldn't lose his balance and pull him over backwards. Tee held this posture for a moment as if posing for a snapshot. But the instant his front feet came back to the ground, he launched himself through the air and bolted out of the ring, crashing through the arena rails as he went.

Everyone at the barn heard the commotion and came out to see what was going on. Audrey and Melissa cantered around from the back ring to see what had happened. They saw Tee running blindly out of control down the front pasture. Chris tried to stop him by using a pulley rein. He shortened his left rein and pressed his knuckles into Tee's neck so he wouldn't turn and possibly slip and fall when he used the right rein. Then with his right hand, he pulled up and back repeatedly and sat back to use his upper body for leverage.

Tee paid no attention to Chris' efforts. He galloped with his nose straight out in front of him. His head was so high that Chris could actually see the whites of his eyes as he tore across the field. They headed blindly toward the solid white fence that enclosed Cherry Hill's property.

Kate and Audrey jumped off and handed their horses to two of the boarders who stood watching in horror at the scene unfolding in front of them. The girls and Ben took off after Chris and Tee on foot.

One of the grooms, Mateo, had seen the commotion and grabbed the farm truck. As he started the engine, Jason hopped in, and they drove across the front field toward Chris and Tee.

"Oh my God," Audrey gasped as they ran. "Will he stop at the fence or try to jump it? Let's hope he stops. If he jumps, he'll land on the pavement on the other side and might slip and fall."

Kate didn't say anything. Couldn't say anything. She just kept running.

The group collectively held their breath as horse and rider approached the fence. Tee didn't stop or try to jump the fence. In his frenzy, he crashed through it, sending splinters and razor-sharp shards of wood everywhere, including into his own body. The force of the collision caused both of them to fall, and Tee rolled over Chris. And then neither of them moved.

When everyone caught up to the pair, they all went to help Chris, except for Jason, who went to Tee to check out his injuries.

Even with his helmet on, Chris had been knocked out. As he came to, he groggily asked about Tee. Kate assured him that Jason had everything under control. She didn't want to worry him about Tee's wounds. Besides, she didn't know the extent of the horse's injuries. And she wouldn't know until the vet arrived. For now, she was just grateful that they were both alive.

Chris looked disoriented and complained about pain in his neck and left arm. They knew he needed to go to the hospital right away. They also knew they could get him there faster on their own rather than waiting for an ambulance. But they worried about moving him because of his neck.

Ben called 9-1-1. He told the operator the location of the farm and what had happened. The operator assured him that an ambulance was on its way. She advised Ben to keep Chris warm and not move him. Kate sat on the ground beside Chris.

Ben's next call was to Dr. Roberts. He was surprised to reach the vet personally in the middle of the day. Ben explained the situation and asked him to come over as soon as possible. Luckily, the vet was in the area; he could be there within the hour.

Jason sat by Tee's head and patted the horse gently as he crooned, "It's okay, boy. We're going to get you some help. You're going to be fine."

As if he understood, Tee lifted his neck and gingerly rose to his feet, looking as stunned and shaken as Chris did.

"I think if we go slowly, I can lead him back through the field," Jason said. "That's the shortest route. He's bleeding a lot from his wounds, but I don't see any blood spurting out, so he doesn't have a severed artery. In his situation, I think it's better to walk him back rather than give him a bouncy trailer ride."

Audrey agreed. "Okay. Melissa and I will go back with you in case you need help."

It took a full twenty minutes for Jason to lead Tee back to the barn. The entire time, Jason comforted him while Audrey and Melissa quietly discussed what could have possibly made this normally obedient horse freak out and bolt the way he had.

Ben called Phillipe on his cell phone and told him to wait by the front gate for the ambulance. Within fifteen minutes it arrived with lights flashing and siren blaring. Phillipe pointed the way to the front field where Chris lay, and the driver immediately drove down the driveway. Phillipe followed on foot through the field.

When they reached the people huddled around Chris, the EMTs jumped out of the truck and assessed the situation. They asked everyone to step back so they could work. They secured Chris's neck first. Then they checked his responsiveness, airway, and pulse. Ben told the EMTs that, even with his helmet on, Chris had been knocked unconscious briefly when he hit the ground. Once the EMTs stabilized him, they knew they needed to get him to the hospital as quickly as possible.

Kate wanted to ride in the ambulance with Chris, but they wouldn't let her. She insisted on going to the hospital anyhow, but Ben told her she couldn't drive in her current state. He asked Mateo to drive her in the farm truck and follow the ambulance.

Kate sobbed as she worried about Chris and Tee. Mateo drove in silence. He didn't know what he could say to comfort her. He didn't know how badly either one of them was hurt.

When they got to the hospital, they had to wait two hours before they got any news. The nurses had taken Chris for a battery of tests. Kate and Mateo had no idea how long it would take before they heard anything. They sat in silence and drank cup after cup of coffee as they waited for some word.

When the doctor finally came out, they stood up like they'd been ejected from their seats. He asked if they were family. Kate lied and said she was. At least in her mind she felt like Chris' family, and that was good enough for her.

The doctor said, "Well, he's a very lucky young man. It's a good thing he had a helmet on. He's awake, but he does have a concussion, a broken collarbone, and some pretty deep lacerations that needed stitches. We did some X-rays and a CT scan of his head and neck. We're keeping him in the hospital for the time being to observe him. I'll let you know how long that will be—it depends on how things go. But tonight is critical because of the concussion, so we'll keep a close eye on him."

Kate breathed a huge sigh of relief. It didn't sound like he had life-threatening or permanent injuries.

"Can we see him?" Kate asked.

"Yes, but just briefly. He's dozing on and off. He's in

Room 206. It's just down the hall to the right. If he's sleeping, please don't wake him. If he's awake, don't stay too long."

"We won't. Thank you, doctor," Kate said. "We just want to see him and let him know we're here, even if we just leave a note."

When they got to Room 206, Kate poked her head into the room to see if Chris was awake. He wasn't, so she and Mateo entered silently and sat in the two hospital chairs near the bed.

Chris' arm was in a sling, and his face, neck, and arms sported several bruises and stitches. Kate had calmed down earlier but had a hard time keeping it together as she watched his still form. She tried to relax by reminding herself his injuries weren't grave although they easily could have been. When you're dealing with a large animal whose instinct is to flee in order to survive, you never knew what potential disaster lay around the next corner. It came with the territory, and they all just accepted the possibility of injury every day when they either worked with or rode the horses.

Kate and Mateo sat quietly and watched Chris for any signs of him waking up. After about a half hour, he turned his head ever so slightly, groaned, and opened his eyes partway. He looked completely disoriented. Kate slid her chair over to the right side of his bed. She took his good hand in hers. "Hi Chris. We're here. It's me, Kate. And Mateo is here with me, too. Can you hear me? How do you feel?"

Chris grimaced. "Where am I? I assume I'm in the hospital, but which one? I don't remember much after Tee and I went down. Just bits and pieces. Ugh! My neck is killing me. I have a splitting headache."

Kate tried to sound matter-of-fact. "You're at Cooley Dickinson Hospital in Northampton. They brought you here by ambulance. You passed out for a few seconds when you fell. That's probably why you don't remember much. You'll have to get the details about your tests from the doctor, but from what I understand you have a concussion, some stitches, and a broken collarbone. We're so happy your neck is okay. You complained about it when you were semi-conscious so they did a CT scan as soon as they got you in here. Luckily, it's not broken."

Mateo stood up and walked over to the bed. "Hey, buddy! You sure put a scare into us. We get enough drama from the Dressage Queens. You don't need to resort to acrobatics to get our attention, you know. Seriously, you look good. I'm going to go out into the hallway and call Ben. They're all waiting to hear."

"Thanks for coming, Mateo. I appreciate it, man," Chris whispered.

Chris then turned his eyes toward Kate and asked, "How's Tee? Is he okay? I'm almost afraid to ask."

Kate said, "I don't really know. Ben put a call into Dr. Roberts right away. But Mateo and I followed the ambulance so we didn't find out anything else. And no one has called us yet with a report. Luckily, Dr. Roberts was in the area and got there pretty fast. I did see Jason leading Tee back to the barn, with Audrey and Melissa following along. So, he's up and walking, at least."

She chose not to tell him about the lacerations on Tee's head and the splinters of wood that had impaled his chest and body. Chris had enough on his plate just processing what had happened to him. He didn't need to worry about Tee right now.

When Mateo came back into the room, he said to Chris, "Everyone sends their best. Dr. Roberts is checking out Tee now. Kate, I think we should leave. The doctor said Chris should rest."

Kate looked at Mateo, saying reluctantly, "I suppose you're right. Chris, I'll be back after work. Do you want anything? How about something to eat? I'm not sure how good the hospital food is. Or maybe some magazines? They want you to stay here for observation at least through tonight."

Chris's eyes started to close again as he drifted off to sleep. "No. I'm good. I can't even think about food at the moment. I'll see you later. Find out what Roberts did with Tee. I'm worried about him. I have no idea what made him bolt like that. I could feel his tension escalate as we came down the centerline to start our test. But I never expected him to go ballistic. I need to figure out what I did to set him off. I don't think I rode differently. All I know is that…"

He didn't get to finish his thought because he'd already drifted back to sleep. Kate looked at him once more and then followed Mateo out of the room so they could head back to the farm. Maybe they could use her help with Tee. She knew Chris would be devastated and blame himself if there was anything seriously wrong with his horse.

⌒ ·

When Kate and Mateo got back to the barn, they immediately went to Tee's stall, but it was empty. They saw several people further down the aisle peering into the wash stall. When they got there, they saw that Ben held a sedated Tee as Dr. Roberts treated him.

Kate found out from Audrey that Tee's injuries weren't life-threatening. The dagger-like splinters of wood hadn't severed anything vital or made deep puncture wounds. Both of those scenarios had been distinct possibilities. But although his wounds and lacerations would take several weeks of care to heal, the vet didn't foresee any permanent problems.

He cleaned and sutured some of the larger wounds. Concerned about infection, he made sure to clean the lacerations to remove surface bacteria and debris. Tee had already been immunized for tetanus, but the vet gave him a booster shot anyhow.

When he finished treating him, they carefully walked a wobbly and semi-sedated Tee back to his stall. Dr. Roberts led him slowly, step-by-step, and Ben held his tail to help steady him as they guided him to his box at the other end of the barn.

The vet reassured the anxious group that Tee would be okay. He suggested that they cold-hose the wounds to reduce swelling and ease the pain, starting the next day. He also gave them some bute for pain and to help reduce inflammation, as well as some ointment to keep the tissue moist and protect it from debris.

Kate asked Ben if she could be responsible for Tee's rehab. She knew Chris would want it that way. And she wouldn't want it any other way herself. Knowing the connection Kate had with Chris and Tee, Ben agreed.

# FORTY-SEVEN

*Chris*

Chris spent two nights in the hospital. The staff wanted to observe him carefully especially at night. Among other signs, they watched him carefully for worsening headache, dizziness, drowsiness, or slurred speech.

Kate came to visit Chris each evening. They mostly held hands and watched television, although that sometimes made his headache worse. When that happened, they switched to discussing Tee's behavior and his injuries. Kate had taken over Tee's care, and Chris trusted her completely. He knew she was more familiar with him than anyone else because of all the work they'd done together when he first came to Cherry Hill.

When the hospital released Chris on the morning of the third day, Kate brought him home and helped him settle in. As they drove up his driveway, Kate once again marveled at the beauty of the stately house and landscaped grounds. Chris had left for a while when he went to college and then worked in New York. But he always returned to Chesterfield—his beloved childhood home.

They stopped at the massive front doors and Kate insisted Chris stay in the car. He reluctantly agreed and waited for her to run around and open the door for him. She helped him out while he insisted he could manage on his own.

As they approached the front door, it swung open to reveal a sprightly woman with silver hair. Her smile could electrify an entire room. She looked to be in her seventies, but her energy and vitality belonged to a much younger woman. Mildred Bates and her husband, Ralph, had taken care of Chesterfield and its residents all of Chris' life. They lived in a comfortable cottage behind the main house. When Chris' parents moved to southern Connecticut to be closer to the city, the Bates chose to stay at Chesterfield and become its caretakers.

Ralph took care of the grounds. He had a crew of people to help him with the heavy work. Mildred kept the house in order and cooked for Chris. She protected her kitchen like a tiger overseeing her territory. No one was allowed in there while she created her gourmet meals or baked her decadent desserts. She was a force of nature, and no one, including Ralph, dared intrude on her domain.

When Chris was growing up, Mildred was his nanny,

and he considered her and Ralph family. He knew they would always be with him, living out their days at the estate.

Mildred seemed delighted to have Chris home from the hospital, but she looked at Kate with suspicion. This was the first time the two women had met face to face.

Mildred had a reputation for having no flies on her. She said exactly what she thought regardless of whether it was politically correct. She'd scared some of Chris' previous girlfriends. It took a lot to pass muster with her. She looked at Kate like a bear protecting her cub and said, "So you're the young woman I've heard so much about. Chris talks about you all the time. Thank you for taking care of my boy."

"Of course, Mildred. It's so nice to meet you. I know you played a huge part in raising Chris. That must be why he's so grounded and kind."

When she heard Kate's words, Mildred's face softened. But she brushed them off and changed the subject by saying, "Well, let's get our young man settled on the couch, and then I'll bring us some coffee and treats. Chris, I made your favorite raspberry squares last night to celebrate your homecoming. I hope you brought your appetite with you, young lady. You look like you could stand to gain a few pounds. Are they working you too hard at that horse stable?"

"No, ma'am. I love it there, and they treat us very well."

Kate took Chris's right arm and Mildred stood by his

left side with her arm around his waist. He chuckled at the two of them hovering over him. Chris knew he didn't need to be coddled, but he enjoyed how much they fussed over him. So, he said nothing and let them do their thing. They settled him onto the couch in the great room, and Mildred disappeared into the kitchen.

Kate took a good look around the beautifully appointed living room. The last time she'd been there was the night Chris picked her up at Chandler House after her fight with John. At that time, she was too upset to take much in.

Rattled by John's cruelty and hasty exit, Kate hadn't been able to think about the way Chris' lived. But now, as she gazed around, she saw it was definitely a man's room that had been skillfully decorated, mostly likely by a professional. It was a luxurious room in a stately home that had been in the family for a long time. Did he own it now, or did it still belong to his parents? She couldn't imagine Chris living in such a grand place on a freelance newspaper writer's salary. Chris had rarely spoken of his background.

Chris looked at Kate with an apologetic grin. "I should have warned you about Mildred. She's a bit of a mother hen, but I love her dearly. I think of her as my surrogate mom because my parents traveled so much when I was a kid. And even when they were home, they went out several evenings each week, so it was mostly just Mildred and me. My folks are good people, but sometimes I wonder why they even bothered to have a child. Growing up, I felt like an afterthought. I rarely remember them coming to school plays or track meets. But Mildred and Ralph always came and cheered me on."

"You're so lucky to have had such caring people in your life."

Chris agreed. "That's for sure. I called my parents from the hospital and they acted concerned, but they've only called back once. They probably thought I was in good hands with Mildred, which of course is true. And in truth, maybe I did downplay the whole thing a bit. Or a lot. But I was hoping they'd want to see me anyhow." He paused. "I know my parents love me in their way. But their own lives come first. Always have. They paid attention to me when it was convenient or when they wanted to put me on display at one of their parties. Once I'd made my trophy-kid appearance, they had Mildred take me to my room so I wouldn't get in the way or annoy the adults. If I ever have kids, believe me, it'll be a different story."

Mindful of the "if you can't say anything nice" idea, Kate kept her thoughts to herself about his parents. "I think Mildred is wonderful," she said. "I'm glad you'll be in such good hands when I can't be here. I can probably get here by around six o'clock most afternoons, and we can have dinner together. But I'll have to leave early when I have night check. Anyhow, don't worry about your folks. You can't change the past. It's totally their loss. In a way I feel sorry for them that they missed out on being a part of your life. At least you had

Mildred and Ralph to love and care for you."

As Mildred returned with a tray, she overheard Kate's last words. By the time she entered the room, she grinned warmly at the girl.

The tray she carried held a coffee pot and three china cups plus her "world renowned" raspberry squares. She poured the coffee and asked Kate how she took hers. When they were all settled in with coffee and delicacies, Mildred said, "Okay. Give me the details on your rehab. What does the doctor want us to do? Do you need anything special for meals? Should we put a bed in this room so you don't have to go up the stairs?"

"The concussion is mild. I do have a headache and I'm a little dizzy when I stand up. They want me to have X-rays every couple of weeks to check my progress. And I have to wear this sling for a while. It's a drag, but I guess I'm very lucky, all things considered."

# FORTY-EIGHT

*Kate*

After a few days, Tee's wounds looked slightly less angry. Kate took him out of his stall three times a day for short hand-walks and to let him graze. While she watched him munching on the fall grass, she worried that he'd get bored because of his extended stall rest and limited time outside. They couldn't turn him out yet because they didn't want him galloping across the paddocks and tearing his stitches open. As she watched him eat, an idea popped into her head. Now all she had to do was run it by Ben and Chris to get their approval.

After putting Tee away, Kate went to find Ben. She found him sitting in the gazebo teaching one of his regulars, Mary Kravis, who trailered in for a lesson once a week. Kate took a seat and watched until the lesson ended. Ben gave Mary some homework to do until their session the following week. As she walked out, she greeted the next rider, Anne Bennett, who entered the ring.

Ben knew Anne would walk her horse for ten minutes before she started her warm-up, so he turned to Kate and asked, "What's up, Kate? Everything okay in the barn?"

"Oh, yes. Everything's fine." Kate said. "I just wanted to run something by you and see what you think. I'm concerned Tee will get bored while he's on stall rest. And I'm worried about why he freaked out and what we can do to help him."

Ben sighed. "I know. I've thought about it a lot. Starting the test triggered him. It would be nice to know more about his history, but apparently his previous owner didn't show him, so I don't think we can get any useful information from her."

Kate nodded and said, "Yeah. It's probably not a good idea to get her involved anyhow. If I were Chris, I'd want to close that chapter."

"Agreed. And it'll be weeks before Chris can ride again. He has to heal from his own injuries first. But once Tee is ready to work, my plan is to start with very small steps and increase my demands gradually. He's obviously had some trauma related to competing. I'm just going to have to take a lot of time to build a new history with him."

"I know you'll put the right plan together for him, Ben. And with your permission, I'd like to add one more thing: clicker training. I can start to teach him in his stall. That'll lay a foundation for rewarding him with the clicker when you start working him under saddle. And it'll also occupy his mind so he doesn't get too bored. The first sessions are only about five minutes long twice a day."

Ben raised an eyebrow and said, "Have you done this before? From the little I know of clicker training, it's mostly used for dogs."

Kate's face lit up. "You can use it for anything! It's all about training through positive reinforcement. I learned about clicker training from a friend who worked at Sea World in California with killer whales, dolphins, and other marine mammals. When she started riding, she brought the same techniques that she used at Sea World to the horses. And she had phenomenal results."

"So, you think clicker training could help Tee?"

"Absolutely! Since horses want to please their people, we can build a relationship based on trust and respect," Kate continued excitedly. "I taught Audrey how to get Bella to sit, stay, lie down, and come with clicker training. Bella thought it was a great game."

Ben laughed. "Now that I'd like to see! I was starting to think that Bella the Boisterous might be untrainable!"

Kate smiled at her mentor. "For the horses you can use it for anything—lowering the head for clipping, loading on a trailer, standing quietly for the vet or farrier, or mounting as well as work under saddle. It's gentle and fun, and it's all based on positive reinforcement.

Can I teach Tee? I'll start on the ground and when he's ready to be ridden, I can get a clicker to attach to the butt of a whip so you can click and reward him whenever you want. What do you think?"

Ben nodded and said, "It sounds like a terrific idea. I'll ask Chris what he thinks. If he's agreeable, go for it. I'll be interested to see how things evolve. Patting, praising, and walks on loose reins are great rewards, but this sounds like another way to reward him exactly at the right time."

Kate rose and said, "Thank you so much, Ben. I can't wait to get started. I won't take up any more of your time. It looks like Anne is ready to start her lesson."

With that Kate left the gazebo. She respected Ben's time and never interrupted him just to chat. If she had questions or issues, she first went to Audrey and Jason to brainstorm. And nine times out of ten, because of their combined experience, they figured out how to solve problems on their own. But this situation was different because she'd be training someone else's horse.

Chris and Ben discussed clicker training and agreed it would be a good addition to Tee's training. They told Kate to go ahead so she ordered a clicker training kit from her friend's website.

The video that came with the kit explained that when a person paired the clicker with food it very quickly took on value in the horse's mind. He learned what to do at the sound of the clicker in order to receive a reward. The clicker made the same sound every time, which was a distinctive cricket-like noise. That sound told the horse, "Yes, you're right." At the same time, he learned to associate the sound of the clicker with a reward—kind of like Pavlov's dogs.

Initially, Kate worried that Tee would think she'd lied to him if he heard the click and didn't get a reward. But the video explained that the click only had to be reinforced with food every ten to fifteen times to keep the behavior-reward connection strong.

Kate started their lessons in Tee's stall with two five-minute sessions a day. She put grain in the plastic container that came with the kit and belted the container around her waist. At first Tee approached curiously and started sniffing around the container. She covered the top of it with her forearm so he couldn't get to the food inside. Tee nudged her arm gently and tried to get his nose inside the box. But Kate stood quietly and didn't allow him to get to any of the grain. Finally, out of confusion, frustration, or maybe by accident, Tee turned his head away from her. As soon as he turned away, Kate pressed the clicker and immediately gave him a handful of grain. They did this several times. Tee learned fast. He soon discovered that if he did the opposite of what his instincts told him to do, he'd get a reward.

Kate and Tee practiced twice a day for two days. Then

Kate introduced the target. The target was a hand-held tool made from a dowel with a marine float mounted on one end. It came with the kit she ordered, but Kate soon realized she could use anything as a target, including the long handled brush they used to scrub out the water buckets.

Next, she taught Tee to focus by touching his nose to the float at the end of the target. She used the target to introduce the idea of performing a task to earn his reward. Eventually, she faded the target out, and the sound of the clicker confirmed that he knew what Kate wanted him to do.

Kate laughed at how quickly Tee learned and how much he seemed to enjoy their interaction. She started by holding the target at arm's length. Tee got curious and ran his nose up and down the handle. Then, when he touched the white float at the end of the dowel by accident, Kate clicked and rewarded him with food. In short order, she was able to do things like tie the target at the far end of the stall, point to it and say, "Target." Tee would leave her side, walk up to the target, touch his nose to it, and return for his grain. Kate giggled to herself that maybe Ben should do some clicker training with Cara to teach her to focus.

After a few weeks, Tee's injuries healed. Ben didn't want to put his staff at risk, so he planned to be the one to start Tee back up and help him work through his competition fear. That was fine with Audrey and Jason. They'd seen Chris' accident and didn't want to be Tee's crash-test dummies. But Kate volunteered to ride him first. She wasn't afraid, and felt she'd developed a strong connection with Tee through clicker training. She wanted to see how it translated to riding. Ben and Chris reluctantly agreed with her, but only if she began within the safety of the indoor arena.

Kate also wanted to do it because she'd watched a confident Tee in the indoor ring many times. Maybe that was because he didn't associate the indoor arena with showing. It wasn't until Chris tried to do the mock show in the outdoor ring that his skeletons rattled out of the closet. Introducing the clicker training work in a safe environment seemed like the perfect solution before they went to the next step.

Kate used the clicker whenever Tee did something well, such as a crisp transition from canter to walk. In the beginning, she stopped him a lot to reward him with a treat. Soon she was able to just click to praise him. That reinforcement helped her keep a strong connection between the sound of the clicker and the reward. Kate was happy that Tee seemed to enjoy their interaction. She hoped that she'd be able to reward him in the same way when they started working through his horse show anxiety.

# FORTY-NINE

*Cara*

Cara's first month at Dietrich's barn flew by. The perks of being Dietrich's lover thrilled her. An excellent one was that he made her privy to all the gossip—both in the barn and in the horse world.

Although they had different agendas, they enjoyed each other's company. Cara adored being wined and dined, and Dietrich loved showing off his glamorous eye candy.

The athletic, creative sex they had in Dietrich's king-sized bed ranked right up there as their favorite pastime. But self-centered people made for selfish lovers; each of them focused on his or her own pleasure rather than satisfying their partner.

After a few weeks, Dietrich grew bored with Cara, particularly when a younger version of her arrived at the barn. Their honeymoon phase came to an end, but that didn't crush Cara. Their relationship had served its purpose. It got her in the door. She really didn't care about having a permanent relationship—especially because she'd begun to find Dietrich, with his sour breath and hairy body, increasingly offensive. But she'd miss the status that came with being his lover.

Every day Cara watched lessons from a bench in the corner of the ring. Increasingly, Dietrich's problem-solving techniques shocked her.

He vented his emotions by using his students as punching bags. Cara could tell how long someone had been in his barn by the intensity of his screaming and the level of his sarcasm. People fell into one of two categories—newcomers and survivors.

Dietrich systematically belittled the newcomers. Then, slowly but surely, he rebuilt them in his own image. When they first came to his barn, he told them they were hopeless, they couldn't ride, had terrible habits, and trained their horses poorly. He was the only one who could save them from themselves. And only he could find them a more suitable mount so they could reach their goals. In truth, he really didn't care if they had good horses or if they ever reached their goals. He just wanted to pad his bank account with training fees and hefty commissions from horse sales.

The people who managed to endure the newcomer phase fell into the second category: survivors. In the beginning, Dietrich tossed out an encouraging tidbit to convince them they'd finally found the true path that he'd laid out for them. After the previous weeks of abuse, they devoured those crumbs like starving creatures.

As a newcomer, Cara fell into the first category. Dietrich no longer praised her the way he had when he'd courted her at horse shows. As far as he was concerned, she couldn't do anything right. Her confidence took a beating, but for once, she worried more about Artie than herself. So far, Artie had escaped Dietrich's cruelty. But Cara was becoming completely neurotic about what each new day might bring.

In the first few weeks of their relationship, Cara tried discussing it with him. But Dietrich had a firm rule. When they finished work at the end of the day, they left all talk of horses behind. It was time for play. Cara supposed that made sense in order to have some balance in life. But she yearned to clear the air about the abuse she saw every day.

After watching Dietrich torment the horses for several weeks, Cara couldn't take it anymore. The final straw came when she saw Dietrich with Teresa Connelly's horse, Alliance. Alliance had a tongue problem. To keep him from sticking his tongue out to the side, Dietrich cranked his noseband as tightly as he could. Despite the tightened noseband, Alliance still managed to loll his tongue out to the side. Sticking the tongue out was the kiss of death in competition. Judges wouldn't give high marks to a horse that showed such blatant resistance. Dietrich was determined to put an end to it that day.

He asked everyone to leave the arena and closed

the sliding door. Cara ran to the stairway that would take her up to the hayloft. From her hiding place she'd be able to see what happened without anyone knowing she was there. She watched in horror as Dietrich rigged up an electrical device to Alliance's bridle near his mouth. The contraption looked like the shock collars some people used to train dogs. Cara overheard Dietrich tell Teresa that the device had two settings on the remote. One button gave off a buzzing sound as a warning. A second button gave an electrical nick. When Alliance put his tongue out, Dietrich told Teresa to warn him with the buzzing sound. If he kept his tongue out, he told her to zap him with electricity.

Cara watched the session with the same mixture of fascination and horror that makes people stare at a car wreck. By the time Teresa zapped Alliance a couple of times, he was in a white-lathered frenzy.

The result pleased Dietrich. He acknowledged his own cleverness and said, "Well, I think I've solved that little problem. He's going to think twice about sticking his tongue out now."

Dietrich's abuse appalled Teresa, but she didn't dare say anything. She loved her horse. And if Dietrich hadn't been yelling at her, she would never have used the device. But she convinced herself that he knew best. She didn't know how to train a Grand Prix horse, while Dietrich had decades of experience.

Cara understood the trap. Ambition or insecurity often got in the way of better judgment. But seeing this poor horse tortured was a huge wake-up call. Before she came to Dietrich's stable, she thought she'd do anything for success. Now she realized she couldn't justify paying such a high price for glory. She planned to talk to Teresa but doubted it would make a difference. Regardless, she had to try. She scurried down the stairs and ran to Artie's stall in tears. She vowed to protect him by getting him out of Dietrich's barn as soon as possible.

Cara needed a plan to get back into Ben's barn. In hindsight, she began to truly appreciate his fairness to both the horses and the riders. And she admired his refusal to play games. Maybe it was time to grow up and stop being so devious. Manipulating people made her feel powerful and satisfied in the moment but left her lonely and without any real friends.

She left Artie's stall, grabbed her cell phone, and headed toward the parking lot, where no one could hear her. Rather than calling Ben, she punched in Kate's number. She decided to test the waters with Kate before talking to Ben.

Kate answered on the third ring. She was surprised to see Cara's name come up on the Caller ID. No one had heard from her since she'd gone to Dietrich's barn over a month ago.

"Hi Cara! What a surprise. We've been wondering how you're making out at Dietrich's stable. How are you? How is Artie doing? Are you loving it at Dietrich's barn?"

Cara dissolved into tears. "Well. That's actually why I'm calling. I made a big mistake coming here. Dietrich is horrible. I'd heard all the gossip about him, but the stories can't compare to the reality. You'd be shocked by what goes on here. But I don't want to get into that now. We'd need at least a whole evening for me to fill you in. I know I should be calling Ben instead of you, but you've always been so nice to me so I wanted to talk to you first. Do you think there's any possibility that I could come back to the barn? Is there any room? Do you think Ben has washed his hands of me since I left? I don't know what I'm going to do, but I do know I can't stay here any longer. The first thing I'm going to do is tell Dietrich I'm not feeling well. Then I'm just going to hack Artie until I have a plan to get us out of there."

Kate felt bad for Cara, but she didn't want to get involved in her drama. And she certainly didn't want to spend an evening with her so she could listen to her trash Dietrich. But Kate thought it might actually be the first time she'd heard genuine emotion from Cara instead of her phony façade.

"Oh, Cara. I'm so sorry to hear it's not working out. I don't know what to tell you about Ben or the stable. The only thing I know for sure is that the barn is filled right now. I have no idea if anyone is leaving. Call Ben. If he doesn't have space for you here, I'm sure he can find you a better situation. Don't worry about him being pissed off. He's not the kind of person to hold a grudge. Just call him."

"I'll do that today. I need to come up with a different arrangement right away. I know I won't sleep tonight if I don't resolve this soon. And if you feel like it, when you see Ben today, maybe you can tell him how awful things are for Artie at Dietrich's. I know how much he cares about the welfare of the horses. Thanks so much, Kate. You're such a good friend and a wonderful horse-woman. I knew you wouldn't want Artie and me to stay in a bad situation."

Kate winced when she heard shades of the old sugary sweet Cara emerge. She'd fawned and flattered her way through life so much that she probably didn't even realize when she was doing it. No. She didn't want Cara and Artie to stay in a bad situation, but she refused to get in the middle of things.

With shaking hands, Cara called Ben that afternoon. He answered right away instead of letting the call go to voice mail.

"Ellis."

"Hi, Ben. It's Cara. How are you doing?"

"I'm fine, Cara. Nice to hear from you. How's Artie doing?"

"Well, that's what I wanted to talk to you about. I know you probably don't want to hear details, but Dietrich's system isn't a good fit for us."

"Maybe you need to give it some time. You haven't

been there very long."

Cara was no fool. She said the one thing she knew would get Ben's attention. "I would, Ben, except that I'm worried about Artie's safety."

Ben was silent for a moment and then asked, "What's going on, Cara?"

"I don't want to say specifically, but I see everything from verbal abuse of the riders to physical abuse of the horses, including electricity. I don't know what hold he has over these people. Or maybe I do. I fell victim to it myself. I'm calling to beg you to let us come back to the barn. Is there any way that would be possible? If you're full, we could go into the quarantine barn that Chris used until something opens up in the main barn. I'll hire someone to take care of Artie so your staff won't have to run back and forth. Please, Ben."

There was silence on the phone as Ben mulled things over. He wasn't sure he wanted the flighty, unfocused girl back in his barn, but he didn't want to abandon her horse to an abusive situation. He didn't say anything for so long that Cara thought he'd hung up on her.

"Ben. Are you still there?"

"Yes, Cara. I'm thinking about what you said. You're right. We are full. I'm sorry to say there's no room in the main barn. And I don't want Artie to be alone in the quarantine barn. He won't be happy without company."

Cara's heart sank as Ben turned her down. She'd been sure he'd let her come back. People always accommodated her needs and desires. Plus, her concern about Artie's safety should have been the final straw for Ben. Besides, why wouldn't he want her back? Sure, she'd bailed on him to go to Dietrich. But she considered herself one of his most successful students. It definitely wouldn't do his stable any harm to have her represent them at shows.

Finally, Ben said, "Okay. Here's what we can do. I'll make some calls and try to get you a stall nearby. I know of several safe places. You can trailer here for lessons when you want help. Then, when we go to Florida for the winter, I'll lease an extra stall for you. We're planning to head down there mid-December. That'll at least take care of your situation for the coming month and a half and give us time to figure something out for the spring. How does that sound?'

Cara was disappointed that she couldn't go right into Ben's barn, but she knew that beggars couldn't be choosers. "Oh, Ben. That would be wonderful. When do you think you could find Artie a temporary home? I'd like to be able to leave Dietrich's house of horrors as soon as possible."

"I'll make some calls tonight and get back to you as soon as I know something."

"Thank you, thank you, thank you! I'm so grateful. And I promise to be a better student. From now on, my middle name is going to be 'focused.' I'm going to make you proud of us, Ben. You'll see."

Ben laughed out loud at that. Time would tell whether or not he'd see a new and improved Cara. Maybe her experience at Dietrich's really did wake her up. With a sigh, he told her he'd be in touch and said good night.

# FIFTY

*Kate*

In the afternoon, Kate started preparing dinner for the horses. She looked up from measuring grain to see John standing in the doorway to the feed room. She hadn't seen him in almost three weeks.

"Hello, Kate."

John seemed relaxed and back to his usual affable self. A relieved Kate said, "Hi, John. Remmy's missed seeing you. We've all missed seeing you. How are you?"

"I'm fine." John said. "When you have a few moments, I'd like to talk to you. Can you fit that into your day?"

"I'm just about done setting out feed. Then I could take a short break."

John nodded and said, "Okay. I'll be out front on the deck watching the lessons. Please join me when you're free."

Kate felt panicky. She had no idea what John wanted. He seemed calm. Maybe he'd come to his senses about her turning down his marriage proposal.

Kate finished her chores and headed out to the deck where John was watching a lesson. When she got there, he stood politely and motioned to a nearby chair. Kate sat on the edge like a young horse ready to bolt from danger.

John said, "You look well, Kate. I've missed you. And I've missed coming to the farm. But I think you needed some time to realize how much sense it makes for us to be together. Now that you've had a few weeks to think it over, I hope you've had a change of heart."

Kate's mouth fell open. She couldn't believe that John actually still thought there was a chance for them to be together as a couple. She didn't want to hurt his feelings again, but she knew she owed it to him to be honest.

"John. You know I've counted on you to be my support system, and you've never let me down. I will be forever grateful to you for that. But no, I'm not ready to get married. Not to you or anyone else."

John narrowed his eyes. "What do you mean anyone else? Is there someone else? Is it that Chris Barton you're always hanging out with? Look. He seems like a nice enough guy, but he can't offer you the lifestyle I can. He's a newspaper writer, for Christ's sake. He probably lives paycheck to paycheck. Is that how you want to live? Haven't you been doing that long enough?"

Kate stared at him. No one, except Audrey, Wheeler, and Peter knew about her feelings for Chris, and she intended to keep it that way. And the last thing she'd ever tell John was that he didn't interest her as a man. She'd already bruised his ego once and had to endure his wrath. She didn't want to go through that again. His rapid personality change at the restaurant had frightened her.

"As I told you before, John, I'm just not in that place in my life right now. My focus is riding and training, and I have very little time or energy left over for a social life or romance. Besides, I've never been driven by money. Although we didn't have much money, my mother always made sure that my sister and I had whatever we needed. We never felt poor or neglected."

He smiled at her indulgently. "Kate, my darling. You're not seeing the big picture. Having money isn't a curse. It can be a wonderful thing. I'll take you away from your working student position and provide you with whatever you need to reach your goals. Where is it written that you have to struggle so hard to reach your dreams? Life doesn't have to be 24/7 workdays with little or no compensation. There's an easier way. And I'm offering it to you on a silver platter. Haven't you missed me these last few weeks?"

"Of course, I've missed you!" Kate practically shouted. "I count on you to be the captain of Team Gage. But no, John, I haven't changed my mind."

John's face darkened like an approaching thunderstorm. He glared at her. Just like at the restaurant, he almost knocked his chair over as he stood up. He clearly wanted to punish her and growled like a tiger, "You

are a complete fool, Katherine Gage. You don't understand what you're giving up. And I warned you weeks
ago that Remmy and I are a package deal. If you're not
willing to accept my proposal, I'm afraid you're going to
have to stop riding my horse as of today. Maybe I'll pay
to have Ben ride him when I'm out of town. Or maybe
I'll turn him over to Audrey. How would you like that?
That should put a little rift in your friendship. I'm sorry, Kate. I really am. For both of us. But especially for
you because you're too stupid to realize what you're
giving up."

John grabbed his coat and stomped off without looking back. He left Kate sitting alone on the deck. In less
than a minute, he'd managed to hurt and insult her
again. After a while she dissolved into soundless tears.
Ben had witnessed the drama from his chair in the gazebo, but he didn't know what was going on. A stunned
Kate sat by herself for several minutes.

When she saw John drive away in his Mercedes, she
slowly got up and walked in a daze to Remmy's stall. He
was dozing with his head hanging over the stall guard.
When he saw Kate, he immediately started molesting
her jacket pockets in search of the treats she always
carried with her. In spite of her grief, she smiled at this
sweet gentle horse that had captured her heart. She
threw her arms around his neck and hugged him as if
her life depended on it.

She whispered into his warm skin. "I'm going to miss
you so much, Remmy. We won't be able to work together

anymore. But I'll always look out for you and bring you special treats. I'm trying not to be sad, but it's really hard. You're the horse of a lifetime, and I'm just so grateful we've had some of that time together."

# FIFTY-ONE
*Kate*

Audrey puttered around in the kitchen, making coffee for herself and Kate. She wanted to help her friend get over the funk she'd been in since losing Remmy. John had indeed handed Remmy over to Audrey. But contrary to what John thought would happen to the girls' friendship, Kate was happy that Remmy and Audrey would have each other.

As she waited for the coffee to brew, Audrey stretched like a cat and said, "Ah. Glorious Mondays! I love days off. What's on your agenda for today, Blister Butt?"

Kate shrugged and said, "Just the normal routine for me—clean my room and the bathroom, pay bills, and, of course, laundry."

"I hear you, girl," Audrey said. "And if that was a not-so-subtle hint, I know it's my turn to do the kitchen and living room. But at least let's do something fun after lunch. They're having a big pre-Christmas sale at

Oakland Saddlery. Let's go pick out our Secret Santa gifts for the Christmas party. We might even have to get something for ourselves. Then we can go for an early dinner somewhere. How does that sound?"

Kate's eyes sparked and she said, "That sounds great. Who did you get for Secret Santa?"

"Duh, Kate! That's supposed to be a secret. That's why they call it 'Secret Santa,' ya know? But since you asked, and I just can't keep a secret. I got Wheeler. It'll be fun picking out something outrageous for him. How about you? Who did you get?"

"I got Melissa. I think I'm going to get her a huge box of Dark Horse Chocolates. Or do you think that's mean? I'd hate to upset her. I'd just like to give her something yummy."

Audrey shook her head and said, "She'll probably just chuck them in the trash. Or re-gift them to someone who'll actually eat them."

"Yeah, maybe I'd better get something noncaloric. I don't want to tease her. She's such a nice person. I wish we could do something to help her."

Kate exhaled. "I know. But that's way beyond our expertise. We can offer our friendship and support but that's the best we can do. She needs professional help. It's weird how she claims she eats a ton and just has a high metabolism. But I think that's what she tells people to get them off her back."

"Yeah. I know," Audrey said. "It's so sad. I still wish I could do something to help her. Anyhow, can you believe that our Christmas party is right around the corner, and then we leave for Florida one week later? I'm so excited."

"Me too! Going to Florida and competing on that circuit is a dream come true."

Audrey's eyes lit up. "You are positively going to love it. As far as the weather goes, living in Florida is like being in paradise day after day. It sure beats New England winters. I think it's hysterical when the weather forecasters down there say something like, 'It's a long-pants day today. The temperature will barely reach seventy degrees. But with the wind chill, it'll feel like the sixties.' Wind chill! That cracks me up. I don't think you can use the words 'wind chill' unless the temperature dips below forty, and there are twenty-five mile-per-hour winds."

Kate laughed. "Their blood must be really thin down there if sixty degrees is considered cold!"

"You got that right. Anyhow, the weather is just one perk. I love how Wellington is wall-to-wall horse farms. It's fun to see people hacking around the neighborhood on the dirt roads. And you can't go into a drug store or Publix or the gym without running into someone in the horse world. I'm not just talking about dressage people, either. I've met so many cool riders from the hunter, jumper, and polo worlds. It's so neat to see and talk to them outside of competition. Everyone is so much more relaxed. And if that's not enough, at the shows you get to see not only some of the top riders in this country but also trainers and riders from Europe. Last year I was a fly on the wall, listening to Klaus Balkenhol and Robert Dover talk about training. I always feel like a kid in a candy shop when I'm there. It's total immersion with the best of the best."

"I can't wait," Kate sighed. "The only sad thing is that I won't be riding Remmy. I miss him so much. Don't give me that look, Audrey. I've told you a million times that I'm not mad at you for riding him. If I can't ride him, I'm thrilled that you have the opportunity. As much as I love Jolicoeur, I'm happy you're riding Remmy instead of Joe. You're going to be a force to be reckoned with. And at least I'll have Tee. I'm so proud of how well he's doing. He loves the clicker training. He thinks it's a fun game. I just hope it translates to the work under saddle. Okay. I'm going to finish my coffee now and start to work on that mountain of laundry. The sooner I start, the sooner we can go play."

Audrey grabbed her steaming mug of coffee and headed out the door. "Sounds like a plan. See you in a few hours."

The girls had a blast at Oakland Saddlery. With its holiday decorations, the tack shop looked and smelled festive. It definitely put them in a joyful mood.

They split up and spent a couple of hours exploring the aisles. Occasionally, they'd meet to get a second opinion on an item. They finally left the store exhausted but satisfied with their purchases.

Audrey said, "That was wicked fun. Let's dump these bags in the car and then go across the street to Brandywines. I know it's early, but it's five o'clock somewhere. We can have a drink and munch on some of their yummy appetizers. I love their mini crab cakes and stuffed mushrooms. Whaddya think?"

"Sounds great to me," Kate licked her lips. "I'm starving. Shopping sure takes it out of you. So many decisions. And my personal wish list is now about a foot long."

They put their treasures in Audrey's old Hyundai, locked the doors, and headed toward the crosswalk so they could walk down the other side of the street to Brandywines.

When the pedestrian light changed, Kate took one step into the crosswalk. Audrey immediately grabbed her arm and yanked her back.

"Whaaaat? What are you doing? Jeez, Audrey. You almost ripped my arm out of the socket."

As Audrey dragged Kate back under the shadow of a nearby shop's awning, she said, "Shhh. Look." She pointed to the entrance to Brandywines, less than a block away.

"Omigod! It's Chris. What's he doing here?"

At that moment, Alyssa stepped out of the pub. She and Chris looked at each other intently and then hugged before walking off together in the opposite direction from the girls.

Kate felt sick. "I knew that Chris and Alyssa had had dinner together a long time ago when he first came to the barn, but I didn't know they were together," she said, not quite believing what she'd just seen. "Obviously, I was wrong. They look pretty serious about each other. I'm such a fool to think we had something special and that he only wanted to be with me."

"Oh, Kate. I'm so sorry. I don't know what to say. It seems totally out of character for him. He just doesn't seem like a player. I guess you never really know. Let's just go home, okay? We can drink and eat and drink some more there. C'mon. I don't think either one of us is in the mood for Brandywines right now."

Audrey took a numb Kate by the shoulders and turned her in the direction of her car as she muttered, "Men. You can't trust any of them."

With tears streaming down her cheeks, Kate nodded. By the time they reached the car, she'd rebuilt the wall around her heart, brick by brick.

Yes, she'd thought she and Chris shared something special. But he'd never said anything about exclusivity. Was it her mistake to assume they only saw each other? She should have known better. He probably thought he hadn't done anything to betray her. He could date anyone he wanted.

In the back of her mind, Kate felt a nagging doubt. *How could the Chris I know do that? How could he be that way? And, seriously, Alyssa?* But she pushed the doubt away. She'd seen what she'd seen, hadn't she?

# FIFTY-TWO

*Chris*

The next morning Chris came to watch Tee's schooling session. He approached Kate as she tacked his horse up in the grooming stall. He greeted her warmly and went to give her a hug, but she stiffened and backed away from him.

A puzzled Chris asked, "Sweetheart, are you okay? What's going on?"

Kate decided to remain professional. She owed that to Ben. She'd continue with Tee's training. But for her, any personal relationship with Chris was over. "I'm fine."

"Well, you don't seem fine. Please talk to me. What can I do to help?"

Kate managed a weak smile and said, "I'm okay really. I've just got a lot on my mind. Let me finish getting Tee ready, and I'll meet you in the indoor so you can watch our session."

Chris shrugged and walked away. He had no idea what was going on, but he could tell this wasn't the time to pressure Kate for answers.

Chris tried to talk to Kate again before he left the barn later that day. He found her just as aloof as she'd been earlier. He invited her to dinner that night, but she politely turned him down. When he asked when they could get together, she explained that they'd see each other when he came to the barn, but other than that, she wouldn't be able to go out in the evenings. She'd be too busy getting ready for Florida, and she doubted she'd have a spare minute. She had to help pack everything so they could set up Cherry Hill Farm South. Plus, she had to organize her personal things for the four-month Florida season.

Chris knew Kate was blowing him off. Like most men, he wanted to fix things. But he didn't press the point. He decided to give her whatever time and space she needed to resolve whatever was bothering her.

Chris waited a few more days, but Kate's attitude toward him didn't soften. Their encounters remained polite and professional. Kate's change of heart bewildered Chris. He couldn't wait any longer to talk to her about it.

He caught up with her in the tack room and asked if he could speak to her. Although Kate felt cornered in the small room, she said, "Of course. What's up?"

"Kate. I don't know what's going on. Why won't you see me or speak to me outside of the barn? Have I done something? Have you met someone else? I'm completely baffled here. If I've done something, please, just talk to me."

Kate measured her words carefully so as not to hurt the man she still loved, despite what had happened. "It's just that I have a lot on my plate. I think we need to take a break."

Chris' eyes widened. "What? A break? Is that what you really want? You can't mean that."

Kate's eyes brimmed with tears. "I can't give you any more than that right now. I'm sorry."

Chris looked at her for a long minute, but Kate had turned back to the bridle she was cleaning.

# FIFTY-THREE

*Kate*

Ben always went full out for his Christmas party. He wanted to show his gratitude to his clients, friends, neighbors, and staff by making this evening special for them. He hired Equifare to cater the event. They provided all sorts of delicacies and made sure that the drinks flowed freely. Maria decked out the lounge with elaborate Christmas decorations and a beautiful eight-foot tree.

The party took place on the fourth of December. Since the Cherry Hill Farm entourage planned to leave for Florida a week later, they celebrated Christmas early. And celebrate they did. People packed the room, and the noise of clinking glasses, boisterous laughter, and happy chatter added to the festive mood.

Ben disappeared at one point and returned dressed in a Santa suit. Maria came as Mrs. Claus. Everyone laughed wildly because dressing up seemed so out of character for the usually conservative couple. Ben had a big sack filled with brightly wrapped boxes, and he and Maria handed them out with great ceremony. The partygoers opened their presents to a chorus of "ohs" and "ahs."

Once Ben and Maria had given out their gifts, Ben went to the tree to gather up and hand out the Secret Santa surprises that his staff and boarders had picked out for each other. Everyone roared with laughter when they got their silly stuff and had fun trying to guess the identity of their Secret Santa.

Well after midnight, the group started to disperse. They hugged, kissed, and wished each other happy holidays. Ben wanted his guests to enjoy themselves without worrying about getting home safely, so he'd hired a car service to drive those who had partied a bit too hard.

As Kate stood in the lounge, waiting for Audrey, Chris approached. "Merry Christmas, Kate. Amazing party, eh?"

Kate was surprised that Chris had come up to her. Beyond what they needed to discuss about Tee, they had barely spoken when they saw each other in the barn. "Merry Christmas to you, too, Chris."

"Well, Kate, I hope you don't mind, but I have something for you. I know things have changed between us, though I still don't know why. Anyway, I got something for you a while back. I hope you'll accept it."

Kate lifted one corner of her mouth in what resembled a smile and tried to change the subject, "Hey! That's breaking the rules. I already got my Secret Santa gift. I'm guessing it came from Ben because it's a book on training. I can't wait to bury myself in it. What did you get from your Secret Santa?"

Chris' cheeks flamed. "I got a pair of red and green bikini underwear with Christmas balls on them. I won't elaborate on the exact placement of the balls, but you can probably guess. I bet they came either from Audrey or Wheeler, but neither one will admit it."

Chris extended his hand toward Kate. In it, he held a small, beautifully decorated box. Kate froze as memories of John giving her that ring at Chandler House flooded her mind.

As she gaped at the box, she repeated, "Chris. You know we're not supposed to give anything extra beyond Secret Santa. You shouldn't have done this."

"Please just indulge me, Kate. I put a lot of thought into this gift, and I hope you love it. I think it's perfect for you."

Kate carefully unwrapped the exquisitely decorated package. She couldn't imagine what Chris gave her. Jewelry? She looked at the size of the sapphire velvet box and thought it could be a necklace or a bracelet.

Just a few weeks earlier she'd have loved having a special keepsake from him. But things weren't the same. Now a piece of jewelry felt completely inappropriate. She started to protest again, and Chris simply said, "Just open it."

As Kate opened the box, she stared down at a small brass rectangle. She squinted at it and asked, "What is this?"

Chris grinned and said, "Turn it over."

A confused Kate turned the brass plate over. It was a nameplate for a halter. Engraved on one line was the word *Chancellor*. Underneath that, it said *Katherine Gage*.

Kate looked from the nameplate to Chris several times. "What is this? I don't understand."

Chris moved closer to her and said, "This is my Christmas gift to you. Please accept it. You and Chance belong together, and I want to be the one to make that happen for both of you."

Kate stared at the brass plate for what seemed like an eternity. When she finally looked up, she was livid.

"I can't accept this Chris. You can't just go out and buy me a horse. And an expensive one at that. You're just like John. You're trying to blackmail me. And what do you expect in return? As much as I love Chance, I can't be bought. You should at least know that about me."

Chris sputtered, "Kate. I'm not trying to blackmail you. Why would I do that? I love you, and I know you love that horse."

"I don't think you know me at all. Or maybe you're just feeling guilty. I saw you at Brandywines, Chris. You and Alyssa. Here. Take it. I don't want it. Or anything else from you, for that matter."

Kate slammed the box into Chris's hand, turned on

her heel, and ran from the lounge. She left Chris standing alone with his mouth hanging open.

# FIFTY-FOUR

*Kate*

For the next couple of days Kate, Audrey, and Jason finished packing, organizing, and clipping the horses for the trek to Florida. Kate did her share of the work but functioned in a semi-daze. Luckily, she had so much to do that she didn't obsess about Chris and what he'd done at the Christmas party. When her mind drifted to thoughts of him, she wondered how she could have been so wrong about someone. He ended up showing his true colors as a spoiled rich man who thought he could buy whatever he wanted—including people. Both Chris Barton and John Davis clearly assumed their fortunes gave them permission to do and get whatever they wanted.

Why did he even have that newspaper job? He never had to work a day in his life. Maybe he used that as his cover story to make sure women liked him for himself and not just his money. And when it came to romance, he obviously fancied himself a player. She'd seen him with Alyssa. He apparently used his charm and good looks to play the field while making each of his conquests feel special. An embarrassed and angry Kate couldn't believe she'd allowed herself to become another notch on his belt. How could she have misjudged Chris so badly? The more she thought about it, the angrier she felt.

As Kate led Celebrity back to his stall, her cell phone vibrated. She took the phone from its case on her belt and glanced at the screen. She saw his name again. Since the Christmas party, Chris had sent dozens of texts and left almost as many messages. They all basically said the same thing. "Please, Kate. We have to talk. Give me a chance to explain."

Kate scanned the message and thought, *In your dreams, Barton. We are so done.*

She ignored the message, stuck the phone back in her pocket and continued down the aisle with Celebrity. She didn't know how to handle seeing Chris at the barn. She wouldn't encourage him. She refused to be manipulated again. *Fool me once, shame on you. Fool me twice, shame on me.*

But her job depended on her being pleasant and professional with the boarders. Being around Chris in Florida would be a challenge. Then again, it probably wouldn't take him long to find a new girlfriend or two to take her place. And then she could simply treat him politely like someone she used to know.

Preparations for the trip south continued like clockwork. Audrey and Jason had done it before so they knew the routine. They started preparing things several weeks early by spacing out inoculations and making sure to give all the horses' shots at least three weeks before the trip. They organized shipping papers and Coggins tests and made them easily accessible for the commercial van drivers. They didn't want them to get hung up at the Agricultural Station at the Florida border because of incomplete paperwork. At that point, the horses would have been on the van for many hours, and they didn't want them on it any longer than necessary.

Kate, Audrey, and Jason continued to pack the trailers and to pile up the trunks and the rest of the equipment at the far end of the barn so it would be easy for Jason, Mateo, and Phillipe to load everything on the commercial van the night before they were scheduled to leave. That way the drivers could get an early start the next morning. They expected to leave by six in the morning. The horses would travel straight through to their southern home at the Winter Equestrian Festival showgrounds in Wellington.

The girls were going to drive Audrey's car with Bella as their co-pilot. They'd leave the day before the horses so they could prepare the barn in Florida. That way everything would be ready when the horses arrived. After the van left with the horses, Ben and Maria planned to leave with his truck and four-horse trailer. They'd filled the trailer with a month's worth of hay to avoid paying the high Florida prices. Mateo and Phillipe organized the farm truck. They'd tow a two-horse gooseneck trailer packed with equipment. Kate didn't know when the rest of the clients planned to arrive. But she knew everyone looked forward to escaping the coming snow and frigid temperatures as well as enjoying life in Welly World.

Kate thoroughly enjoyed the road trip to Florida. Except for the Devon Show in Pennsylvania, she'd never been outside of New England. She loved seeing new parts of the country. When she wasn't taking her shift driving, she practically pressed her nose against the window to see the sights. Bella did the same thing. The Golden Retriever did her job by barking at cars to keep her people safe from potential intruders. No one seemed to mind the wet nose prints on both backseat windows. It came with the territory. If you had horses, you had dogs. And nose prints.

On the other hand, Audrey had made this trip three times and didn't enjoy the traffic or the monotony of the drive. But she liked having Kate and Bella along for company and laughed at their unbridled excitement. As a seasoned road tripper, she'd packed the car with all kinds of drinks and junk food and special dog treats for Bella. The two girls ate, talked, and laughed their way down I-95.

Of course, most of the conversation revolved around the horses, Ben, the Florida circuit, and the latest gossip from other stables. They also talked a lot about Chris. The girls disagreed about his motives and they almost had a fight over it.

Audrey told Kate she should talk to Chris and hear what he had to say before condemning him. "C'mon Kate. I think you're jumping to conclusions. Give the guy a break and hear him out. He's obviously nuts about you."

"He's not nuts about me. He's trying to control me the way John did. They both know that I love Remmy and Chance, and they figure I'll sell my soul to have those horses to ride. Well, I'll probably never be able to afford horses of that quality, but I refuse to prostitute myself to get the ride on them. I'll learn from the Jolicoeurs of the world. You know me. I love all the horses. I'm just as happy riding a school horse as I am riding a fancy horse. I don't need to make an Olympic team to feel successful. Plus, you saw Chris with Alyssa outside Brandywines. In hindsight, I think of the times he was unavailable, or I couldn't reach him by phone. He was probably busy with her. I know I'm old-fashioned, but if I ever get in a real relationship with someone, I expect it to be exclusive. How can you claim you love someone and then be seeing someone else?"

Audrey countered, "You really don't know any of this for sure. You keep making up stories and condemning Chris without really knowing what's going on. I think you do that because you're afraid of getting too close to anyone. You push him away before he can hurt you. Maybe you couldn't reach him those times because he was volunteering at the animal shelter. That sounds more like the Chris I know than the womanizer you're turning him into. You're beginning to sound more like me, the cynic."

Kate gritted her teeth. "I'm not cynical. I'm realistic. If he's doing something like that, why didn't he just say something? We're supposed to be a couple. Don't couples share everything?"

"You're asking the wrong person," Audrey laughed. "Let me think about my serious relationships. Joel Greenberg invited me to his Bar Mitzvah at 13. I think we lasted a week. He moved on to Amy Cohen because she had bigger boobs. Since then I've enjoyed playing the field and having fun while I'm footloose and fancy-free." Audrey turned serious. "Look. I have no idea why Chris wouldn't mention doing something like volunteer work. He's a humble guy. He didn't broadcast it to the world when he saved those horses. Maybe he likes being anonymous. Just promise me one thing, and I'll never bug you about this again. Talk to him. Call him. Text him. I think you owe it to both of you to know what really happened. At least that way you can stop torturing yourself with all these stories you keep making up."

Kate turned to look out the window and said, "I'll think about it. But at the moment I have a splitting headache. Can we drop the subject for now?"

To break the tension, Audrey said, "Okay. Okay. Hey! I have a great idea. When we get farther south, let's stop at South of the Border. You and Bella will love it. It's so much fun. It definitely gives new meaning to the word 'tacky.'"

Kate cocked her head. "What's South of the Border?"

Audrey raised her eyebrows and said, "Oh, I don't want to spoil the surprise. Pretty soon you'll start seeing billboards with "Pedro" on them. You'll recognize him by his sombrero, his poncho, and his philosophical musings that are quite profound, I must say. Pedro won't let us forget to stop and get our tacky fix. He has a billboard every half mile or so. There's even one to remind you to go back if you miss the exit. You're required to visit South of the Border on your first trip to Florida."

The girls headed back to the South of the Border parking lot, giggling the entire way. Bella bounded happily beside them. To her, everything was an adventure and every adventure deserved a celebration.

Kate said, "Look at all this junk we got!"

"See. I told you that we had to visit Pedro's South of the Border."

Kate threw back her head and laughed, "And as always, you're right."

After Audrey put Bella in the back seat with one

of her new toys, the girls climbed in the front. Kate checked her cell phone, which she'd left in the car. Chris had left another message.

"It's Chris again," Kate said. "He called and left a message this time instead of texting."

Audrey rolled her eyes and said, "Just answer him, Kate. Get it over with. You can't avoid him forever. You're going to see him every day in Florida. Not only will he be in our barn, but you'll still be riding Tee until we know he's safe for Chris. I know you've asked Ben if I could take over grooming and riding Chance. And that's fine. But you can't keep avoiding Chris. Think of the rest of us too. We want a nice atmosphere in the barn. We don't need or want tension because of a lovers' quarrel. Go on. At least listen to what he has to say."

Kate played Chris's message. He apologized yet again and said he really needed to talk to her to clear the air. Could they at least do that?

"C'mon, Kate. Put the poor guy out of his misery."

Kate took a deep breath, and then sent a short text back to Chris. It simply said, "Yes. We can talk."

Chris must have had the phone in his hand because seconds later he replied. "Great. See you soon. I'll be down next week after my doctor's appointment."

# FIFTY-FIVE

*Chris*

Chris was thrilled. It seemed like an eternity since he and Kate had spoken.

He hoped he could say the right things to clear the air. He needed to set Kate straight about Alyssa. And she had it wrong about Chance, too. He didn't know which one she was angrier about.

But the one thing he was sure of was that he couldn't imagine a life without her. He'd do whatever it took to win her back.

The time dragged by. The day after his doctor's appointment, Chris flew to West Palm Beach. He'd shipped his car down the week before and had it delivered to the barn. As soon as he got off the plane, he collected his bags and took a cab to the Winter Equestrian Festival showgrounds where the staff from Cherry Hill Farm had set up their winter quarters a few days earlier.

When Chris arrived at the stables, he greeted everyone and then went to check on Chance and Tee. His horses came to the front of their stalls to see him, and he spoiled them with a few Mrs. Pastures Cookies that he'd brought in his carry-on bag.

After spending an hour at the barn, he announced his plan to get settled at home and come back later. He'd rented a house in the Polo Club so he'd be less than ten minutes from the showgrounds.

Before Chris left, he tracked down Kate. At least she'd agreed to talk. That was something.

Chris found her in the wash stall, scrubbing shipping boots. "Hi Kate. When do you think we could get together? Dinner? Lunch? Coffee? I'm up for anything you feel like doing."

Kate swallowed hard. "Well, as you can see, we're pretty busy. There's a lot to do to get settled into a new place. Why don't we go for a quick coffee at the concession stand? I'm almost done here, and that's really all I can do right now. I don't want to abandon Audrey. She'll end up doing all my work, too."

Chris shook his head side to side and said, "Of course not. I'll go back and hang out with Chance and Tee until it's a good time for you to take a break. Come get me when you're ready.

About twenty minutes later, Kate found Chris in Tee's stall. He was working with Tee by doing some of the tricks he'd seen Kate teach him.

Kate smiled when she saw Tee bow. "He sure learned

his lessons well. He loves performing and having people fawn all over him."

Chris grinned. "Yes. It was a stroke of genius for you to start clicker training with him. He looks more secure under saddle, and I'm sure learning tricks kept him from going stir crazy during stall rest."

"Well, I hope so."

Chris said, "Are you ready to go? I could really use some coffee. I had to get up at four this morning to catch my flight."

They headed to the concession stand, bought two coffees, and found a table in a far corner. At this time of day, few people took breaks, so it was pretty deserted.

Chris gazed at Kate, feeling forlorn. He knew she thought he'd tried to blackmail her with Chance. He didn't know how to make things right except to simply tell her the truth.

Chris took a sip from his coffee and said, "Thanks for seeing me."

Kate drank her coffee, saying nothing.

"I think we need to talk about what happened at the Christmas party," Chris said. "As a matter of fact, what did happen?"

Kate steeled herself for what was to come. "You tell me."

"Kate. I've loved you from the first moment I saw you. I've never met anyone like you. I've never been happier than when I've been with you, and I thought we'd be together always. Isn't that what you wanted, too? What changed?"

Kate lifted one shoulder and said, "Maybe at one time. But what about other women? Silly me, I thought we had an exclusive relationship. And I hate being blackmailed with a horse. Been there, done that with John. You know that about me. I lost Remmy because I refused to be manipulated."

A dumbfounded Chris said, "Wait a minute! What in the world makes you think I'm seeing other women? Sure, I've dated in the past. I imagine you have too. But since I met you, I haven't seen anyone else."

Kate's voice rose an octave as she said, "Oh, c'mon Chris. Do you really think I'm that much of an idiot? Stop lying to me. That's pretty insulting. What about Alyssa?"

"Alyssa? What about her? We're just friends."

Kate pursed her lips and said, "Oh, so that's what they call it now. Is that why you want to be 'friends' with me?"

"Kate! What are you talking about? I had one date with Alyssa when I first came to Cherry Hill. She asked me out to discuss training. I didn't know many people here so it sounded like a good idea. We went to the Rusty Scupper. We had a good meal, talked a lot, but quickly realized that there'd be nothing romantic between us. It sounds weird, but our backgrounds are too similar for anything to work between us even if we wanted it to. We laughed about it and agreed to just be friends. That was the end of it.

Kate stared at Chris. "Is that so? When are you going to stop lying to me? Deny it all you want, but I saw you with her. Audrey and I went shopping before the Christmas party and were going to have a drink at Brandywines. We saw you and Alyssa come out of the pub. Judging by the way you hugged her and she clung to you, it sure looked like you two had something going on. I mean it's totally understandable. She's gorgeous, smart, and wealthy. She knows what clothes to wear and which fork to use. She'd fit right in at all your fancy parties and not embarrass you in front of your rich friends. Why wouldn't you want to be with her? I screwed up thinking we had anything exclusive. I guess I'm just ridiculously naïve. Of course, you'd want someone more worldly."

"Kate! Stop," said Chris. He held up both hands, palms toward her. "Oh my god. So that's why you shut me out. I wondered what you meant by feeling guilty when we talked at the Christmas party. I'm telling you, Kate, there is nothing going on between Alyssa and me. We hugged because we'd just sealed the deal for me to buy Chance for you. She was happy to find a solution for her dilemma. Those two just didn't have the right chemistry. Riding him made her nuts. And she knew he hated it, too. It's a win-win situation for everyone. Alyssa doesn't have to torture herself or Chance anymore. Chance gets a person who adores him, and I'm able to give the love of my life a special gift that she very much deserves—with no strings attached, by the way."

Kate listened to Chris, but five words got most of her

attention. After hesitating for a long moment, she said, "The love of your life? Really? Is that how you honestly feel?"

Chris didn't answer Kate with words. Instead, he enveloped her hand in his, leaned across the small table and brushed his lips over hers with all the love and tenderness he felt. As he reluctantly pulled away, they gazed at each other. "I love you so much Kate. As long as we're honest with each other, and don't keep secrets, nothing can ever separate us."

Kate looked at the ground and said, "Chris, you know my history. I'm damaged goods. I'm never going to feel whole. I'm always going to doubt and second-guess myself. Without meaning to, I'll destroy us sooner or later. You've just had a perfect example of how that could happen."

Chris shook his head. "No, my darling. I won't accept that. I can't remember when I've felt more complete than when I'm with you. I want to make you as happy for the rest of your life as you make me."

Kate shook her head. "You have no idea what you'd be getting yourself in for. I don't think I'll ever be the woman you want me to be."

"I don't believe that for a second. Here's what we'll do. We'll get you some professional help to help you work through your trauma. It may take some time, but I have all the time in the world. Eventually you'll see yourself the way the rest of us see you—loving, compassionate, kind, and capable. Not to mention beautiful," he added, grinning at her.

Kate looked at Chris. "I'm amazed that you see me that way, and that you'd take a second chance on me despite the way I've treated you."

The look in Chris' eyes told Kate what he felt in his heart. He smiled and said, "Second chances. That's perfect. We have a second chance together and you have a second chance with Chancellor, too. Let's go tell him the great news."

They stood up and moved into each other's arms. Neither one of them pulled away for what seemed like the longest time. Then Chris stepped back and extended his hand. They laced their fingers together and walked hand in hand back toward the barn, and toward the journey that lay ahead.

# ACKNOWLEDGMENTS

Thank you to my family, friends, and students for encouraging me to venture into the unknown territory of fiction. It takes a village.

# ABOUT THE AUTHOR

Jane Savoie is one of the most recognized names in the equine industry and for good reason. Her accomplishments and the breadth of her influence are impressive. As a dressage rider, she was a member of the United States Equestrian Team, competing internationally, including a position as the reserve rider for the bronze-medal-winning team at the 1992 Olympics. Savoie was the dressage coach for the Canadian 3-Day Event Team at the 1996 and 2004 Olympics, and coached a number of dressage and event riders at the 2000 Olympics. She is the author of many bestselling books and video programs on riding, training, and sport psychology, and is a popular motivational speaker. Savoie splits her time between Vermont and Florida.